# TARGET DECK

A BREED THRILLER

CAMERON CURTIS

*To Michael Crichton*
*A rational man*

*Our deeds still travel with us from afar,*
*And what we have been makes us what we are.*

*- George Eliot (Mary Ann Evans)*
*Middlemarch*

# MAPS

**Yunnan Province and Jiang Shi**

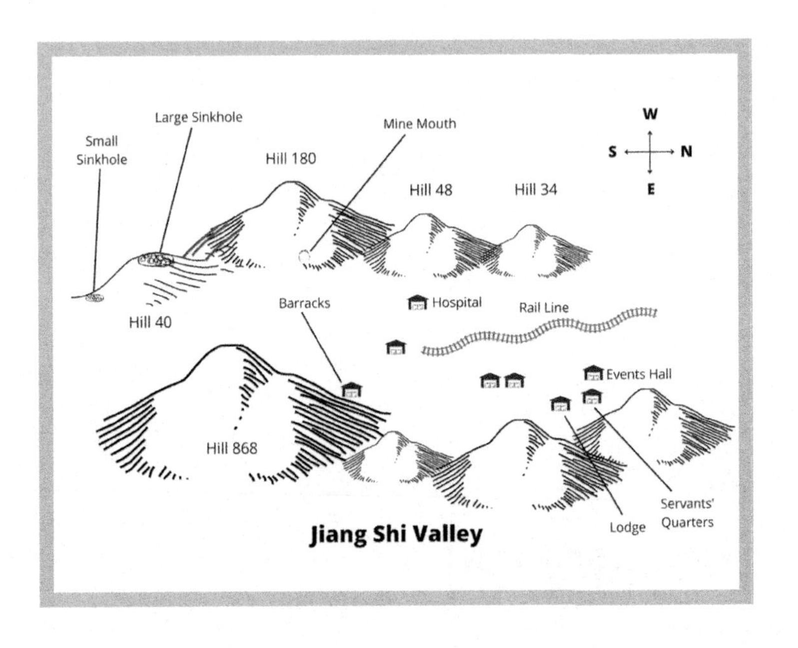
Large Sinkhole
Small Sinkhole
Mine Mouth
Hill 180
Hill 48
Hill 34
W
S
N
E
Hill 40
Barracks
Hospital
Rail Line
Events Hall
Hill 868
Servants' Quarters
Lodge
Jiang Shi Valley

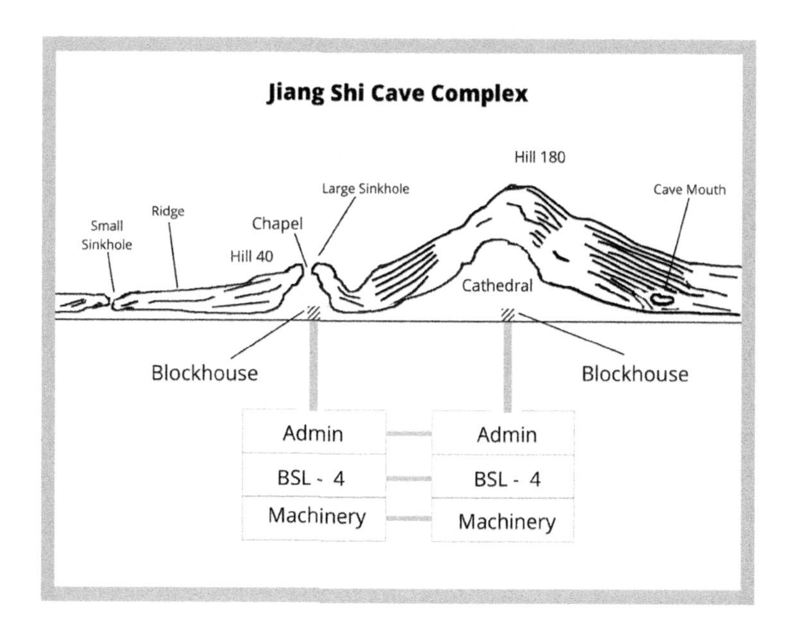
Jiang Shi Cave Complex
Hill 180
Large Sinkhole
Cave Mouth
Ridge
Small
Sinkhole
Chapel
Hill 40
Cathedral
Blockhouse
Blockhouse
Admin
BSL - 4
Machinery
Admin
BSL - 4
Machinery

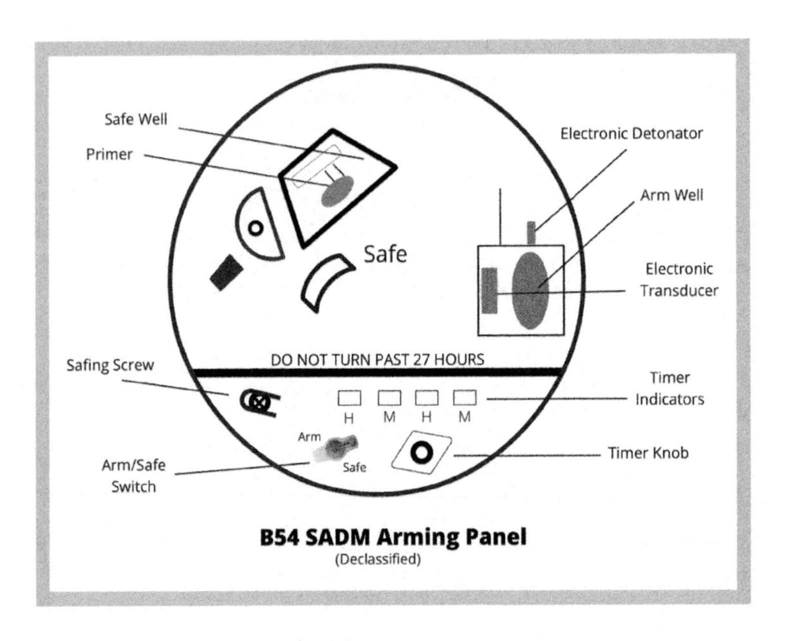


**B54 SADM Arming Panel**
(Declassified)

# 1

## TANDEM

**Afghanistan, 2006**

"He's never jumped out of an airplane."

We are standing at one end of a briefing hall. The air, warmed by electric baseboard heaters, smells of stale dust kicked from rough plank floors. A photograph of an Afghan village has been projected on a screen at one end. Other screens display maps. PowerPoint slides present weather forecasts and wind conditions.

The briefing has broken up. Most of our Rangers and ANA—Afghan National Army—troops have shuffled out. Delta Force operators and officers remain. They stand in small clusters, discussing the mission.

"That's alright." Lieutenant Koenig sounds relaxed. "*You* have."

I stare at an ANA captain standing at the front of the room. He is conversing with Captain Bois, our commanding officer. The Afghan is tall and sharp, with aquiline features. He sports a perfectly trimmed beard and pressed camouflage fatigues. My blood boils.

"Forget it."

"Breed, you've done a thousand jumps, you're tandem qualified, you are our most experienced jumper. Civilians do tandem jumps all the time. No experience required."

I look around the room. A short distance away, my team stands together talking. They carry rucks packed with spare magazines, Claymores, and two-quart camelbacks. Their helmets and NODs—Night Optical Devices—hang from their packs. I catch Ortega staring at me, troubled. My friend turns away.

"That has nothing to do with it," I tell Koenig.

"Your job is to work with our partner force and bring them up to speed."

"I will be happy to take Captain Rahimi on his first jump next week—in daylight."

"He wants to go on *this* mission."

"The captain wants to pad his resume." Rahimi is greedy for advancement. The more senior the officer, the greater the proceeds of corruption. "Why doesn't he go in a school bus?"

The evening's mission is a raid on an Al Qaeda cell. They operate from a Taliban-controlled village high in the mountains. The "school buses" are CH-47 Chinook helicopters, each carrying thirty-five Rangers and ANA. These men will back up Delta Force operators leading the assault. In the event the bad guys run, my platoon of Deltas has been tasked to land by parachute on the far side of the mountain. Our blocking position will cut off their escape.

"It's not the same." Koenig shrugs. "He wants to jump."

"Tough shit."

"Breed, the general has approved Rahimi's jump—provided *you* take him."

Koenig's playing his last card. He knows how much I respect the general. We have a good relationship, I've been his shooting companion for years. He's playing politics with the partner force. Sees this as a small give, expects me to do it for him.

I scowl. "I want Ortega to be my jumpmaster. And another jumpmaster to check Rahimi."

Jumpmasters are specially trained to ensure jumps are concluded safely. There are jumpmasters among aircrew. In each team or platoon, two or three Deltas are jumpmaster qualified.

"*Two* jumpmasters? For God's sake."

"This is *not* routine. We're jumping from thirty-five thousand feet, in the dark, and my passenger doesn't know his ass from his elbow."

"Fine. Whatever you need, but Rahimi is *your* responsibility."

Koenig turns on his heel and crosses the room. Joins Rahimi and Bois. A brief exchange and the three men turn to look at me. The lieutenant has assured them I'll play ball. The Afghan officer flashes me a charming smile, nods his head.

*Motherfucker.*

THE CARGO BAY of the C-130 is cold and noisy. Every thousand feet, the temperature drops two degrees. At thirty-five thousand feet, it's minus forty. I'm wearing gloves and the warmest clothing I own. In his camouflage uniform, Captain Rahimi shivers. Captain Bois and Lieutenant Koenig didn't tell him to bring his warmies.

We sit in two rows of twelve men each. Rahimi, seated across from me at the back of the plane, is odd man out. He makes our complement twenty-five. He and I will jump together. We are furthest from the tail ramp, which will lower to allow the platoon to egress. Above the ramp, a traffic light glows red. When it flashes green, we will jump.

Ortega, jumpmaster-qualified, sits next to Rahimi. Our eyes meet and he slides his gaze toward the Afghan. The reason for Ortega's concern is obvious.

Rahimi is hyperventilating.

We're all equipped with helmets, goggles, NODs, and oxygen masks. The masks have been strapped tightly to our faces. The NODs have been flipped up on our helmets, and we stare at each other in the red ambient light of the transport.

We've been pre-breathing aviator-grade oxygen for the last hour. Moisture-free, to prevent valves and hoses from freezing. More important, the exercise squeezes nitrogen from our blood and tissue. It prevents us from getting the bends—the condition that plagues divers who surface too quickly. The plane's cabin has been depressurized. To an inexperienced jumper, the whole situation feels claustrophobic.

Rahimi grew tense during the pre-breathing preparation. Minute by minute, he climbs a ladder of anxiety.

Ortega lays a reassuring hand on Rahimi's shoulder. The Afghan looks at him with terrified eyes. My friend motions the captain to mellow out. Extends a gloved hand palm-down, makes a patting motion. If Rahimi doesn't slow his breathing, he'll pass out.

A perfect excuse to leave him behind.

I look down at the navigation board strapped to my chest. Altimeter, compass, GPS. I've dialed in the key waypoints. Primary, secondary and tertiary drop zones. All I need to do is press the requisite buttons and the device will guide me to a perfect landing.

The crew chief and an Air Force jumpmaster enter the cabin. The chief goes to the ramp and holds up his hands. Signals six minutes.

No point shouting. The noise from the engines drowns

out every word. The men in our Delta platoon wear earphones and short-range radios. Line-of-sight, it is easier to communicate with hand signals. Once out of the aircraft, we will free fall for five seconds, open our chutes, and form up. For twenty minutes, we'll navigate under canopy to Drop Zone One. Our blocking position will be set up long before the main attack begins.

Hydraulics lower the ramp. The red light of the plane's cabin gives way to the night sky. Above, a field of stars. Below, the dark bulk of the Hindu Kush.

His back to the ramp, the crew chief motions for us to stand up.

As one, we rise to our feet and face the open door. Each Delta checks the equipment of the man in front of him. Parachute harnesses, main and reserve trays, ripcord cables and pins.

Immediately, Ortega and the Air Force jumpmaster begin their work. Rahimi is wearing a tandem harness, and they snap it to the front of mine. There's a lot of tugging and cinching. A civilian tandem harness has four points of attachment. The one Rahimi is wearing has more in front. Rahimi is strapped to me. We each carry our personal weapon, but Rahimi has to carry *two* oxygen bottles *and* our rucksacks. He carries his own bottle and air hose, *plus* mine.

Ortega slaps my back. Keys his mike. "You're good, Breed."

Normally, the slap would be enough. Ortega knows I'm not happy about this jump. My passenger is on the verge of panic. Ortega's words are meant to be reassuring. He takes his place behind me and holds my drogue chute in his hands. Waits for the Air Force jumpmaster to check his gear.

I'll jump with Rahimi, and Ortega will set my drogue. Hold it out and deploy it once my passenger and I have cleared the aircraft. The drogue, a small pilot chute, will open and orient us in free fall. When we are properly aligned, I will pull the main.

The crew chief flashes a hand signal.

*30 seconds.*

The Air Force jumpmaster slaps Ortega's chute.

First at the door, Koenig flashes the crew chief a thumbs-up.

The traffic light turns green.

Koenig dives into space.

The two sticks of Deltas rush to the ramp and jump. Rahimi hesitates, and I prod him in front of me. Together, we waddle forward. The C-130 is moving so fast, every second between jumpers translates to a physical separation of a hundred yards. Twelve jumpers in each stick means three quarters of a mile between the first man and the last.

Ahead of us, one after another, men disappear into the night.

It's our turn at the door, and—

Rahimi freezes.

*Motherfucker.*

I shove him. "Let's go."

Rahimi tries to turn around and go back inside. Of course, he's strapped to me and I refuse to budge.

Ortega stands behind us, holding my drogue.

I bear-hug Rahimi and manhandle him to the open door. The crew chief stares at us, wide-eyed. The Afghan captain digs his heels into the roller system built on the ramp.

"Breed," my radio crackles. "Jump!"

It's Ortega. The seconds are ticking by. We're half a mile behind the group and the gap is opening fast. Rahimi struggles to break my grip. Twists and turns. Claws at me.

I lift him bodily and dive into the night. Rahimi's scream is so loud I hear it over the howling wind.

We're inverted, spinning like a top. The stars and mountains swap places in my vision, a ride in a kaleidoscope. I feel the drogue tug at my back. God bless Ortega, we have a chance. The drogue flips us belly-to-earth. We're still spinning, but I deploy the main. Air rushes into the cells. Like an inflating mattress, the high-glide chute ripples open. There's a crack of nylon and I'm bounced back and forth like a rag doll. I tuck my chin, try to keep my face from slamming into the risers.

The Army used G-Force meters to test the opening shock of the parachute. The meters all broke. They maxed at 10 Gs, or ten times the force of gravity. The Army didn't want to know, threw them away. The harness connection points have been stress-tested to five thousand pounds each. We've never had a harness fail. Teeth, shoulders and collarbones, but never a harness.

Rahimi kicks and struggles. I look up. Our spin caused the cords to twist halfway to the canopy. Ahead of us, I see the shadow of another parachute deploying. A glimpse is all I get, then it's gone. Thank God, Ortega got out.

Rahimi thrashes against me as I work to straighten the lines. I grab the risers and kick my legs from side to side like a child playing on a swing. I remember as a kid, twisting the chains on the playground ride. This is the same principle, but far more difficult.

"Team." Koenig's voice crackles in my ear. "This is Five-Five Actual. Check in."

One by one, the men in the platoon transmit their call signs.

"Five-Five Sierra," Koenig calls. "Check in."

"Five-Five Sierra," I respond. "I have an issue."

"What kind of issue."

I wrestle with the lines. Slowly, I straighten them. Like a drowning man, Rahimi grabs my mask. I push his hand off.

"This is Five-Five Kilo," Ortega calls. "Sierra has a reluctant passenger."

"Understood," Koenig says. "Form up."

"Actual, we are at least a click behind you. Maybe two."

"Do your best."

Koenig transmits his bearing to the platoon. I reach for my navigation board, but it is securely pinned between Rahimi's back and my chest. I squeeze my eyes shut, memorize the figures.

I feel like a heifer is strapped to me. Hanging from the harness, the captain's head is level with my throat. Rahimi twists, elbows the side of my head, and grabs the right brake with both hands. Tries to pull himself up.

*You son of a bitch.*

The brakes are toggles. Handles attached to cords that allow a jumper to deform the trailing edge of the canopy. Pull on *both* toggles and the parachute slows down. Pull *one* toggle, and that side drops. The parachute turns in that direction.

That's what happens. As Rahimi pulls on the right toggle, our chute turns sharply right and loses altitude. We're spinning—falling out of the sky. The spin can accelerate on itself and become impossible to recover.

Rahimi is going to kill us both.

Of course, I can kill *him*. I can twist the fucker's head right off his neck. Explain *that* to a court martial.

My wrist altimeter reads thirty thousand feet. I tear Rahimi's mask away from his face. At this altitude, without oxygen, an untrained man has a minute of useful consciousness. Rahimi's arms lose their strength. I pin them easily.

In his harness, the captain slumps.

For the first time since leaving the airplane, I have time to evaluate the situation.

We jumped close to the Pakistan border. I have no idea

which direction we're facing. Looking down, all I see are snow-capped peaks and carpets of forest.

I drop my NODs, free my navigation board, and consult the GPS. The adventure with Rahimi pinned the device between us. Pressed a bunch of buttons. The device has reset. All the points I stored before boarding the plane have been erased.

I key my mike. "Actual, this is Five-Five Sierra."

"Go ahead, Sierra."

"I've lost GPS. Will try to catch up."

"Very well. RV at blocking position."

"Understood. Sierra out."

I shift my attention to the compass. How long have I been struggling? I'm a mile behind the platoon, a good twenty minutes from the drop zone. I have Koenig's bearing, but no easy way to determine where I am. With the compass, I know east from west. For the next twenty minutes, my best course of action is to follow Koenig.

It's a lonely flight. I check my altimeter. At 12,000 feet, Rahimi starts to come around. Twitches against me. Turns and gropes for the left-hand risers. I pound the heel of my hand against the side of his helmet.

Rahimi holds his head in his hands, hangs helpless. I turn my attention to the terrain below. Viewed through NODs, it's a ghastly green and black landscape. I've given up on reaching the DZ. Once on the ground, I'll break out maps and navigate by compass.

There, below us. A dry riverbed. I should land into the wind and flare for a gentle landing. To do that, I'll have to make extra turns, but we're too low to execute them safely. We have to go in hot.

The riverbed's a carpet of stone. Rahimi doesn't know what to expect. As we approach for landing, I pull hard on the rear risers. We're going too fast, the chute doesn't respond. We hit hard and I land on Rahimi like I'm falling on a cushion. He pancakes, arms and legs splayed, dragging our rucks between his legs. Digs in face-first and eats rocks.

*Sorry about that.*

I unclip Rahimi's harness from my D-rings. Stand up and stretch, suck cold mountain air into my lungs. I reach down and help the captain to his feet.

It feels good to be alive.

# 2

## STEIN

### Georgetown, Present Day

Warm sunlight bathes the patio at Gilbert's. Halfway between Georgetown and Foggy Bottom, the restaurant serves a mixed clientele. Up-and-coming government functionaries and students sip their drinks. Chase their ambitions while admiring everything the opposite sex has to display.

Anya Stein stares at me. "Did you deliberately use Captain Rahimi as a landing cushion?"

Waiters in white shirts, striped aprons, and straw boaters make their way among the tables. I feel relaxed and mellow.

"Of course not. It happened to work out that way."

I can't understand Stein's obsession with my file. In the two years I've known her, she's become a senior executive at the CIA. Casually referred to, by those who know, as "the Company." I don't know exactly what her job is, and that's the way she seems to like it. On the other hand, she dissects my service record with a scalpel. Probes me every time we meet.

"The Afghan National Army wanted you court-martialed."

"Stein, that was fifteen years ago. Who cares?"

"Our deeds still travel with us from afar, and what we have been makes us what we are," Stein recites.

"I'm supposed to ask who said that?"

"George Eliot."

Attractive woman. Mid-thirties, looks younger. Smooth skin, white as ivory, like she's spent her whole life in libraries. Her dark brown hair falls straight to the shoulders of her signature black suit jacket. Creases sharp enough to cut. Harvard Law staring at me.

Stein cleans her laptop keyboard with a Q-Tip.

"Right. I'll put him on my reading list."

"George Eliot, pen name for Mary Ann Evans. One of the leading Victorian writers." Stein's expression softens. "Breed, you spent fifteen years in the Army trying to get kicked out. I'm amazed you lasted as long as you did."

"Well, they didn't court-martial me."

"No. Captain Rahimi was so damaged by the experience he asked to be reassigned."

"See? Everyone's a winner."

"You had other close calls. At one point, you were counseled for disrespect."

"I call things the way I see them."

"Yes." Stein sips her wine. "Special Forces, and Delta in particular, look for independent thinkers. Men who operate outside the box."

"Nothing came of that counseling. It was filed in the bottom drawer. For some reason, only *you* seem interested."

"Because the country needs men like you." Stein leans forward. Her brown eyes hold mine. "Now more than ever. The last incident—shooting Afghan women who were torturing American POWs—couldn't be filed away. Unless you resigned."

Bad dreams. Stein doesn't understand the buttons she's pushing.

"So I resigned. Made everyone happy."

"It would seem so," Stein says thoughtfully. "Are you happy working for Long Rifle Consultants?"

Working for an executive protection company pays well. You land some cushy gigs. "The leftovers from the cocktail parties are great."

Stein shakes her head. "Breed, you are a racehorse pulling a plow."

"Oh my God." I laugh. "Stein, what do you want?"

"I want you to consider working for the Company. There are a number of standard arrangements we can customize. You would be responsible only to me."

I don't like the sound of *that*. "I have problems with authority."

"It wouldn't be that way." Stein hesitates. "You'll have unlimited rules of engagement."

"You know what that means?"

"Give me credit, Breed."

Stein has paid her dues.

"I'm taking time off, Stein. Let me think about it."

My eyes sweep the patio in search of our waitress. There's a big guy standing next to the outdoor bar. Mid-thirties, he wears an expensive, hand-tailored suit. Cut to disguise his bulky biceps, chest and shoulders. On the street sits a black, up-armored, Chevy Suburban. A second man waits beside the vehicle.

I signal our waitress. She's a rosy-cheeked young girl, wearing a blue-and-white apron. Lovely in her straw boater. Long black ribbons hang from the pretty hat, down the nape of her neck. Her smile generous, she holds my eyes. Long enough to convey interest. I ask for another beer, another glass of wine for Stein.

Stein and I watch the girl leave. Her white trousers are skintight. She walks like she knows I'm staring at her. Enjoys the attention.

"For God's sake, Breed."

"She's a nice girl."

Stein scowls. "I wanted to speak before you flew out to Montana."

The waitress returns with our drinks and I lean back in my chair. Watch her set Stein's glass of wine on the table. The girl takes my beer glass, tips it, and pours carefully. I thank her, turn to Stein.

"What's going on?"

Stein stiffens. "Why does anything have to be going on?"

"I've never known you to circulate with bodyguards."

Stein carries a SIG P226 Legion in a handmade holster. Double-action, loaded and de-cocked. She by God knows how to use it.

"What bodyguards?"

I tilt my head. "The one at the bar—him, *you* told to be unobtrusive. The one by the car didn't get the memo."

That earns me a flash of irritation. "We have a situation. Certain people at the Company have been tapped for extra protection."

"What kind of situation?"

"I can't say."

"I still have my clearances, Stein."

"I know, Breed." Stein looks worried. "But you don't need to know, and it's better you don't."

We're sitting in the middle of Washington D.C. If the CIA is afraid senior officers' lives are in danger, this is serious.

I signal the waitress for the check.

"How long will you be in Montana?" Stein asks.

"At least a couple of months." I tap my credit card on the reader. Wait for the machine to spit out the receipt. The girl tears it off with a flourish and hands it to me with the bill.

*Tracy*

The girl's name has been automatically printed on the bill. Underneath, she has scribbled a phone number. I fold the paper in half and slip it into my shirt pocket.

"How can I reach you?" Stein asks.

"Try carrier pigeon."

"Be serious."

"I am. There's no mobile reception where I'm going."

"Give me your landline."

"Don't have one." I take out my phone, search my contacts. "The closest is at Sam Crockett's place. Leave a message with him."

Stein's eyebrows edge closer together. "Sam Crockett."

"A friend of my father. When Dad passed away, Sam and I spent a lot of time together."

Stein stores the number. "How can you *not* have a landline?"

"I haven't been in the place more than two weeks in fifteen years. Why pay for something I don't use?" I squint. "You're awful nervous, Stein. Are you going to need help with this situation of yours?"

The woman doesn't sweat.

"We don't know enough yet."

A large group of students is making its way toward the restaurant. Loud, boisterous laughter. The university football team.

I drain my beer. "Alright, Stein. I need to exfil."

Stein gets to her feet. In her black pantsuit, she looks like a model cut from the glossy pages of a magazine.

*That* is a perfect resting bitch face.

"Can I give you a lift?" she asks.

"Thanks. I'll walk a while."

We wind our way to the patio steps. The big guy at the bar speaks into a collar microphone and pushes off to follow us.

The students rush up the stairs. I grip Stein's upper arm and hold her back as they pass. The woman stiffens at my touch, turns her head to look at me. I sense the acceleration of her heart.

"We're in no hurry," I say.

My eyes sweep the street. The man by the Suburban has opened the front passenger door. Maybe her guards are used to Stein's independent approach, but I think she intimidates them. They should have cleared her way to the vehicle the moment they saw us get up.

Exec Protect requires a different mindset from Direct Action. A bodyguard is, by definition, defensive. That doesn't mean you always let the bad guy get off the first shot. It means you work twice as hard to be proactive, so he doesn't get a chance. That means you control your principal. No matter how senior she is.

I quarter the ground. My eyes flick across the hands of people on the street. I check the high places. The open windows. If he's good, I won't see a rifle, but I look anyway.

Nothing. I escort Stein down the stone steps. Walk her to the waiting Suburban, let go of her arm.

Stein gives me a strange look. "Does this meet with your approval, Breed?"

She must be referring to her security arrangements.

"Depends on who's out to get you."

Stein mounts the Suburban and the bodyguard slams the armored door.

I turn and walk away.

# 3

## CROCKETT

**Ronan, Montana**

The sky stretches ice-blue all the way to Canada.

Sam Crockett pulls goggles over his eyes. The pair of us crouch at the open door of the airplane while the wind rushes by at ninety-five miles an hour. To the north lie the wilds of Glacier National Park. To the east lie the Rocky Mountains. Twelve thousand feet below spread the impossibly blue waters of Flathead Lake.

I motion Sam to go ahead. He's seventy-two years old, but it's impossible to think of him as an old man. A former Green Beret, his tall, rawboned frame looks hard and wiry. The eyes staring at me through the goggles are alert and sharp with intelligence.

A thumbs-up, and Sam steps through the door. Without hesitation, I follow him out.

The prop wash rocks my body. I spread my arms and legs, arch my back. Flat and stable, I plunge into free fall. The wind thunders in my ears. This jump is pure joy, and I catch myself smiling. For a few joyous seconds, I can savor the experience of flight.

Military static jumps are physical abuse. Paratroopers are light infantry. They fight with what they carry on their backs. A mass airborne drop is meant to seize an objective and hold until relieved. If air resupply fails, or relief is delayed, paratroopers run out of food and ammunition. For that reason, they jump with all the weapons and ammunition they can carry. Landings are not pleasant. The sound of bones detonating on impact stays with you.

As Special Forces, I was more often involved in military free fall insertions. High Altitude Low Opening (HALO) and High Altitude High Opening (HAHO) maneuvers are meant to avoid detection. The night Captain Rahimi almost killed me, we were attempting a HAHO insertion. I usually enjoy those jumps, though there is a lot on my mind. The procedures for jumping from high altitude, and the nuances of navigation while flying a nylon wing.

Compared to military work, civilian skydiving is fun.

I join up with Crockett at six thousand feet. I wear three altimeters. The first is a big, square, analogue gauge on my left wrist. With screws at each corner of the cover plate, it looks like a vintage aircraft instrument. Another altimeter is strapped to my chest, and a third is attached to a device on my reserve. The latter will deploy my emergency chute if I have not pulled the main above a thousand feet.

One in eight hundred jumps results in a failed main parachute deployment. A reserve chute has not failed in over twenty years. Yes, parachutists die. They die all the time, but few die from catastrophic double failures. Most deaths are caused by parachutist error.

That's why I love skydiving. If you know what you are doing, it's safe.

Below us, the drop zone is a wide field, a mile outside the

Ronan Airport. I signal Crockett I'm leaving him. Open some distance, pull my ripcord. The pilot chute pops. I feel a gentle tug, then hear a flutter and whistle as the canopy billows out and the cords pull the risers from the tray.

There's a whack as the canopy inflates. The risers grab the straps of my harness. They were tight to begin with, but now they slam my shoulders and jerk my crotch. My chin bounces on my chest and my legs kick high. I look up. Two hundred and fifty square feet of nylon wing open over my head and the slider descends. Lines fan out from my risers to the canopy.

My heart swells.

I look for Crockett. We can glide together for a while, line up our approach.

There. Crockett's red jumpsuit. Bright against the green and tan squares of the fields below. He's flat and stable, arms and legs outstretched. I see the airport and its runway. Falling at a hundred and thirty-five miles an hour, Crockett plunges toward the drop zone.

My throat closes. I want to scream at Crockett to pull, but we have no radios. He's a tiny red speck now, easily below a thousand feet. He must not have an emergency trigger on his reserve.

A puff of white from Crockett's back. His pilot chute blooms like a flower—in a heartbeat, the wing deploys. It's hard to judge altitude from the air, but I swear he pulled at five hundred feet.

Crockett turns into the wind and brakes. The chute flares, and he lands feather-light in front of a red-and-white Hilux pickup. A tiny, dark-haired figure steps away from the vehicle. Helps him gather the folds of nylon.

I'd planned on soaring for a while, but Crockett's stunt has shaken me. Now all I want is to get down as fast as possible. I plan my approach. At nine hundred feet, I touch my left toggle. Dip the wing, ease into a two-hundred-seventy-degree turn.

Approach errors kill jumpers all the time. They turn too quickly, at too low an altitude. Before they know it, they've bled so much energy they can't recover. They pull on the lines and the canopy refuses to respond. I've seen it happen. Heard the flutter of the wing, the whistle of the wind through the cords. Known right away something was wrong. Then—the *smack* of a carcass hitting the earth. At seventy miles an hour. Most jumpers die under perfectly functioning equipment.

I sail over the pickup. Crockett and Heth stare at me. From sixty yards, the young girl's electric blue eyes are piercing.

I've turned into the wind. Pull on the right brake, straighten the wing, flare. Three feet from the grass, I'm this side of stalling. My boots touch the earth and a feeling of sadness sweeps over me. I am no longer a creature of flight.

"Textbook landing, Breed."

Crockett and Heth help me gather my chute. The older man's words don't sound like a compliment.

"You got a death wish, Sam?"

"Are you kidding?" Crockett laughs. "If I wanted to kill myself, I'd have gone long ago."

"That so?"

"Ground's gonna smack you at a hundred and fifty miles an hour. All you have to do is *close your eyes*."

Heth lays her hand on my shoulder. Her touch is electric. "Breed likes to figure all the angles."

Crockett's granddaughter is twenty-four years old and pretty enough to take your breath away. Slim and dark-haired, with high cheekbones. Half Salish, half white. Fair-skinned, with a trace of olive. Her striking eyes make her look like a witch. Heth's name comes from the Gaelic word for fire. It suits her nature.

The Indians talk about Heth in whispers. Crockett taught her to shoot when she was a child, but Heth was born with a gift. She reads the wind like no one I've ever met. She calls its speed within a mile an hour, its direction within fifteen degrees.

Crockett throws his arm around my shoulder. Pulls me toward the truck while Heth stows our gear. "Breed knows you can't do everything with math," he says. "Sometimes you have to roll with your gut."

This man has been like a father to me. I lower my voice. "Sam, I don't want Heth to watch you burn in."

"Breed." Crockett squeezes my shoulder. "You think too much."

"No one's told me *that* before."

# 4

## HETH

### Breed Home, Flathead Lake

My father left me and Mom a low ranch house on the east side of Flathead Lake. Two miles south of Crockett's larger spread, the land it sits on occupies four acres. Like Crockett, my father was a Green Beret. My mother worked as a receptionist at a doctor's office in Pablo.

Crockett pulls up next to a gray Ford Bronco parked in the gravel drive. He's loaned me the truck. Heth and I jump out and drag my parachute gear from the back of the Hilux.

"I'll stay and help Breed clean up the place," Heth says.

"Make sure you're at the lodge by six," Crockett tells us. "I'm going to pick up Butler at the airport. He's joining us for dinner."

Crockett drives away. Heth shoulders my parachute gear and follows me through the front door.

I gesture toward my father's den. "Put it on the floor in there."

Heth sniffs. "You've been back a week, and you haven't done any dusting. You need a woman, Breed."

"Got anyone in mind?"

The girl's smile is wicked. "You don't know what you're missing."

I'd been in the Army four years when the towers fell. Already, I had my Airborne, Ranger, and Special Forces tabs. I'd been selected for Delta, but there was nothing going on. I was on leave, having dinner with Mom, Crockett, Tall Deer, and Heth's mother. Crockett and Tall Deer—Heth's two grandfathers. Both were tall, rangy men. Crockett's light-colored hair and blue eyes contrasted with Tall Deer's dark, craggy features.

We heard the news, and right away I knew my life was going to change.

I watch Heth carry the parachute into Dad's den. She shuts the door, faces me.

"You'd better behave," I say, "or I'll spank you."

Heth's piercing blue eyes lock on mine. "That might be fun. I didn't know you were kinky, Breed."

"You have no idea," I say. "And you don't want to know."

For ten years, the war kept me away from Flathead. It felt like the mountains of Afghanistan were home. My team were my family. I spent my leaves in Fayetteville, thinking about my next deployment.

Cancer took Dad when I was five. He'd served with Crockett in Vietnam. Crippled by an AK47 round, he came home. The army said he'd taken the hit in Vietnam. Only later did I learn from Crockett that Dad had been shot in Laos. A helicopter dragged him out of the triple canopy jungle, dangling from a rope.

Heth goes to my refrigerator, opens it, and takes out two cans of beer. Opens one with a pop, hands it to me. Takes the other for herself. She sips the beer, licks her lips. "What if I do?"

When Dad died, I heard Crockett talking with Mom. They figured he'd gotten the cancer from orange shit the army sprayed all over the jungle. While I was deployed to Afghanistan, Mom passed away. I came back for the funeral. Found that Heth, who had been only five when the towers fell, had grown into a pretty girl of sixteen.

After the funeral, Heth helped me pack away Mom's things. Being around the empty house hurt. I stayed at Crockett Lodge for the rest of my leave. Returned to Afghanistan in time for the final surge of fighting.

For years, I stayed away from Flathead. Found excuses not to visit. Shared the odd email with Crockett. He talked about Crockett Lodge, and how proud he was of Heth. She'd left home for college, but he knew she would come back.

I wasn't sure I ever would.

"Everybody wants what isn't good for them," I say. Throw myself on the couch, put my feet up on the coffee table, take a long drink. I point to an easy chair. "Go on, take a load off."

Heth stares at me. Looks like she's going to throw a leg over, straddle me, and look into my eyes as we drink our beers. Or something.

Instead, she drops into the chair and pouts.

Heth Crockett. Twenty-four years old and nubile. Ripe, ready, and not one bit shy. I'm not made of iron. I lie awake at night in my old bedroom. Allow myself to imagine what it would be like to sleep with her.

And there, I stop.

I don't know what she would do if I ever took her up on that childlike flirtation. She might run scared. More likely, she would sleep with me. However it went, our relationship would never be the same. Crockett wants me for Heth. But that's a responsibility I'm not ready for.

"Drink it while it's cold," I say. "Then we should do some dusting. I appreciate your help."

"No problem." Heth winks. "I'm a terrific Hoover."

God, she's asking for it.

HETH and I drive north on Highway 35 until we come to a big wooden sign that reads *Crockett Lodge*. I pull into the drive and we roll up to the main building.

It's grown over the years. For a long time, Crockett had trouble making ends meet. Against the odds, he built the lodge into a profitable business. Guests occupy private cottages and two wings of the main building. Large duplex apartments for Crockett and Heth occupy a third wing. There is a big restaurant with picture windows that face the lake.

"Mr Butler's arrived," Heth says.

Crockett's Hilux is parked in a private space. He's back from the airport.

I park next to Crockett's truck and we get out.

Our last year of high school, Crockett's son got Heth's mother pregnant. Crockett made Patrick marry the girl. Patrick took his new wife and baby Heth to university. There, he got an architecture degree. The responsibility cramped his style. After graduation, the girl took Heth back to Flathead. Patrick took a job in San Francisco.

Never to be heard from again.

We slam the Bronco's doors shut and walk to the lodge. The restaurant's big windows have been swung open. Patio tables are full of guests enjoying the afternoon sun.

The manager at the front desk greets us with a smile. "Good afternoon, Miss Heth. Mr Breed."

I give a low whistle. "*Miss* Heth?"

"You get used to it," Heth says.

She leads me to the ground floor of the private wing.

Devoted to a large living room and library. The walls are lined with photographs, bookshelves, and antlers. A fireplace occupies pride of place against one wall. The iron bucket of pokers lies at one end, and a steamer trunk of firewood rests at the other. The sofa and easy chairs are deep and cozy.

An all-purpose table with seats for four occupies the other end of the room. A young man in a waiter's uniform is setting it for dinner.

"Mr Crockett and Mr Butler will be down shortly, Miss Heth."

"Thanks, Thomas." Heth strolls around the room. Stretches.

The pictures on the wall fascinate me. Black-and-white memories of the Vietnam war. Hung behind the table, a large photograph, shows six men in tiger stripe camouflage. They wear no badges of rank or unit insignia. Most carry CAR15 short-barreled carbines. Ancestors of the modern M4, these have older twenty-round magazines. One man carries a Soviet RPD light machine gun with a drum belt-carrier. The barrel has been cut down and the weapon has been stripped of its bipod.

I recognize Crockett in the center. Tall and rangy, he wears a cocky grin.

The picture has been around a while. Before Crockett renovated the place, I saw it in the lodge. I'm struck by how large the lodge has grown. Crockett must have been sitting on these photographs for years. Only recently built the space to display them.

"Your grandfather's team."

"Yes. During the final years."

Heth didn't say it was taken after Dad was sent home.

"Do you recognize them?"

"Yes. That big man is Mosby. The man with the machine gun is Stroud. The one with the Dragunov is Appleyard. The porn mustache is Spears. The bandana next to grandfather is Butler."

I squint at the photograph. Young men, all of them. In their early twenties.

"Grandfather was the 1-0," Heth continues. "The team leader. Mr Butler was the 1-1, the assistant team leader. Come look at these, Breed."

Heth motions to a row of photographs that adorn the wall. A neat row arranged beneath a line of antlers.

A photograph of four men in front of a helicopter. Two Americans, two South Vietnamese. The helicopter is an old HC-34 Kingbee. The type with an elevated cockpit and a bulbous nose. A single cargo door on the right side. The Americans are Crockett, and—my father.

"Dad."

"Yes." Heth grips my arm. The four men are smiling. Crockett is blond-haired and blue-eyed. Dad is dark-haired, with a neatly trimmed mustache. Average height and build. Apart from the mustache, I could be staring into a mirror.

Crockett's voice startles me. "That was one of the last photographs of us together."

He's standing at my shoulder. Butler stands behind him. A much older version of the young man wearing a bandana in the other photograph. Still lean, he wears khaki trousers, a polo shirt, and an expensive linen sport jacket. "Breed, this is Will Butler. He was my 1-1, second in command."

Butler and I shake hands.

Crockett points to the photograph. "That's Captain Tran and his copilot. Heroic sons-of-bitches, the best pilots I've ever seen. Tran's twenty-three in this photograph. He flew our team on your father's last Bright Light mission."

"Bright Light?" I ask.

"Yes. Our teams went into Laos to locate enemy supply depots and troop concentrations. Planted sensors and wiretaps. When a team was compromised, the North Vietnamese Army threw everything they had at them. Bright Lights were rescue missions."

"Leave no man behind."

As I say the words, I know the sentiment is as unrealistic as it is noble.

"That's the idea," Crockett says. "But—sometimes it can't be helped."

# 5

## BRIGHT LIGHT

**Laos, October 1971**

Crockett invites us to sit at the table. Thomas brings us bottles of wine and pours.

"I was in France last week," Crockett says. "Picked up this wonderful Pauillac. Château Lafayette. Try it."

I taste the Cabernet. "That's very good."

Butler smiles. "It's a masculine, sophisticated wine. Smooth, but unafraid."

*Right*. Bourbon would better suit my palate. "What were you doing in France, Sam? Retiring at last?"

Crockett laughs. "No, I'm selling Montana hunting trips. Very little open space remains in Europe. Everything is crunched together. Discriminating European outdoorsmen want to visit a real wilderness."

"I'm sending my clientele this way," Butler says. "They're all executives and celebrities. Love to hang out with their exec protect staff. Deep down, all these Hollywood and corporate types want to jock-up and do the guns thing."

Butler owns an executive protection company. Much like Long Rifle.

"Next week," Crockett says, "Heth will guide a rock star."

My attention strays to the photograph on the wall. Maybe I should grow a mustache. Then I'd look like Dad did in 1971.

Crockett reads my mind. "You look like your old man."

"Was that really taken right before his last mission?"

"Yes. I think it was the day before."

"What happened?"

Crockett tells us about October 9, 1971. My father's last mission.

CROCKETT SAT in the stripped cabin of a South Vietnamese Air Force CH-34 Kingbee. Opposite him, the door gunner racked the M60 machine gun. Breed sat on the floor to Crockett's right. They stared out the cargo door at the carpet of jungle, three thousand feet below.

Somewhere in that green hell, the men of RT Utah were fighting for their lives. Shortly after insertion, the team had been compromised. The 1-0 called for extraction. A Kingbee had been sent. The team popped red smoke, but the NVA popped their own smoke grenade to confuse the rescuers. The Kingbee attempted to land in the wrong place and was shot down. Crockett and Breed were ordered to mount a Bright Light rescue.

The noise in a helicopter is too loud for normal conversation. The crew wear helmets with an internal comms system. Unless they are handed a headset, passengers are out of luck. The crew chief slapped Breed on the shoulder, leaned close, and yelled in his ear.

Breed nodded. Turned to Crockett, held up one finger. They had grown adept at communicating nonverbally.

*One minute out.*

Crockett felt his stomach flutter. Gripped his CAR15 more tightly. Passed his free arm through a cargo strap fastened to the cabin wall. Breed did the same. They knew what was coming.

The pilot pushed the collective, leaned on the right pedal, and put the chopper on autorotate. With a sickening lurch, the machine fell out of the sky. Legs dangling over the jungle, Crockett and Breed hung by the cargo straps. Stomachs in their throats, they dropped like they were sitting in a two-bit carny ride.

Captain Tran's move came just in time. Green tracers arched from the jungle, streamed harmlessly over the Kingbee.

Two hundred feet above the jungle canopy, Tran hauled on the collective and threw on power. The rotors clawed the air. Crockett felt the helicopter level off. Craning his neck, he could see the fast-moving river below.

The crashed Kingbee looked like a dead whale. The machine's tail boom had broken off and lay on the riverbank. The shattered cabin lay in the river, and rushing water was breaking over it. The fire had been doused, but the wreckage was still smoking. There were no signs of life.

Huey gunships raced back and forth, spraying the tree line with machine gun fire. The Americans fired red tracers, the NVA green. The tracers crisscrossed. Tran had no more tricks, the NVA had the Kingbee in their sights.

Breed threw four McGuire rigs through the cargo door and over the side. Each was a 120-foot length of rope weighted with sandbags. Each rope was strung with canvas loops for a man to throw a leg or arm through. One end of each rope was secured inside the helicopter. A Huey could lift three men in McGuires. The Kingbee was older, and not as sexy, but it could lift more. The rigs were used to extract soldiers when it was too dangerous for a helicopter to land.

The triple canopy was a hundred and fifty feet high and the tree line reached to the river's edge. The survivors of RT Utah were in an arc with its ends anchored on the riverbank. There was no room for the Kingbee to descend. It could not get low enough for the McGuire rigs to reach the trapped men. The only clear area was over the river, and that was no good.

Breed grabbed Crockett's arm, pulled him close, and hollered in his ear. "We need to blow a landing zone."

Crockett nodded. Four South Vietnamese Rangers completed their team. Crockett motioned for them to get ready. They were going down. Breed pulled his gloves tighter, grabbed one of the ropes, and swung himself into space. The McGuire rig had not been meant for rappelling, so he lowered himself hand-over-hand. Crockett slung his weapon and took another rope. The Rangers followed them out.

The pilot descended so the ends of the McGuire rigs reached to the river. The clattering machine was now thirty feet *below* the jungle canopy. Crockett and Breed could look directly across at trees and foliage.

The NVA lit up the Kingbee with every gun they had. Tried to knock the men off the strings. Tran held the helicopter steady, taking fire. Bullets looked like clouds of colored fireflies swarming toward them. The thin skin of the chopper offered no protection. Bullets went in one side and out the other. Tracers raked the chopper and passed between the ropes. The door gunner returned fire. Hot shell casings showered the men. One of the Rangers fell.

Crockett watched Breed let go of the rope. Fifteen feet above the riverbank, Breed picked a spot and jumped. Fell heavily onto his side and crawled behind a rock. Crockett gritted his teeth. He couldn't see any place level enough to jump to. The rope swung him over the river. He closed his eyes and let go.

There was a smash and water closed over his head. The weight of his rucksack and weapons pulled him straight down. God smiled on him. The water was deep enough to break his fall, yet shallow enough to not drown him. His rucksack and weapon, seventy pounds of dead weight, kept him from being swept away.

Bullets cracked. Burning tracers slapped the water and sizzled. Two of the Rangers descended the ropes into the water. Under fire, they splashed toward dry land. Only one bullet in five was a tracer. There were five times as many bullets snapping through the air than Crockett could see.

Choking and sputtering, Crockett struggled to the riverbank. The Kingbee was gone. Tran had held the platform steady long enough to deliver the team. He had pulled back and was orbiting the battlefield a mile away. A third Kingbee joined the orbit.

At the edge of the jungle, a figure waved. Breed.

Breed and the three surviving Rangers had joined the remnants of RT Utah at the tree line. One American and three ethnic Chinese Nung mercenaries. Another American, RT Utah's 1-0, lay dead. The door gunner of the crashed Kingbee had a compound fracture of his right femur. The team had given him as much morphine as they dared, but he twisted in agony.

Breed's team had doubled the firepower of the small band. Through an interpreter, he instructed the Rangers to reinforce the defensive perimeter.

"Where do we set up the LZ?" Crockett asked.

"Right here," Breed yelled. "We can't move anywhere else."

"We can't leave the perimeter."

Breed grinned. With a cry, he leaped to his feet and charged into the jungle.

The two SOG teams followed, firing on the run and throwing grenades. The shock of their attack threw the NVA back. After fifteen minutes of bitter fighting, they pushed the perimeter forty yards into the jungle.

Breathing space. Crockett and Breed fell back. They would blow a semicircular area clear of trees.

Crockett opened his ruck and hauled out det cord. Breed did the same. While the others held the perimeter, the two men wired an arc of trees for demolition. They wound explosive cable around the trunks, two feet from the ground. Joined the trees in a net.

"This better work," Breed said.

"Fire in the hole."

"*Fire in the hole!*"

The det cord exploded. Across a two-foot high belt, tree trunks burst into a hail of matchsticks. Black smoke squirted horizontally between the remaining trees. For a mile around the blast, flocks of birds took flight.

There was the crack of splintering wood. The crushing sound of branches and foliage rubbing shoulders. The tall trees collapsed in a wave. First, those closest to the river fell into the water. Then, those further away toppled onto their fallen comrades.

Crockett made his way to the American manning the radio.

"Bring them in," he said. "Call for extract and gunship support."

Breed ran to the perimeter, grabbed the interpreter. "Pull back when I give the word," he said. "When the NVA see us withdrawing, they'll attack."

"Talon Four from One-Three Uniform," the comms sergeant yelled into the handset. "We are withdrawing for exfil. Once on strings you're all we got. Give us gun runs on the tree line."

"Roger that, One-Three Uniform. Guns on the tree line."

Captain Tran brought his Kingbee in low over the river. The third Kingbee remained in orbit. With the trees blown down, Tran had a clear zone into which he could descend.

The volume of fire increased. Green tracers flashed toward the chopper, red tracers streamed toward the jungle. With its north and south ends anchored on the riverbank, the perimeter described an arc. In the center, Breed popped a green smoke grenade. Rangers at either end did the same. Smoke billowed over the team's positions.

"Talon Four from One-Three Uniform, we have marked our perimeter with green smoke. Look for green smoke."

"One-Three Uniform, we see green smoke."

"Bring it, baby. Give us everything you got—*outside* the smoke."

"Roger. Outside the smoke."

Huey gunships roared in and sprayed the jungle with machine gun, rocket, and automatic grenade launcher fire. Red tracers and orange fireballs lit up the jungle ten yards in front of the team. The Green Berets and Rangers could hear screams and shouts in Vietnamese.

"Now," Breed yelled. "Every second man, fall back to the river."

Crockett and a Ranger supported the wounded door gunner. Together, they stood in the Kingbee's rotor wash. From the riverbank, grit and spray kicked up around them. Crockett grabbed a rope. Together, he and the Ranger strapped the gunner into a McGuire rig. Crockett lifted him up and the Ranger stuck the man's good leg through a loop. Crudely splinted, his broken leg dangled like a wet noodle. The man shrieked with pain. Crockett pushed the man's arm through a canvas strap.

"Get on," Crockett ordered the Ranger. "Hold him."

There was no guarantee the wounded man wouldn't let go. He was so deranged by the pain, he could barely cling to the rope. The Ranger mounted another rope and linked arms with him.

A green tracer flashed through Crockett's ruck and knocked him down. Splattered against a rock on the riverbank. Stunned, Crockett watched the bullet fragments burn. Forced himself to his feet, waved another man over—one of the first team's Nung mercenaries.

Two Rangers, a Nung, and the man with a broken leg. The three others linked arms and crushed the wounded man to them. They might spend an hour in flight, dangling from the ropes. Together, they would try to keep him from falling.

Crockett looked up at the Kingbee's crew chief. Flashed the man a thumbs-up. Tran increased power and climbed above the canopy. Pitched nose-down and left the area, dragging his bizarre cargo. Four men on strings. Later, they would count over six hundred bullet holes in the aircraft. All the pilot's windows were shot out. It was a miracle Tran was not hit.

The eighteen echo was working the radio. Two A-1E Skyraiders had joined the fray. Armed with 20mm cannon and five-hundred-pound bombs. These planes, affectionately called "Spads," were propeller-driven bombers of World War Two vintage. They were known for their ability to carry ordnance and loiter for hours over a battle.

"We can't take the body with us," Crockett said. "It's too hot."

He scanned the perimeter, looking for Breed.

The third Kingbee thundered into position. The crew chief kicked McGuire rigs over the side. The sandbags plunged to earth, trailing coils of nylon rope.

"Hawk One from One-Three Uniform. We are abandoning the perimeter. Give us gun and bomb runs. At will, outside the smoke."

"Roger, One-Three Uniform. Guns and bombs outside the smoke."

"Bring it. We're pulling out."

The NVA charged. The remaining Ranger on the perimeter ran back toward Crockett. They raised their rifles and covered his withdrawal. Breed stayed at the perimeter, firing. NVA passed him on either side. He was being overrun.

"Go." Crockett pushed the radio operator toward the dangling ropes. The prop wash was a ferocious blast of shredded vegetation and grit. There was no leaving radio equipment to the enemy. The comms sergeant dropped his ruck, shouldered the radio, and grabbed the McGuire rig.

The Ranger reached the ropes. Dropped to a kneeling position, turned, and fired to cover Crockett and Breed.

The Spads swooped into action. The muzzles of their 20mm cannon flickered. Breed was at the very edge of the perimeter. The NVA were rushing him. Cannon shells struck ten feet away, breaking the NVA charge. Breed raised his arm to shield his eyes from shrapnel.

The planes disappeared in the distance. Nothing remained but the faint Doppler of their engines. Bowels and body parts draped the foliage. The enemy's sons and brothers, human animals defiled by the destructive technology of modern warfare. Breed turned and ran toward the riverbank.

The Ranger stuck one leg through a loop, grabbed a strap with his left hand.

The enemy swarmed toward them. NVA ran through the smoke, firing.

Crockett fired his CAR15.

The Spads banked, dove for a second pass.

With a spike bayonet, an NVA thrust at Breed. Breed deflected the weapon with the foregrip of his CAR15.

Smashed the receiver into the man's face. Jabbed the muzzle into his throat with such force the muzzle punched a hole in the man's trachea.

Breed ran toward Crockett. Bullets cracked, and he jerked in mid-stride. Tumbled on the riverbank.

Crockett got to his feet, ran to Breed.

The door gunner sprayed the NVA swarming the landing zone. A scythe of red tracers cut them down.

The Spads cut loose with cannon and dropped five-hundred-pound bombs. The tree line disintegrated into geysers of black earth, splintered trees, and foliage. The shock waves were so powerful the concussion knocked Crockett flat. He could see parts of Wilson Circles—condensed humidity—radiating from the explosions. A second later, the air rushed back to fill the vacuum. Sucked the breath from his lungs.

Crockett dragged Breed to his feet. Breed's tiger stripes were soaked black with blood. From his right hip, all the way down his leg. Crockett lifted him in a fireman's carry, ran toward the ropes.

They thrust Breed's good leg through a loop. The other three men clutched him in case he lost his grip. Crockett signaled the crew chief to climb.

The Kingbee began to rise. Crockett looked down as the riverbank fell away. He could see drops of blood trickling from the toe of Breed's jungle boot. Falling. Whipped away in the wind.

"YOUR FATHER WAS one heroic son of a bitch," Crockett says. "But he was well out of it. None of us thought we'd see the end of the war."

"But you did," I say.

"Yes. We all got hit more than once. Call it luck, divine intervention, whatever you like—we shouldn't be here."

Thomas rolls a cart into the sitting room. Sets huge plates of steak before us. In the center of the table, he sets out more plates. Piled high with roast potatoes, peas, and other sides.

We're a long way from the jungles of Laos and Vietnam.

# 6

## THE BLACK SHEEP

**South Vietnam, May 1972**

The late hour and Bourbon work their magic.

Heth excuses herself and goes upstairs to her apartment. Come morning, Crockett and Butler will hunt elk. The elk population has grown thin, but Crockett likes a challenge. If anything, he is intimately familiar with the animals. He spoke with Tall Deer, agreed to leave Big Black Leg alone. Two more seasons and the bull will be ready for harvest.

Crockett and Butler sit back and reminisce. Share their adventures. How many remain untold after fifty years? I sip my drink while they talk about what it was like to work for the CIA.

The old-timers look at me kindly.

In May of 1972, Crockett's life changed forever.

The Quonset hut squatted in the middle of Da Nang air base. Hidden among a hundred like it. Crockett sat at the back of the room, looked around at two dozen men. They sat in straight-backed chairs, classroom-style. A raised plywood dais occupied the front of the room. A single regional map of southeast Asia was pinned to the wall.

Most of the men wore tiger stripes. All were armed. The median age of the group was twenty-two. Not one was a day over thirty. Crockett knew them all. They were members of the recently disbanded MACV-SOG. The Military Assistance Command Vietnam – Studies and Observations Group.

The unit's name was meant to sound nerdy. It conveyed an interest in ethnology and culture. In fact, every man in the room was a Special Forces gunfighter. Every one had been wounded at least once, most several times. That boy over there, twenty-two years old, had five Purple Hearts. Three more than Crockett, who was the same age. Both were 1-0s, recon team leaders.

A man walked to the front of the room and stepped onto the dais. "Don't get up, gentlemen."

None of the soldiers were inclined to rise in the presence of a civilian. The man on the dais wore khaki trousers, a short-sleeved dress shirt, and an olive drab utility vest. Round, wire-rimmed glasses. Thin and hollow-chested, he looked like an academic.

"My name is Martin Fairchild." The man stood in the center of the dais, feet planted shoulder-width apart. He might have been thirty, an old man compared to those he was addressing. "I'm with the embassy. I'll keep this short and sweet."

Butler was among the men in the group. He caught Crockett's eye and winked. Fairchild had CIA written all over him.

"The United States is withdrawing from South Vietnam," Fairchild announced. "The South Vietnamese cannot win this war on their own."

"Look at that." Fairchild gestured at the map. "French Indochina. Vietnam looks like a long finger running north-to-south. Bordered by China to the north and the Gulf of Tonkin to the east. To the west are stacked Laos and Cambodia. Neutral, but the North Vietnamese use them freely. Run weapons and supplies down the Ho Chi Minh Trail. NVA regulars conduct attacks all along Vietnam's western border."

Crockett closed his eyes. Relished the frigid air conditioning. Fairchild wasn't telling them anything new. But it was over a hundred degrees outside. Crockett was in no hurry.

"You have all been drawn from MACV-SOG," Fairchild continued. "You have conducted deniable operations across the fence into Laos and Cambodia. Now MACV-SOG has been disbanded. You will be reassigned. How does a vacation in Bavaria sound?"

Crockett opened his eyes slowly. The men in the room were silent.

"I am here to engage in a little sheep-dipping," Fairchild said. "We cannot give the South Vietnamese official assistance. I am here to invite you to resign from the United States Army."

Fairchild paused.

"The Army and CIA have collaborated in the past," he said. "That won't do any longer. Deniability has to be absolute. This is voluntary, gentlemen. If you accept this option, you will never return to your military careers. If you do not want to be part of this program, leave now."

Not one man rose.

"Alright." Fairchild clasped his hands behind his back. "You will resign from the Army and sign contracts with shell corporations. Untraceable, controlled by the CIA.

"As soldiers, you were subject to the Uniform Code of Military Justice. As civilian contractors, the UCMJ will not apply to you. Understand the deep significance of these words, gentlemen. You will no longer be subject to military law. You will fall under civil law, such that exists.

"If you've had enough, walk away. There is no going AWOL from the CIA. Maintain your silence and quit. Your paychecks will stop. Your bonus will be forfeited. The Company will claw back payments you have not earned. Under certain circumstances, we may ensure you never work again. If you violate your secrecy agreement, you will be prosecuted. The Company pursues civil, not military, remedies. Any questions?"

Fairchild's words had sucked the air from the room. The men would abandon their military careers to pursue a new calling. They could not go back the way they came.

"You will operate under unlimited rules of engagement." Fairchild took a deep breath. "You operated that way in SOG. But you were Army. Did you wonder… What if they hang me out to dry? Not a pleasant thought, is it? The distinction between Title 10 and Title 50 accountability is not academic. It has real legal consequences. Title 10 of the US Code governs the military. Title 50 governs the CIA and covert operations.

"Under this arrangement, you are civilians. Military courts have no jurisdiction over you. When you are in the field, anything that moves is the enemy. You are free to kill any perceived threat. You all speak three languages. If you are captured, you will not speak English. You will find no help from the United States. But neither will you face American retribution. I think that's fair, don't you?"

I'M AWARE OF SHEEP-DIPPING. In Afghanistan and Iraq, I met civilian contractors. Former operators. After they retired, a number of my friends signed contracts with the CIA. Some deliberately resigned so they could work for the Company. Lots of handlebar mustaches and cowboy boots. 1911s stuffed in hip pockets.

Some things never change.

Crockett and Butler touch their glasses and grin at me.

"We went back into action," Butler says. "Didn't miss a beat."

"Why?" I ask. "Were you that committed to the cause?"

"We all had our reasons." Butler pours himself another glass of Bourbon. "We believed in the war, we believed we would win. When they pulled us out, it was a kick in the balls."

Crockett leans forward. "We were integrated with the indigenous troops. Montagnards, South Vietnamese Special Forces, Nung mercenaries. We owed our lives to South Vietnamese Air Force Kingbee pilots. On strings and ladders, they dragged us from the jungle. Under fire. When the high command pulled us out, we left them to fight and die alone. It was a betrayal."

When the chips are down, you don't fight for God and country. You fight for the men to your left and right. Every man in a shell hole is a brother. I know exactly what Crockett is talking about.

"I couldn't live with myself if I took a post in Bavaria while our little people were massacred." Crockett looks to Butler for confirmation.

"That's the long and short of it." Butler drains his Bourbon. "By joining the Black Sheep, we could stay in the fight."

"The Black Sheep?" I ask.

"Can you think of a better name?" Crockett laughs. "We didn't exist."

# 7

## THE ELK HUNT

**Salish Rock, Montana**

"Breed, come in."

Heth's voice crackles from the walkie-talkie on my kitchen table. I haven't heard from either her or Crockett for two days. Figured they were busy with Butler and the lodge.

I pick up the handset, key the transmit button. "Hi, what's up?"

"I need your help, Breed. Mr Butler's been shot, and grandfather's missing."

"What happened?"

"They went hunting yesterday. Grandfather and I check in with each other by ham radio twice a day. He didn't check in last night. When he didn't check in this morning, I called the police. They found his truck out by Salish Rock. Found Mr Butler shot dead in the woods. No sign of my grandfather."

"I'll be right over."

. . .

Salish Rock, a brooding outcrop of granite, towers over the tall fir trees that cover the mountainside. The road is dark and heavily shadowed by forest. I see black-and-yellow police tape before I see vehicles.

"There," Heth says.

I pull over and park the Bronco next to the cordon.

Without waiting for me, Heth gets out and strides to a Sheriff's deputy standing by the road. "I'm Heth Crockett," she says. "My grandfather is up there."

The deputy holds up his hand. "Wait a minute. I'll get someone to take you up."

Heth kicks at gravel. The young man raises a walkie-talkie to his ear. Turns away to speak.

It's cold and damp in the shade. I thrust my hands deep in my jacket pockets. On the other side of the cordon, I see a small clearing. Sam's red Hilux, an ambulance, two Sheriff's cruisers, two Tribal Police cruisers. The grass has been crushed flat into the mud.

I look up and down the road. It's impossible to tell how many vehicles have driven this way and parked in the clearing.

Paramedics slam the rear doors of the ambulance, get in, and start the engine. Heth looks anxious.

"They're taking the victim away," the deputy explains. "Everyone is still up there, looking for you grandfather."

"Who do you think did the shooting?" Heth asks.

"Hunting accident," the deputy says. "The pickup was the only vehicle parked when we arrived. If the shooter was here, he's gone. If he parked somewhere on the other side of the rock, he might still be out there."

I lift my face to the sound of helicopter rotors. A twin-bladed Huey with police markings thunders overhead. Sheriff's deputies with binoculars sit at the open doors.

The minutes tick by. The deputy hasn't been to the crime scene. He has nothing more to tell us.

"For heaven's sake," Heth fumes. "How long is it going to take to get us up there?"

I check my watch. We've been waiting an hour.

At last, a young Tribal Policeman steps from the tree line and approaches. Good-looking kid. Mid-twenties, in dark pants, blue shirt, and a dark jacket. Daniel Running Bear. Went to high school with Heth. He joined the Tribal Police, she went to college. He acknowledges me with a nod, turns away.

"Heth."

"Dan."

The Tribal cop raises the police tape so Heth and I can cross. "We haven't found your grandfather yet. Captain Morris wants to speak with you."

"I want to speak with him."

Running Bear leads us into the woods. When I was younger, I hunted around Salish Rock. This side of the rock, close to Flathead Lake, is steep and heavily forested. The rock itself is flanked by ridges that slope down to the Swan River Valley. Beyond the river, more woods. Slopes that mount in elevation until one finds oneself among the Rockies.

Elk, deer, and other animals are drawn to the river and adjacent ponds for water. A patient hunter can stake out the ground from the ridges, or stalk his prey in the woods. Heth's the best hunter in the valley because of her talent for reading the wind. She understands its capricious nature, anticipates its gusts and reversals. Maneuvers to stay downwind of prey that can smell her at three hundred yards.

People give Heth their elk and deer tags so she can put food on their table.

Running Bear leads us through the woods. Heth follows him, and I bring up the rear. I've spent my life in the woods. I can sense the slope of the trail. I know where to put my feet, how to maneuver while leaving minimal trace of my passage. Heth amazes me. She moves with the fluidity of a ghost. I find myself working to keep up.

"How long ago was Butler killed," I ask.

"At least twenty hours," Running Bear says. "There was no rigor."

Rigor mortis is complete eight hours after death. The condition might persist for another twelve before disappearing. The county medical examiner will develop a more precise estimate.

It took Running Bear an hour to reach us. It'll take an hour for him to lead us to the scene. I decide to save my breath.

We step onto the ridge and break into daylight. High on our left looms the bulky shoulder of Salish Rock. Sheriff's deputies and Tribal Police have formed another cordon. Technicians from the Montana Highway Patrol forensic lab are photographing the scene.

Above, the Huey runs a search pattern. It's covering the slope between the ridge and Swan River.

Running Bear leads us to a middle-aged man in Tribal Police uniform. Introduces us to Captain Morris.

"Miss Crockett." Morris greets us. "Mr Breed."

"Have you found my grandfather?" Heth asks.

"I'm afraid not," Morris says. He looks uncomfortable. "Look, I don't want to worry you, but we think he's wounded."

"Wounded." Heth stares incredulously. "How many shots were fired?"

The captain rubs the back of his neck. "At least two. One shot killed Butler instantly."

"And the second?" Heth is trembling.

"Butler died *here*," Morris says. He points to a two-foot long plastic stake driven into the forest floor near the edge of the ridge. A stain darkens the earth for several square feet beyond the chalk boundary. "We've found blood on the ridge and the foliage over *there*."

Forensic technicians are photographing the brush. Vegetation that lines the ridge between us and Salish Rock. Heth and I walk cautiously toward them. We move along the edge, careful to avoid white circles drawn on the ground. Technicians spray luminol on the foliage. A wide swath extends down the reverse slope. They are picking their way from the ridgeline into the forest and toward the Swan River.

Heth's voice is clotted with emotion. "A second shot hit my grandfather."

"Was Butler's rifle fired?" I ask.

"No," Morris says. "He dropped it when he was hit, a .308 Remington Model 700."

"Crockett carried a .308 Winchester Model 70," I say. "A Pre-64. Did you find it?"

"No. We reckon he was hit by the second shot, crawled through the brush, carried the rifle with him."

Heth's eyes burn with rage. "Any sign of the other party?"

Morris shakes his head. "No. They've had twenty hours. Could be long gone."

"Grandfather was lying here," Heth says to herself. "Mr Butler had his rifle out. They were looking down-slope to the east."

"So?" Morris frowns.

Heth points at the tree line a hundred and fifty yards down-slope from the ridge. "We've hunted here before. You find elk or deer at the edge of the forest. But if the wind shifts on you, they're gone. The other hunting party wouldn't be stalking in the woods this time of year. Back in bow hunting season, but not now."

I see her point. Bow hunters will be looking for kills

inside sixty yards. It's unlikely rifle hunters would stalk in the woods when a clear shot is available from the ridge.

A switch clicks in my mind. I look at the field like a soldier.

"Butler was killed with one shot," I observe.

"Got him through the chest," Morris says.

"Okay. So a mistake has been made. Butler falls dead. What does Crockett do?"

"Identify himself." Morris squints at the tree line. "Yell for the other guys to cease fire."

"Exactly. Instead of putting up their rifles, they fire a second time, and Crockett is hit."

"The other bunch are panicky."

I shake my head. "Crockett hits the dirt. Checks Butler's condition. He should look for cover, retreat toward the road."

"The bloodstains..."

"...lead along the ridge, then through the brush down the reverse slope."

"Yes, that's why we've got the chopper searching between here and the river."

Heth stares at me. "Breed?"

I step off the ridge and walk toward the tree line. A hundred and fifty yards. It's not far. An easy shot unless an elk catches wind of you. Heth, Morris, and Running Bear follow me.

At the tree line, I stop and turn. Squint at the ridge. Salish Rock to the right, it's like I thought. The ridge runs north-south above the forest. Figures on the ridge are silhouetted from below. Not a concern for a hunter. Deadly for a soldier.

It's not hard to follow the tree line. I walk a hundred yards north to the shadow of the Rock, then turn and slowly make my way back. The police should have done this hours ago, but the ground looks undisturbed.

"Here," I say.

Took me a while. I had to travel a hundred and fifty yards back the way I came, but I wanted to be thorough. I point to a spot inside the tree line where the brush has been flattened. Already, the brush and long grass are resuming their undisturbed shape. I bend and look at the forest floor.

"The other party was here," I say.

The flattened brush lies next to a sapling. I examine the trunk. Shoulder-height, the bark has been scraped.

"One man," Running Bear says.

"Yes," Heth agrees. "But no shell casings."

"The shooter stopped to pick up his brass."

"He decided to run," Morris says, "rather than call for help."

I say nothing. Turn and start back toward the ridge.

"Breed, where are you going?" Heth runs after me.

"Back to the lodge. If we start now, we'll get back before dark."

Heth grabs my arm. "We can't leave grandfather out here!"

My voice is gentle. "He's not out here."

# 8

## THE CHASE

### Crockett Lodge

We retrace our steps and return to the Bronco. I get in, slam the door, and start the engine. Frowning, Heth piles into the passenger seat.

"If Grandfather isn't out there, where is he?"

I back around with a crunch of gravel. Throw the truck into gear and head for the highway. Keep my eyes on the road, focus on getting us to Crockett Lodge in one piece.

"That was no hunting accident," I say.

"What?"

"You heard me. Butler was shot by a sniper in the tree line. The shooter stalked them. Waited till they presented a nice target silhouetted on that ridge."

"Why do you think that?"

"It's the only theory that fits the facts. The killer stood by the tree and fastened a cord around the trunk. Might have been his belt. Stuck his rifle through, twisted it in place to provide tension. I'm guessing Sam and Butler saw an elk at the tree line. Maybe they didn't have a good angle, maybe the wind shifted. In any case, they didn't take the shot. Butler stood up, rifle in hand, and the gunman took him out."

"In cold blood."

"That's what snipers do. Sam thought it was another hunter. Dropped down, probably yelled a warning. The killer fired again, but Sam was already a difficult target. The killer only wounded him.

"Sam knows the difference between cover and concealment. He crawled along the ridge, a bit back off the edge and out of sight. That way, the ridge offered protection and the shooter couldn't tell which way Sam was going. When he'd gone about twenty-five yards, Sam stopped. He tied a tourniquet around his wound and started crawling *toward* the shooter."

"That's why the blood trail extended toward the river."

"Yes. But the blood trail will peter out, because Sam got the bleeding under control. He had his rifle, he was maneuvering for a shot."

"So why isn't he out there?"

"I don't have all the answers, because I don't know why someone was trying to kill him. I don't know if Butler was the primary target or if it was the other way around. I don't know if the killer was trying to get them both."

I glance at Heth. "In any event, Sam must want to get the killer himself, rather than wait for the police. I think the killer got away, and Sam headed back to the lodge."

"Why wouldn't he take his truck?"

"There was a risk the killer staked out the truck. The killer's vehicle may have been parked in the same clearing. For his own reasons, Sam might have wanted to leave everything a mystery to buy time."

Heth stares straight ahead. The sun is low. The forest cloaks the road in shadow, and I flick on the brights. "Time for what?" she asks.

"I don't know. But Sam has had plenty of time to hike back to the ranch. Without a ruck, carrying a rifle. Off-road, he could have made the twenty miles in eight hours."

"Wounded."

"The wound wasn't serious, he got the bleeding under control. In Laos, your grandfather survived terrible wounds."

"Why didn't you tell this to the police?"

"First, it's *their* job to put evidence together and draw conclusions. Second, there is a more important question."

"What's that?"

"Why didn't *Sam* go to the police? Assuming he escaped, he's had ample time to reach out to them—by telephone or radio. Sam's *my* friend and *your* grandfather. Whatever Sam has going on, I don't want to sabotage him by acting rashly."

Troubled, Heth falls silent. I turn onto Highway 35 and head south. Crockett Lodge is minutes away.

"There's something else you haven't mentioned," Heth says.

"Tell me."

"Breed, if you're right, Grandfather returned to the lodge before I called you."

I PULL the Bronco into the parking lot of Crockett Lodge. It's early evening, and most of the bungalows are dark. The guests are out dining. Some have gone into Pablo, others are at the lodge restaurant. It's open for dinner, and guests are enjoying the night air on the patio.

"What now?" Heth asks.

"I think you're right," I tell her. "Your grandfather returned to the lodge long before the police called you. That means he snuck in. Had any of the employees noticed him return, they would have said something. Either to him, or to you. Your apartments are duplexes. Accessible either from the lodge, or by private entrances.

"Let's say Butler was killed noon yesterday, though it could have been earlier. You called the police first thing this morning. The police were on the ball and found Butler's body by noon. That means your grandfather could have returned to the lodge as early as last night. Long before you reported him missing."

"I looked all over for him."

"Yes, but did you really *look*? Did you open his bedroom door and go inside? Check the bathroom? Did you look inside his study, or open the door and call his name? I'm saying you *looked*, but you didn't *search*. There are different kinds of searches. There's a search meant to find a person who is preoccupied. Another meant to find a person who is injured and unable to call for help. Yet another search is meant to find a person who does not want to be found. Which one did you conduct?"

"Not the last kind." Heth looks miserable. "But why would grandfather hide from me?"

"That's another mystery, isn't it? Another reason we're not telling the police anything until we've spoken with him."

Heth dismounts from the Bronco and slams the door. "Okay," she says. "Let's do the search I should have done in the first place."

"ANTONIO," Heth snaps.

"Yes, Miss Heth." The night manager rushes to the front desk.

"I'll be with Mr Breed in our living quarters. See that we're not disturbed."

"Yes, Miss Heth."

The girl takes the stairs two at a time. Leads me to the

north wing of the lodge. Her apartment is on the east side, facing the mountains. Crockett's apartment is on the west, with a lake view.

Heth opens the door to Crockett's rooms.

Before us stretches a comfortable library and den. A big mahogany desk faces picture windows that look onto Flathead Lake. Against one wall stands a mahogany gun cabinet. Against another wall, a steel gun safe. Through a door to the right is Sam's bedroom and private bathroom. On the left, a set of French doors open to a sunroom and balcony.

We enter Sam's bedroom. King-sized bed, walk-in closet. Nothing looks out of place.

"Breed."

Heth has lifted the lid on a hamper in the bathroom. Inside are a blood-stained shirt and jacket. Blood-soaked bandages. Needle and thread.

"Looks like Sam stitched himself up."

"Shot in the arm," Heth observes. She holds up the bloody shirt with a torn sleeve. "You were right."

I go into Sam's study, survey the gun cabinet. "What's missing?" I ask. "Do you see his Winchester?"

Heth scans the shotguns and rifles. The chain strung through the trigger guards is secure. She takes a set of keys from her jeans pocket and unlocks the cabinet drawers. Inside are boxes of ammunition. "I can't be sure," she says, "but I think he's taken a box of .308 and fifty rounds of .45 ACP."

The gun safe is secured by a combination lock. Heth's fingers spin the dial. She turns a handle and hauls the door open. Inside are an array of automatic weapons. An M110 sniper rifle, an M4 carbine, a suppressed M3 grease gun. Magazines of ammunition and stripper clips.

"His 1911 is gone," Heth says. "So is his SOG knife."

SOG operators were issued special Bowie knives. Blades

that could not be traced to their country of origin. Not many SOG knives made it home. Those that did are treasured collector's pieces. My father's sits in my footlocker.

Heth closes the door and locks the safe.

Crockett has taken a long rifle, a sidearm, and a knife. A hundred rounds of ammunition. Not much ammo, but both .308 and .45 are easy to come by.

"Your grandfather's ready to go to war," I tell Heth.

"But why?"

I step to Crockett's desk. On the desk is a black-and-white photograph of Crockett and five other men in tiger stripes. The same photograph blown up and hung on the wall of the sitting room downstairs.

Crockett, Butler, Mosby, Spears, Stroud and Appleyard.

Appleyard—missing in action, presumed dead.

The rest of the men, a hundred and ten percent casualties. Each wounded more than once. MACV-SOG, then the Black Sheep.

My eyes stray to Crockett's landline. I press a button and a display lights up with recent incoming calls. Nothing today.

"Do you have your own landline?" I ask Heth.

"Yes. I moved into the lodge on the condition Grandfather allowed me privacy."

Of course. That's why her police call didn't come through Crockett's phone.

I press another button and the display pages to outgoing calls. Conveniently, it shows the contact's name and the time of call.

Mosby – 0635
Spears – 0647

"What is it?" Heth asks.

"Your grandfather made two phone calls this morning.

One to Mosby, another to Spears. Do you know where they live?"

"California. Mosby is in San Francisco. I'm not sure where Spears is. He owns a knife-making business and a dojo. A small town near San Luis Obispo."

I look for Crockett's mobile phone, it's nowhere to be found. It's unlikely to be much use. With spotty mobile reception, we rely on landlines, walkie-talkies, CB, and ham radio.

There is a laptop.

"Do you know his password?" I ask.

Heth shakes her head.

I scan the desktop. There, in one corner, a leather address book. Trust a seventy-year-old to have low-tech habits. I flip the pages, find Mosby and Spears, copy their details onto a piece of paper. Fold it and put it in my pocket. Stroud is not listed.

"Six men," Heth says.

"Four," I correct her. "Appleyard and Butler are dead."

"Grandfather telephoned two of them."

I search the landline's contact list. "Stroud isn't stored in either the phone or the address book."

"Grandfather and his friends talked about him as though he was difficult."

"In what way?"

"They thought he was involved in illegal activities."

"Interesting crew," I say. "It looks like Mosby is closest to us, followed by Spears. Care to bet your grandfather is on his way to visit them?"

"No bet," Heth says. "But why?"

The photograph, I fold into my pocket. The frame, I stow in a desk drawer. I punch buttons on the phone. Find "clear" on the menu, erase the phone's memory.

I look into Heth's blue eyes.

"Let's ask him."

# 9

## MOSBY

### Kalispell to San Francisco

"We can beat Sam to San Francisco," I say.

"How?"

"We have to fly." I look about myself. "The lodge has internet. Can we use yours?"

Heth leads me to her apartment. The floor plan is a copy of Sam's but there is more space. Heth has fewer things. A bookshelf with schoolbooks from her college years. Mostly books on engineering and ballistics. A handful of novels. An open laptop rests on a table by the window.

In common with Crockett, Heth owns a collection of rifles and a locked cabinet. She has a Remington Model 700, an M4, an M14, and a Winchester '96 lever action. A selection of shotguns. All have been racked with a chain through their trigger guards.

"Sam's not carrying weapons and ammo onto a plane," I tell her. "That means he's driving. I'm guessing it's an eighteen-hour drive to San Francisco. Twenty-four, because he had to hike off-road to Pablo, steal a car, and get some rest. If he left right away, he'll arrive eight o'clock tomorrow morning. We have to get out of here tonight."

Heth fires up her laptop and we browse flights to San Francisco. There aren't many. Most fly out of Kalispell, on the northern tip of Flathead Lake.

"This flight leaves in an hour," Heth says. "If we miss it, there isn't another till six tomorrow morning."

I buy the tickets, ignore the "non-refundable" warning. No time to pack. Heth takes Crockett's bloody clothes and bandages out of the hamper. She wraps them in towels, and stuffs them in a garbage bag. Takes them into her bathroom and locks the door to the apartment.

We hurry downstairs, get in the Bronco, and race over Highway 35 to Kalispell.

IT WON'T TAKE LONG for the Sheriff's department and the Tribal Police to figure we're gone. They'll phone the lodge, then visit. Then they'll put two and two together. Figure Sam's alive and we've either joined him, or gone looking for him.

They won't know what's going on. Only Crockett knows that. But they will revise their assessment of the incident. Butler's death will be moved from the "hunting accident" file to "homicide." They won't necessarily suspect us, or Crockett. Their lab will determine it was his blood on the ground at Salish rock. They will consider us persons of interest in a wrongful death.

We deplane at Terminal 1 in San Francisco. I half expect to see police waiting, but there isn't a badge in sight. I lead the way past the car rentals and into a big parking lot. Uncomfortable, Heth stands watch as I hot-wire an old Taurus sedan. It's only nine-thirty, so I drive to Mosby's address.

Mosby is on the top floor of a small, three-story building

in the Outer Richmond district. I park in an alley off the main street and we stare at the lights.

I look at Heth. "Let's try calling Sam."

"You think he has reception now?"

"I'd bet on it," I tell her. "That's not the question. He's probably gone silent."

Heth hits a speed-dial, lifts the phone to her ear. She shakes her head. "Straight to voicemail."

I exhale, puff my cheeks, and fish the phone numbers out my pocket. "We have to do it sometime. Call Mosby."

"Can't *you* do it?"

"Mosby doesn't know me from Adam. You're Sam's granddaughter. He'll speak to you."

"Can't we do this tomorrow? Grandfather will be in town then."

"Sam's driving because he's carrying weapons. If the killer wanted to beat Sam here, he'd travel by air like we did."

"He could be here already."

"That's the math."

Heth squints at the paper. Punches numbers into her phone.

"Mr Mosby? I'm Sam Crockett's granddaughter. Something terrible has happened. Mr Butler's been killed in a hunting accident and my grandfather's been shot. We think he's coming to see you."

There's a muffled voice from the other end of the connection. Heth's brow furrows.

"I know it's not a convenient time, Mr Mosby. Please. I'm very worried about my grandfather."

I assume Mosby is giving in. "I got your address from my grandfather," Heth says. "I'll be there in a few minutes."

Heth disconnects the call, stuffs the phone into her hip pocket. "He's not happy, but he'll see me."

"Was it Mosby's voice?"

"I don't know. I've never heard Mosby speak."

"How old was the person speaking?"

"Middle-aged. Not a boy."

That tells me nothing.

Heth looks worried. "You think the shooter might have Mosby's phone?"

"We can't rule it out. He's had plenty of time to get here."

I open the door of our stolen Taurus, step into the alley. If I'm right, and the shooter took a plane to San Francisco, he's probably unarmed. That's a comforting equalizer.

On the other hand, this is America. You can pick up a gun anywhere.

"Let's go."

Heth unbuckles her seat belt, gets out of the car, and slams the door.

I quarter the ground. Scan the cars parked on either side of the street. Check the dark alleyways, the high places. Nothing.

Heth and I are wild cards. The killer may or may not know who we are. Either way, he's not expecting us.

We cross the street and climb the stoop. There are buzzers and six mailboxes. Two apartments to a floor. Number five has Mosby's name on it.

A strong voice answers Heth's buzz. "Come on up."

There is a metallic click as the front door is unlocked. I pull on the handle and we step into the foyer. There is a staircase and a small elevator.

We take the elevator to the third floor, find ourselves in a hall. At one end is the interior stairwell. To our right, at the far end, is a fire exit. Between the elevator and the stairs are doors to two apartments.

A large copper numeral 5 is screwed to the face of one door. Below the number is a small fisheye lens.

"Stand to one side," I tell Heth, "then knock on the door."

Heth follows my instructions to the letter.

The doorknob turns, and the wooden slab swings open.

The interior of the apartment is dark. A hulking figure has opened the door and stepped back into the shadows. This man knows what he is doing. Heth and I stand lighted in the hall, he has the cover of darkness.

More than that.

In the man's hand is a pistol, a Colt 1911.

# 10

## COMING HOME

### Mosby's Apartment

"Stand in the light, girl," the man says. "The big guy, too. Keep your hands where I can see them."

We stand side by side.

"I'm Heth."

"Sure enough, you have Crockett's look." The man points the 1911's muzzle at my chest. "Who's he?"

Heth swallows. "Breed's helping me find Grandfather."

"Breed." The man squints at me. "You the son of Crockett's friend?"

"Yes."

"Damned if you don't look exactly like him."

The man raises the 1911, brushes the thumb safety into place. The single-action Colt remains cocked and locked. "Come inside," he says. "Close the door behind you. Light switch on the wall."

Heth locks the door behind us, puts on the chain. I reach for the switch and flick on the lights.

Mosby is a large man, over six feet. Whereas Crockett is

rawboned and rangy, Mosby is big and barrel-chested. His hair has gone white, and he has a hint of a spare tire that stretches his white Polo shirt. His right arm is covered by a sleeve of tattoos. His wrists are thick, the forearms muscular.

"Sit down," Mosby says. He gestures us to a sofa, goes to the kitchen. "Offer you a drink? Whiskey or beer."

"Beer sounds good," I tell him.

"Same, please." Heth's voice is small.

Mosby stuffs the 1911 into his waistband. He takes two cans of beer out of the fridge. For himself, he finds a whiskey glass and a bottle of Crown Royal. Carries the lot to the living room and sets them on the coffee table. "Help yourselves."

Mosby takes the pistol from his waistband, sets it on a side table, and lowers himself into an easy chair. He sits kitty-corner from the sofa.

"Sam told me he wouldn't get here before morning," Mosby says. "It'll be a long night."

On his right hand, he wears a diamond pinky ring. Picks up the whiskey bottle, squints at it, and uses the ring to scratch the glass. The line is a quarter of the way down from the neck.

"Not one drop more." Mosby winks at me, pours himself three fingers.

"What did Crockett tell you?" I ask.

Mosby shrugs. "Someone shot Butler and tried to kill him too."

"Did he say why?"

"It's because of what the Black Sheep did in 1974."

"What did the Black Sheep do in 1974?"

Mosby squints at me. "That's classified, son. Besides, it isn't obvious to me why anyone would want to kill us *now* over what happened in 1974."

"Crockett knows."

"He has a theory, but he wouldn't tell me over the phone. He said he would fill me in when he got here."

"You have no idea why your lives are in danger?"

"Absolutely not. I haven't thought about that mission in fifty years. Ran through it in my head all day."

Desperate for answers, I grasp for more. "When you got back, you must have been debriefed."

"Yes, we were."

"Didn't anything stand out?"

"Details surfaced that were relevant to the military situation of the day. Nothing that would be pertinent fifty years later."

We've hit a dead end. There's nothing to do but wait for Crockett.

I pop my beer and drink. Get to my feet, step to the window. With two fingers, I lift the curtain an inch and peer into the darkness.

Mosby sips his whiskey. "No need to worry, Breed."

"No?"

"No taller buildings in the vicinity. We occupy an elevated position."

"But not a 360-degree view."

"No," Mosby concedes. "But no one can take a shot through that window, and no one is climbing through."

I'm not so sure about that. Were I instructed to take Mosby's apartment, I would send a team to the roof and rappel to the window.

"Did you come home in 1974?" Heth asks.

"Yes." Mosby relaxes. "We were all wounded. Spears and I were sent to the hospital at Fort Miley. Crockett was in better shape. He was treated briefly at Fort Lewis. Butler and Stroud went to Fayetteville."

Heth leans forward. "Did you leave the Army?"

"We'd *all* left the Army in 1972. We received medical treatment by special arrangement as veterans. The Company made certain no questions were asked. I'd been shot twice and had shrapnel all across my back and legs. The worst was shrapnel that fractured my hip. Did you know pain has colors? I saw colors. They gave me morphine. I went through a dozen surgeries. Doctors couldn't believe I walked out of the jungle."

Mosby drains his glass, pours another four fingers. Stares at Heth. "Don't look at me like that, girl. I made my mark and I will drink no further."

"I believe you," Heth whispers.

I study Mosby. The old man looks sober.

"I lost it for a while," Mosby says. "The morphine took over. Halfway through the physiotherapy, I decided to recover without the morphine. That's when I started drinking."

Heth sits quietly. I cast my eyes over the apartment.

Two bedrooms. Kitchen, dining area, and living room. Clean and tidy. It looks like he lives alone. A vase of flowers on the dining table provides a feminine touch. A girlfriend, perhaps. One who visits, but doesn't live here.

Mosby looks at me. "You know about drinking, Breed?"

"Some."

Delta was fun. Drink till six in the morning, go for a ten-mile run at seven. It was part of the culture. You can do that in your twenties.

"Holly waited for me. When I got back, I couldn't live with her. Doctors said I would never be the same, and Holly said she'd take care of me. I couldn't accept that. I'm not a mean drunk, but I'm an angry drunk. I had to be mad to do what I had to do. I worked my ass off to get my arm back and walk normally. Holly walked, too."

"Maybe," Heth says, "you could have asked her to leave until you got through it. Then she could come back."

Mosby smiles ruefully. "I wish I had. But I wasn't thinking straight."

"No one thinks straight when they're in that place," I tell him.

"I suppose not. When Holly left, I drank more. I was discharged, got a job. Got fired, found another job. Lost that one. Spears came to see me. Told me I was a fuck up. Told me he could smell fuck up all over me. I punched him and he kicked my ass. Made me go to therapy at the Fort Miley VA."

"You quit drinking?" Heth looks skeptical.

"As a matter of fact, no." Mosby cracks a smile. "I took one-on-one therapy. I was drinking because of some really deep shit. No twelve-step program would get to that."

Makes sense to me. Maybe I should talk to someone about my dreams.

What am I going to say? *Hey, man. I shot some women who flayed our POWs alive. The Army suggested I leave.*

Fuck that noise. I'm not talking to anyone about that.

Mosby drains his second glass.

"MACV-SOG operators were killed in Laos and Cambodia," Mosby says. "Their families were told they died in Vietnam. We took the war to the enemy. Came back and couldn't talk about it. Not to a shrink, not to a priest. We fought for our country and they called us baby-killers."

Troops came home from the first Gulf War and the country threw them a parade. Guys who came home from Vietnam were hated. MACV-SOG guys like Mosby and Crockett disappeared in silence.

Mosby fondles the 1911. "Hey, Breed."

"Yes."

"A PKM crew is slaughtering your platoon. Would you shoot a ten-year-old carrying their ammo?"

I say nothing.

"I thought so." Mosby laughs bitterly. "Welcome to the

self-help generation. Everybody's an expert. I told my doc I wasn't going to quit drinking. He told me that was fine. We negotiated this system. I make my mark and that's my limit."

"Dude," I say. "If you're strong enough to kill the enemy and teach yourself to walk all over again, you're strong enough to do anything."

"Fuckin' A." Mosby caps the bottle. "I squared my shit away. Used the GI Bill to get a degree. Now I counsel at the VA."

I take another look out the window. Traffic passes. On the sidewalk, a couple walk arm-in-arm. I wonder who killed Butler. It must have been a professional like myself, Crockett, or Mosby. On any number of sides. The question is which side and why.

Mosby takes out his wallet. Inside is a picture of an attractive woman. He holds it up for us to see. She's forty years old. Brown hair, open features.

"I have a thing for Hollies," Mosby laughs. "This is Holly 2."

I smile. "She's nice."

"I made my peace with Holly One," the old man says. "We're close, but it'll never be the same. We send each other cards at Christmas."

"No going back," I say.

"No. I won't fuck it up with Holly Two." Mosby turns from me to Heth. "She'll move in next month. The place needs a woman's touch."

Shouts echo from the hall. As one, our heads jerk toward the door.

There's a gritty smell in the air. Smoke.

The fire alarm goes off.

# 11

## KANG

### Mosby's Apartment

The fire alarm whoops.

It's so loud you can't hear yourself think. Mosby snatches his pistol from the table and rushes to the door. I grab him by the arm. "You know what this is, don't you?"

Mosby turns to me. "We need to assess."

"Let me go first," I say. "Cover me."

I step to the door. Already, it's hot to the touch. Tendrils of smoke curl from the crack at the bottom. I undo the chain and pull the door open.

The hall and staircase are in flames. A young couple have frozen in the doorway of Apartment 6. The woman is screaming. A sharp smell permeates the air. Volatilized accelerant.

"The staircase is on fire." I slam the door shut. "We have to run for the fire escape."

"Metal stairs. Through the fire door."

I rush into Mosby's bedroom, find the toilet. Grab as many towels as I can and soak them in water from the bathtub tap. I must have half a dozen. Throw two to each of Mosby and Heth, drape the others over my head and shoulders.

"He'll pick us off on the steps," I say. "I'll draw his fire. Mosby, you follow. When he shoots, spot his muzzle flash and get him."

No time for a decision tree. I throw the door open. A blast of heat flares in my face. Flames consume the wallpaper, fed by accelerant and ancient glue that has impregnated the walls. I cover myself with the soaking towel and dash to the left. I catch a glimpse of the man from Apartment 6 falling down the staircase, a human torch. There's no sign of the woman.

The fire door is steel. It has one of those long metal handles you open with your elbows. I bang through and a blast of cold air hits me in the face.

Screams.

The fire stairs are mats of iron bars with less than an inch separation between them. Tenants from the second floor are scrambling to safety. I glance over my shoulder. Mosby is there, Heth right behind him. We cast aside our wet towels.

In the distance, I hear the sound of sirens. I rush down the stairs. Hit the second floor, grab a metal rail, swing myself onto a switchback. Keep going. As I hurry down the fire escape, my eyes sweep the street, the alleys, the cars. I'm looking for any sign of a gunman. I expect the impact of a bullet any second.

Nothing.

One last switchback and I hit the pavement of the alley outside. Dark, shadowy, deserted. Parked cars and dumpsters. Twenty feet away, a crowd has gathered on the street. Swallowed the tenants from the second floor. People stare at the burning building, point at the upper floors. Roaring flames engulf the wooden structure. Timbers split with cracks loud as gunshots... The roof falls in.

Behind me, a cry. A blur of motion, the thud of a body hitting the pavement. Heth's been flung aside like a rag doll. Her head hits the metal side of a dumpster.

Mosby swings around, raises his pistol.

In the garish light of a street lamp—a figure in a dark suit. Broad Asian features, wavy black hair. Not more than five-ten, but muscular. Built like a tank. He seizes the wrist of Mosby's gun hand. Pounds the heel of his free hand into Mosby's nose. The veteran's head bounces like a flower on a stalk.

The Asian twists the 1911 out of Mosby's grasp and turns it on him. Before Mosby can react, the killer shoots him twice in the chest.

Mosby's down. I'm staring over the black bore of the 1911. Behind it, the killer's dead eyes. I dive behind a car parked at the side of the alley. Squatting with my back to the vehicle's grille, I chance a look back. The killer stands in the middle of the alley, feet shoulder-width apart.

"Breed, I'm not here for you and the girl." The killer's voice is calm, conversational. He speaks with a flawless American accent. "Stay away."

He fires a third time into Mosby's face.

Nothing I can do. Heth is slumped against the dumpster. The killer turns and strides back along the alley. Disappears around a corner.

I get to my feet, walk to Heth. She's groggy, supports herself against the dumpster. I help her stand. The people on the street are preoccupied with the fire. They haven't noticed the action in the dark alley. Three shots. They sounded like backfires, lost in the whooping of the fire alarm, the roar of the blaze, the cracking of timber.

"Let's go," I say.

Mosby's a crumpled sack on the pavement. Two bullets in the chest and a third, execution style, in the face.

"Why didn't he kill us?" Heth asks.

Heth and I lose ourselves in the crowd, make our way to the parked Taurus.

"He's a professional," I tell her. "Mosby was the target. He could have killed us, but we weren't on his list. He saw no benefit in our deaths."

Heth gets into the car, slams her door shut. "He was so cold," she says. "The way he went about killing was so cold."

I climb in behind the wheel, repeat the hot-wiring process. The engine rumbles to life. With the headlights off, I back the car out of the alley and drive away.

"There's no question," I say, "he's out to eliminate Sam's entire team. He's killed Butler and Mosby. Spears and Stroud have to be next. Sam is a moving target. This guy's good. He'll improvise."

"Why didn't he wait for Grandfather to arrive?"

"The odds were stacking against him. He knows who we are. He staked out Sam and Butler before following them into the woods. We'll find he was a guest at another lodge in the area around Flathead. He might even have been a guest at Crockett Lodge. Do you remember seeing any Asian guests in the past week?"

Heth shakes her head.

"Had Sam shown up, the killer would have had three trained opponents to cope with, two of them armed. He decided to take out Mosby while he could. This guy's very deliberate. He won't make another move until he knows exactly how he is going to achieve his objective."

I pull into the parking lot of an all-night diner. Allow the engine to idle. I need to think.

Mosby is dead because of me. I failed to anticipate the killer's resourcefulness. In the burning hall, I smelled the sharp odor of accelerant. No fire could have spread so quickly without it. Gasoline thrown against the walls and down the stairs. The killer had all the time in the world to buy a gas can at Walmart. Buy gas at a nearby station or siphon it from cars parked on the street. We trapped ourselves on the third floor. Had we burned alive, the killer's job would have been done. But he anticipated we might escape down the fire stairs.

I made my second mistake. Assumed he had acquired a gun and would pick us off. He took us on bare-handed. Disarmed Mosby and turned his weapon on him. Now the killer has a 1911, and he can buy ammunition anywhere.

"What next?" Heth asks.

"Sam warned Spears," I tell her. "When Sam finds Mosby dead, he'll make for Spears's place."

I take the paper from my pocket and check Spears's address. He lives in San Cristos, an hour east of San Luis Obispo.

"He was going to be happy," Heth says.

"Who?"

"Mr Mosby. He had such a sad life, and he was finally going to be happy."

I pull into the traffic. For the first time, I reflect on Mosby's story. It's a story told hundreds of times over. I know scores of vets, many of them friends, who fell victim to substance abuse. We're the 9/11 generation. We played hard in the paint from the moment the towers came down. It was game on. Work came first, family second. We were driven, and we lost sight of things that really mattered.

From what they've told me, the Black Sheep were no different. Like us, they played a competitive game for the highest stakes. Whatever their motivation, they wouldn't have traded it for anything.

There is nothing worse for a war dog than sitting idle. Each of us, in his own way, was taking advantage of an opportunity to test himself. To engage in a contest we chose to spend our lives training for. I don't have a family. I hurt myself by missing opportunities to raise one. My friends and I put the job first.

We were having too much fun.

# 12

## THE LEGEND

### San Cristos

How long before I need to steal another car?

I park the Taurus behind a gas station, out of sight. If our luck holds, we'll get to Spears's place without trouble.

"Why don't you go inside and get us some food?" I suggest. "I need to make a phone call."

Heth looks drawn. She undoes her seat belt, gets out of the car. Walks around to the station entrance. I lean against the hood, take out my phone.

I punch a speed-dial.

Stein answers the first ring. Her voice is all business. "What's up, Breed?"

"Stein, I need your help."

A moment's hesitation. "Wonders never cease. Alright, what is it?"

I relate everything that happened in the last twenty-four hours. Has it been that long? Neither Heth nor I have slept. No surprise she looks exhausted. I must look like hell.

The tension on Stein's end is palpable. "Is that everything?" she asks.

"Yes. I need you to find out what the Black Sheep did in 1974 that's getting them killed today."

"It's a bit of a story," Stein says.

I suck a breath. "Tell me what you know."

"I'll tell you what I can."

"Stein, people are getting killed."

"I don't have the full story." Stein makes no effort to disguise her impatience. "The situation is fluid."

"Update me on the fly."

"Who called who?" Stein's tone could freeze the fires of hell. "I repeat. I'll tell you what I can."

Fucking typical.

STEIN LAUNCHES INTO HER STORY.

In 1972, the North Vietnamese Army launched its Easter Offensive. The attack was repelled only through massive use of American air power. Nixon was determined to extricate the United States from Vietnam.

The United States and North Vietnam signed the Paris Peace Accords. In February of 1973, North Vietnam released American prisoners of war. By the end of March, the United States withdrew its ground troops. Turned the fighting over to the ARVN—the Army of the Republic of Viet Nam.

Cambodia and Laos were too important to concede. The CIA organized the Black Sheep to continue the work of MACV-SOG... under more stringent conditions of deniability.

The South Vietnamese continued to lose. The constant flow of men, weapons and supplies down the Ho Chi Minh Trail overwhelmed the ARVN. Worse, the United States Congress blocked the use of American air power. By 1974, the North Vietnamese were ready to mount their final offensive.

General Vo Nguyen Giap was North Vietnam's hero of Dien Bien Phu. His name was synonymous with victory. It is not widely known that, by 1974, Giap had fallen out of favor. Planning of the final offensive was assigned to a less-well-known general—General Van Tien Dung.

The CIA learned that General Dung was to meet his Chinese counterparts in the fall of 1974. The objective of the meeting was to finalize plans for the spring offensive.

The meeting was to take place twenty-five miles across the border in China. Yunnan Province bordered North Vietnam and Laos. The planners selected Jiang Shi. The village lay close to a rail line that provided easy access for delegates.

There, the legend began.

The mission was a desperate throw of the dice.

Six Black Sheep were selected to penetrate China. Their mission was to assassinate General Dung. The highest authority approved the killing under Title 50. The objective was to decapitate the NVA leadership.

Codenamed Guillotine, the mission was conducted under conditions of maximum deniability. The six Americans were former MACV-SOG operators. They would wear uniforms with no badges of rank or identification. They would use weapons manufactured in communist countries.

All six had been sheep-dipped. They were employed by shell companies whose ownership was untraceable.

Crockett was the team leader and primary shooter. Butler was his second-in-command. Appleyard was the backup shooter.

From its inception, MACV-SOG had been plagued by leaks. Many teams disappeared, never to be heard from again. Others were hunted by battalions of NVA, often with bloodhounds. The source of the leaks could not be found.

Guillotine was organized under total secrecy. The Black

Sheep were smuggled into northern Thailand. The team would march through northern Laos, then China. They would hike to the target, assassinate Dung, and exfil.

Stein pauses, waits for me to react.

"Guillotine was a suicide mission."

"That's the kind of men the Black Sheep are, Breed." Stein's voice is sober. "Twenty-year-old kids who volunteered to fight. They knew the chances of being wounded or killed exceeded a hundred percent. Your father and Crockett are true heroes."

"Did you know this when we spoke in DC?"

"I learned more later. Special people attract special people, Breed. Put the most expensive marbles in a bowl and they're bound to bump into each other. Your father and Crockett were the best. From what I hear, you are the very incarnation of your father."

The kindness in Stein's voice makes me uncomfortable. She's sincere, but I like her better cold. "Alright, what developments?"

"Last week, Martin Fairchild was murdered."

"The man who recruited the Black Sheep."

"Yes. Fairchild was one of the longest-serving officers in the CIA. Our Gray Eminence, our expert on China. A senior officer in Saigon during the MACV-SOG and Black Sheep periods. Guillotine was his baby."

"The Ugly American."

"I hate that book. We've identified the killer and his accomplice. Two men, seen separately in the vicinity of Fairchild's house. Tried to burn it down."

"Our killer likes to play with matches."

"They both do. You've met one of them. Chinese, educated in the United States, Switzerland, and the UK. Speaks English and several other languages. In the US, he's a visiting lecturer by the name of Kang. Works for Pacific

Crossing. It's a Non-Government Organization that fosters goodwill between Asian countries and the United States. The demands on his time are flexible. He has enormous latitude to travel."

"A valuable chess piece. Where did he get his training?"

"The PLA Special Forces."

"Who's the other man?"

"The other man killed Fairchild and his two bodyguards. An older man, very professional. He tortured Fairchild. Got what he wanted."

"How do you know?"

"The killer finished him off with a suppressed .45. Then he disposed of Fairchild's two bodyguards. Shot one man in the living room. Killed the other with a knife—an SOG seven-inch recon."

"That's pretty specific."

"That blade has a distinctive shape. The killer stabbed the bodyguard in the chest. The fight was messy. The killer broke the knife pulling it from the body."

"Did you recover all the pieces?"

"No," Stein says, "the killer took the handle and tang with him. But the blade was buried in the bodyguard. A modern knife, not old enough to be original issue."

"You said you identified the killer."

"Yes. It was Appleyard."

"I thought Appleyard was dead."

"No, he was left for dead."

The story is moving too fast for me. "Slow down, Stein. How did Appleyard go from dead in the jungle to murdering Martin Fairchild fifty years later?"

"We aren't sure. I'll tell you what I can, because you might run up against him. You have already encountered Kang."

"Yes, he's resourceful."

"So is Appleyard. He was Crockett's backup shooter on

Guillotine. The plan was for the two men to establish their firing position. A third man would spot while both lined up Dung. Crockett would fire first, followed by Appleyard. They couldn't miss.

"The team never got a shot at Dung. They were surprised by Chinese security forces and had to fight their way out. The railroad junction and village were located next to an old copper mine. The railroad had been built to transport ore.

"Crockett led the men on a fighting withdrawal. More Chinese troops joined the chase, and the team ran to the mine.

"By this time they were all wounded, Appleyard worst of all. Crockett gambled they could elude their pursuers in the mine. Appleyard was too badly wounded to move. He offered to remain and delay the enemy."

I frown. "I can't imagine any of those men allowing themselves to be captured alive."

"No," Stein says. "Crockett and the others fled into the cave. Behind them, they heard shooting and the explosions of hand grenades."

"Most operators save the last grenade for themselves."

"Crockett and the others assumed Appleyard went down fighting." Stein pauses. "Following the team's debriefing, Fairchild thought the same."

"What changed?"

"In the late seventies, we detected a pattern of assassinations in Asia. In every case we were agnostic about the result."

That's unusual. "You didn't care about who got hit?"

"No. It was like the targets were selected to not piss us off. But—our job is intelligence. We wanted to know who was at work. Everything pointed to Appleyard. An American who could speak French, Vietnamese and Chinese. Knew his way around Asia. Fairchild announced that Appleyard had survived."

"How did he come to that conclusion?"

"Fairchild had a vast network in Asia. They told him about Appleyard's work.

"As early as 1977, Appleyard led Chinese Special Forces in Cambodia. Worked with the Khmer Rouge. They formed an effective force against the Vietnamese, and Appleyard was well paid. As Fairchild put it, Appleyard fought our old enemy. In China, Deng Xiaoping had taken over from the Maoists. He was trying to impress America and the West with his pro-capitalist outlook.

"Then came the Sino-Vietnamese War of 1979. The Chinese paid Appleyard to assassinate high level Vietnamese political and militia leaders. We had no dog in the fight. If anything, we favored the Chinese."

Stein pauses. "There is another critical data point."

"Tell me."

"In 1996, the Chinese inserted a team to assassinate President Lee Teng-Hui of Taiwan. In the event, the mission was called off. Appleyard kept his fifty percent advance."

"Why is it important?"

"Appleyard's partner was a twenty-four-year-old PLA Special Forces officer—Kang."

"For God's sake. Did Appleyard and Kang become an item?"

"No. As far as Fairchild was able to determine, they never worked together again."

"Why would Appleyard switch allegiance?"

"Appleyard played the middle. He accepted jobs that showcased his talent, paid well, and didn't put him on our hit list. The Chinese made him rich."

Heth has returned with bags of food. I acknowledge her

with a nod, and she gets in the car. I stroll to a chain-link fence at the back of the parking lot.

"Two valuable assets committed to this mission."

"Quite the team. Appleyard is in his early seventies, Kang in his early forties."

I shake my head. "It doesn't make sense. Why is Appleyard killing his old team members now?"

"So far, it's Kang who is killing them. We think Appleyard is still in DC."

"Where he killed Fairchild. Surely *that* is detrimental to US interests."

Silence.

"Stein?"

"That's all I can tell you, Breed. Do *not* push me."

I would shake Stein if I could. Instead, I say, "Okay. Help me find Stroud."

"My team is working on it. He's somewhere in Colorado."

"What is it about this guy?"

"Stroud's shady. He doesn't have a legitimate phone or mailing address."

"Of course. Not even his best friends know where he is. Right now, that might be the only thing keeping him alive."

"I'll share Stroud's location when we find him," Stein says. "Meanwhile, be careful—Kang and Appleyard are top-flight."

Stein disconnects the call. I pocket my phone and walk back to the car.

What did Stein say?

*Certain people at the Company have been assigned special protection.*

Stein, Fairchild and others. Targets.

That's why Appleyard is still in DC.

## 13

## SPEARS'S KNIFE COLLECTION

**San Cristos**

"There's nothing to worry about," Spears says.

"This man killed Mr Butler and Mr Mosby."

Heth has her mobile phone on speaker. She's set it on the molding between us in the Taurus. We sit, heads bent together, straining to listen.

"I hear you." Spears's voice is confident. "If he comes around here, he's going to get his ass shot off."

"Have you heard from Grandfather since yesterday morning?"

"No. He warned me that we were in danger. That's all."

"He's going to visit you," Heth says. "We'll come up and wait for him."

"This isn't a convenient time." Spears's tone is firm. "Crockett said nothing about coming to see me. If he comes by, I'll call you."

Spears disconnects the call. Helpless, Heth stares at the dead phone.

I cast my eyes over the street, the front of Spears's closed dojo. The sign in the window proclaims evening hours six nights a week and an afternoon session on Saturdays. A Boy Scout and his mother walk past. The boy peeks in the window. I look at the Scout's uniform and merit badges. Think of the similarity they bear to my Airborne, Ranger, and Special Forces tabs. It's nice to know *merit* still means something.

Small-town America. Cut from the 1960s. The kind of town a man like Spears would settle in.

"Something's wrong," I say. "We're going out there."

Spears's house and knife workshop are located a mile out of town. Nestled among rolling hills in the countryside of the central California coast. A white mailbox marks a gravel lane that leads from the main road to the residence.

I pull into the lane and stop. There are low hills on either side. Green with shrubs and copses of trees. A corner of the house is visible, about a quarter of a mile away.

"What are you doing?" Heth asks.

A thicket chokes the space between two hills to our right. I turn off the lane and drive the car deep into the brush. Look into the rearview mirror. I stop when I am satisfied the car cannot be detected from the lane.

"Wait here," I tell Heth.

"No, I'm coming with you."

"Spears's behavior is bizarre. I'm sure Sam would have contacted him as soon as he found Mosby dead. Spears should have made more time for Sam's granddaughter. He's expecting trouble, wants to keep you out of it."

I get out of the car and close the door. "I'll call you as soon as I know anything," I promise.

Heth sits in the car, fuming.

I climb the nearest hill. Stretch my muscles, enjoy the burn in my legs. When I get to the top, I cast my eyes around.

Our car is invisible, submerged in the thicket. Around me,

the landscape is lush with green hills. The vegetation is shiny under an expanse of blue sky. The lane, a brown ribbon, winds toward the house.

The house.

A two-story, ranch-style structure. Sprawling. There's a two-car garage attached to one end, and a low, single-story extension at the other. Behind the house, set off by about fifty yards, is a low, wooden building. A single story, it covers four or five times the area of the garage. That must be the workshop.

There are no cars occupying the broad parking space adjacent to the garage. I doubt Spears has employees working today.

Ten minutes' hike brings me to Spears's front door. Three sharp knocks and the door opens.

Spears is an older version of the man in the picture. A long face with craggy features. Clear, intelligent eyes. A lean, hard frame with wide hands and strong fingers. His hair, including the porn mustache, has turned pure white.

"You must be Breed's boy."

Spears's smile flashes rows of strong teeth set like bricks in a wide mouth. He is not happy to see me.

"I am."

"Damn. If someone put a mustache on you, I'd think you were his ghost."

"I had to come," I tell him. "Crockett warned you the Black Sheep are being targeted."

"He did," Spears replies. "But it's none of your business."

"He's my friend."

Spears holds my gaze for a long moment, then steps aside. "Okay, Breed. You came all the way out here... You might as well stay a while."

The living room could be a weapons museum. The wall above the fireplace is adorned with crossed spears and a five-foot-tall wooden shield. Against another wall hang two sets of three samurai swords each. Katana, Wakizashi, and Tanto. One set bears original handles. The other set displays custom handles of gold and malachite.

"Come on in," Spears says. "Have a look at my collection."

"Did Crockett tell you why the Black Sheep are being targeted?"

"Only that it had to do with what we did in 1974."

Stein's given me part of the picture. I want more. Different people often remember events differently. Cross-checking stories is fundamental to intelligence gathering.

"What did you do in 1974?"

"That's classified."

"Classified. That was fifty years ago."

Spears shrugs. "If it makes you feel better, I can't think of a reason anyone would want to kill us."

A long glass case has been set against the living room wall. Thirty knives are set on plastic blocks on a long shelf draped with crimson velvet. The naked blades gleam under concealed ceiling lights. Above the shelf are black-and-white photographs, much like those on Crockett's wall.

Spears opens the hinged lid. Picks up a long, wicked blade. It's been well-used. Its edge bears the marks of sharpening stones.

"That an original SOG knife?" I ask.

"This is *my* SOG knife. There aren't many left." Spears points to a photograph of himself in tiger stripes, carrying a CAR15. He wears a knife in a leather sheath, high on the left side of his chest.

"Is that the same knife?"

"The very one," he says.

"Handle down."

"And blade inward. That way, when you draw it, it comes down naturally to your hip, blade-up."

"Not everyone thinks to carry it blade-up."

"We all loved the SOG knife," Spears says. "But it was a compromise. True killing knives are pointed and double-edged. Some committee in the Pentagon decided everyone should have a utility knife. So every grunt was issued a K-Bar or Special Forces knife to open C-rations. No multi-purpose knife is optimized for killing."

"SOG knives *are* well-loved," I say. "I still have my father's."

"I made reproductions for the Black Sheep. They all use my Spears Specials."

The old man lifts a beautiful blade from the case. "The original has a blued finish to reduce glare. That finish wears quickly. I make mine with a proprietary Parkerizing process."

I turn the knife in the light. The blade looks matte black.

"That finish will hold up much better than the original bluing. I'll make one for you, if you like."

"Thanks." I hand the blade back to him. "I appreciate it, but I carry a Cold Steel."

"OSS?"

"Yes."

Spears smiles. "That's a true killing knife. Double-edged, eight inches. Long enough to punch through heavy clothing in the winter. No serrations."

The old soldier picks up a K-Bar. "This was the compromise that started it all," he says. "A single edged blade, and a thicker spine to pound on for chopping wood. But now the direction in which you hold the blade matters. *If* you're a knife fighter, it's clumsy. In a fight, you have to consciously hold it blade-up. To attack the throat from behind, you hold it normally. To tear out a throat from the front, you reverse your grip."

Spears closes the case. "Come on," he says. "Let's take a look at the showroom."

Beyond the kitchen, a door opens into a vast display room. It's the single-story extension I saw from the hill. Spears flicks a light switch and the room is flooded with light. There are no windows. Only another door at the back that leads to the workshop.

The walls are richly paneled. Decorated with endless rows of knives and photographs. Glass cases like the one in the living room occupy the floor. Close to the kitchen door stands a card table and a set of straight-backed chairs. On the table lie product catalogues, meant to exhibit Spears's wares. To the right, a comfortable sofa, coffee table, and books about knives and knife-making.

"When I got back from the war," Spears says, "I didn't know what to do with myself. Didn't have any college. When I was young, I hunted with my father. We made knives for skinning game. I decided to keep myself busy by making knives—for myself and my SOG buddies."

"That's how businesses get started."

"The dojo was my business. I rode the martial arts craze in the seventies. Knives were a hobby. I was surprised when knife-making brought in more money than the dojo."

"Is that your factory out back?"

"It's a workshop. More space than I need. Eight guys work for me, all vets."

"Full time?"

Spears gives me a sharp look, nods. "Every model is sold out the minute we hang it on the web. Our chef's knives are back-ordered for a year. I'll grow the business, but I want to keep the custom aspect. And I want to provide jobs for vets."

As far as I can tell, no one has come to work, and today is a weekday. Spears must have given the men the day off.

"You'll appreciate this," Spears says.

He opens a glass display case, reaches in, and hands me an eight-inch blade. Double-edged, razor-sharp. Black Parkerized finish. The scales that adorn the tang are a beautiful dark green.

"That blade's modeled on your Cold Steel OSS," Spears says. "I experimented to get the scales right. They're micarta —grippier when wet."

It's beautiful. I turn the knife over in my hands, test the grip. The texture of the handle makes the blade feel part of my hand. The last thing you want is for a bloody knife to slip.

"Keep it," Spears says. Reaches into a drawer underneath the display case, hands me a leather sheath. "Veterans made this in the USA."

I don't know what to say. Came here suspicious of Spears's behavior. I'm not prepared for his generosity.

"Don't say anything," Spears says. "I heard about you—your father would be proud."

A voice booms from the kitchen door. Echoes in the closed space.

"That's right, Breed. Don't say anything. Put the knife down on the case behind you."

Spears and I whirl. It's Kang, standing at the kitchen door.

Kang is holding Mosby's 1911 to Heth's temple.

# 14

# DEAD END

### San Cristos

Kang is holding Mosby's 1911 to Heth's temple.

The girl stares at me with terrified eyes. The killer's left arm is wrapped around her chest, crushing her to himself. "I warned you to stay away," he says. "Don't move, or I'll kill her."

Spears and I face Kang across the long axis of the room. We're separated by seven yards of open space between the display cases. I set the knife down on the case next to me.

Kang came for one thing. He extends the 1911 and shoots Spears twice in the chest. The vet crumples. Kang shoots him a third time in the face.

Heth twists free of Kang's grip and throws herself against his gun arm. Knocks it aside. In a heartbeat, she's free. Dives for the floor and scrambles for cover behind a row of display cases.

I snatch the knife from the case and hurl it with all my strength. The blade flashes through the air. I launch myself at

Kang before the knife finds its mark. He swings the 1911 to cover me.

The knife buries itself high on the left side of Kang's chest as he pulls the trigger. In the closed space, the crash of the shot stabs my ears. The slide reciprocates and the bullet blows past. I grab his wrist and bear down. Step left, club the outside of his elbow. Hard enough to snap a man's arm. The joint hyperextends, but does not break. Kang's arm is made of concrete.

Kang grunts with pain, drops the pistol. He twists into me, breaks my grip. A striking snake, his left fist crashes into my right cheek. There's an explosion in my head. I stagger against the wall. With a grunt, Kang pulls the knife from his pectoral muscle. Slashes.

Back to the wall, I throw myself sideways. The blade slices across my chest. I stumble, recover, and snatch one of the straight-backed chairs from the card table. Like a lion-tamer, I parry Kang's thrust. The point of the blade splinters the seat of the chair.

I ram the chair into Kang, snatch the gun from the floor. The hammer's cocked. I swing it around. He dodges through the back door as I fire.

*Miss.*

Kang's gone. I scramble to my feet, run hard.

I burst into the bright sunlight, blink. The workshop is fifty yards away. Kang runs past it, heading for the cover of brush at the base of the hills. I raise the pistol, but the slide's locked back.

*Shit.*

The pistol's a paperweight. I drop it and start running.

*Crack.*

A rifle shot.

*Where the fuck did that come from?* I saw neither muzzle flash nor bullet splash. I throw myself to the ground, scramble back inside the display room. Kang disappears into a thicket.

"Breed."

It's Heth.

"Stay back," I say. "Sniper."

Appleyard? Covering Kang?

He's supposed to be in DC.

Heth stares at me. "Breed, you're hurt."

The engagement happened so fast, I felt no pain. I look down, find the front of my shirt wet with blood. "Oh, shit."

"Let me look at that."

"Not now," I tell her. "We don't know who's out there."

I bend to check Spears's pulse. Nothing.

*Way to go, Breed.*

I fucked up again. Kang, of course, was the consummate professional. He didn't kill me and Heth in San Francisco. We weren't on his list. More important, the time might come when we might prove useful.

Kang needed an edge against me and Mosby. He set a fire.

He needed an edge against me and Spears. He used Heth.

I take the sheath from the top of the display case. Pull the knife from the chair and slide it into the scabbard. Stick it in my belt.

"How did he get hold of you?" I ask.

"I was sitting in the car. He hauled me out, held a gun to my head."

"Come on, let's get out of here."

We find Spears's bedroom and I take a pair of shirts from his closet. Take mine off, tie it around the cut on my chest. Shrug on one of his.

It takes us twenty minutes to make our way back to the car. I lead the way, through the brush and over the hills. Can't take a chance Appleyard is waiting for us. Worse, Kang might have doubled back.

We reach the thicket and wait another half hour, watching the car.

Nothing.

I get in the car and start the engine. Wave Heth over.

"We've hit a dead end," I tell her.

"What now?"

I twist in my seat, back the car out of the thicket.

"We regroup."

# 15

## THE BACKWARDS FLAG

### San Cristos

When I graduated jump school, each platoon held a secret ceremony. The barracks windows were shut and blacked out. For most of the night, we endured the usual hazing. We knew we were waiting our turn while other barracks received the honors.

Our turn came, and we stood at attention at the foot of our bunks, clad only in our skivvies. I was frightened and excited at the same time.

When our turn came, a dozen Black Hats—airborne instructors—entered the barracks. One carried a box. They slowly made their way up one row of troopers, then down the other. They stopped at each man. The senior sergeant took a gold parachutist's badge from the box and pinned it to the graduate's bare chest.

"Now you're airborne."

"Yes, sergeant airborne."

The first two Black Hats stepped to the next man. The others formed a line. Stopped at the first man they had pinned. Then they pounded the badge into his chest with their fists.

I bore the pain with joy.

Years later, there was a stink when the practice was made public. I can only say that those who have endured it are true brothers.

"DON'T YOU FEEL ANYTHING," Heth whispers.

"I feel everything," I tell her.

I'm sitting in bed, bare-chested. Heth has taken off her boots, climbed on the bed, and straddled me. Surgical needle and thread in hand, she stitches the cut that stretches across my chest. I feel the bite of the needle. The tug as she cinches the lips of the open wound together.

Heth looks in my eyes, trembles.

I take her wrist in my hand. "Focus."

Without another word, she bends to the task.

We left Spears's house and returned to San Cristos. Heth bought medical supplies at a drugstore, changes of clothes at the local Target.

The motel is comfortable. A good place to take stock. The room is clean and cool, arranged like a million other motel rooms across America. Two single beds, a table, threadbare furniture. The lights are on in the bathroom and over the dresser. Dim twenty-five-watt bulbs. The floor lamp by the window burns brighter.

When she has finished, Heth sits back on my thighs. Examines her work. Studies the scars on my body. The AK47 entry wound in my right side. "What happened here?" she asks.

"Bad guy got lucky."

Heth bends forward, traces the smooth, hard flesh with a finger. Reaches behind and feels the exit wound.

I'd gotten lucky, too.

Heth's voice is hushed. "I've never been hurt."

"See? We're all lucky."

Heth leans to one side. Examines the black-and-white tattoo of the American flag on my right shoulder.

"Why is it the wrong way around?" she asks.

The flag has been tattooed with the field of stars facing forward, the stripes facing toward my back.

"The flag-bearer leads the charge. If he's shot, another man picks up the flag before it falls. The flag flies in the wind, and if you look at it from the right side—that's what you see."

Tears in her eyes, Heth strokes my shoulder. She bends to kiss me.

God, how I want her. I feel my body respond.

I put my hand on her chest. Stop her.

"Heth, this isn't a good idea."

"Breed, I know what I'm doing."

"When this is all over."

Heth sits back, wipes the tears from her eyes. "Okay."

She gets up from the bed. Laces up her boots, steps to the door.

"Where are you going?"

"There's Bourbon in the trunk. *That's* something we can do together."

Heth closes the door behind her.

"Goddamnit." Heth's voice carries from outside.

*What now?*

I swing out of bed, pull on my boots, and go to the window. Part the curtain and peer out. Heth reaches into the driver's compartment of the Taurus. Pops the trunk. Walks around the car and rummages in the back.

When Heth straightens, she's wielding a tire iron. She strides down the street. I turn my head and catch a glimpse of several men turning a corner.

I pull on a clean shirt and follow her.

Heth calls, "Hey, asshole, give me back my shit."

The alley's dark. Three tweakers. One wearing jeans and a white sleeveless T-shirt. Another with a ragged jean jacket. A blond guy in a mullet is carrying Heth's canvas haversack in one hand. They've turned to face her. Heth's carrying the tire iron behind her back.

"Fuck you, cunt. What else you got?"

The guy in the white T-shirt steps toward Heth. In one motion, she stoops and cracks the tire iron against his knee. He howls and falls to the pavement. Heth straightens and boots him in the face. There's a sound, something between a crack and crunch.

One hand occupied with loot, the mullet steps forward. Heth whirls and backhands him with the tire iron. There's a thud as it connects with the side of his head. The mullet crumples like an empty suit of clothes.

I step into full view. The guy in the jean jacket looks uncertain. Turns and runs.

Heth stands looking down on the mullet. He's on his knees. Blood pours from his scalp and soaks his shirt. Like she's driving for a hole-in-one, Heth draws the tire iron back with both hands.

My God, she's going to knock his head off.

Engine rumbling, a car pulls up behind us. Its headlights bathe the alley in white light. Heth and I turn around.

"I think you got your shit back." The driver leans out the window. "Maybe we should leave."

It's Crockett.

# 16

## CROCKETT'S STORY

### Las Vegas

Heth and I collect our things, wipe down the room and the Taurus. We pile into Crockett's shiny black muscle car, a '72 Dodge Charger. The paint job gleams in the street lights. He must have had it washed after the drive from Montana.

"Could you possibly have stolen a more conspicuous car?" I ask him.

"Always wanted one of these. Couldn't resist."

We don't know how long it will take for Spears's body to be found. It could be as early as the following morning when his workers return.

"Where's Stroud?" I ask Crockett.

"Somewhere near Denver," he says.

"Not good enough."

"You don't get it, Breed. Stroud doesn't want to be found."

"Looks like we're going to Denver."

"That's at least eighteen hours."

"We'll take turns at the wheel." I fish a quarter out of my pocket. "Loser drives as far as Vegas. Call."

Crockett hesitates. "Heads."

I flip the coin, catch it on the back of my left hand. "You're driving."

Heth stretches out on the back seat. I climb in next to Crockett, fashion a pillow from my jacket, and slump against the passenger window. Close my eyes.

For six hours, we drive east.

Crockett stops at a Denny's the other side of Vegas. We go inside for a late dinner.

I go to the washroom and splash water on my face. When I return to the table, I decide to confront Crockett.

"Three of your friends are dead, Sam. Tell us about it."

"Not much to tell, Breed."

"Try me."

"Butler and I were stalking a bull elk. It was Butler's tag, but he couldn't get the angle. He passed on the opportunity, stood, and somebody shot him.

"I yelled that we were hunters. Whoever was at the tree line fired again and clipped me. I knew right away he was trying to kill us. Butler was dead. I took my rifle, displaced. Tied off my wound, maneuvered for a shot. The bad guy was gone."

"You had CB and ham radios in your truck," I say. "You could have called for help."

"Whoever shot at us wanted both me and Butler dead." Crockett sips his coffee. "There's only one thing of any significance that connects us."

"The Black Sheep, 1974."

"Yes."

"Don't you think that's a bit of a stretch, Sam? You and Butler were only two data points."

"But significant ones. You weren't there, Breed. That was

no hunting accident. It was a deliberate hit. I made my way back to the lodge and took care of myself. Called Mosby and Spears."

"Packed an arsenal, stole a car, headed for San Francisco."

"Yes. I was too late to save Mosby."

"And Spears? He behaved strangely."

"Spears and I planned to set up the killer. He would play the tethered goat. I would set up a firing position on the hill with my long rifle."

"That's why Spears didn't want us around."

"Exactly. He told his men not to come to work. Imagine my surprise when I saw *you* knock on the front door. Then, worse. The killer approached with Heth. He held her close, at gunpoint. Very careful. I couldn't get a clear shot. There was no way I was going to risk hitting Heth."

I had killed Spears. Ruined the ambush. Worse, I left Heth vulnerable. "Kang must have staked out the lane."

"I knew there was trouble inside," Crockett says. "But I didn't think I would get there in time. I heard gunfire. Saw the killer run out the back, saw you chase him. I took the shot, but he was running across my line of fire. I didn't allow enough lead."

"I couldn't tell who you were firing at."

"I wasn't sure what to do. Exfiltrated, tried to think things through. Decided to find you and join forces."

"What happened in 1974, Sam? What do you know the others don't?"

"Nothing. All I have is a theory."

"You promised to tell Mosby and Spears—now tell me."

"It's classified, Breed."

"Bullshit. I'm tired of people yanking my chain. SOG's nondisclosure agreements ran out in the nineties."

"But not those for the Black Sheep."

"I don't give a damn. Cough it up."

## 17

## JIANG SHI

**Yunnan, December 20, 1974**

I fold my arms on the table. Hands on her lap, Heth sits quietly. Crockett reclines in the booth and sips his coffee. He gathers his thoughts, and tells us about Christmas, 1974.

CROCKETT STOOD atop the mountain and looked down at the valley of Jiang Shi. It was a plain, surrounded by mountains and low hills. The slopes were lush and green, the valley carpeted with tan elephant grass. The tall blades swayed in the sultry breeze.

The mountains and hills were granite and limestone, camouflaged by vegetation. The team had left the deepest triple canopy jungle behind in Vietnam and Laos. In Yunnan, the top layer was relatively sparse because the province lay on the northern fringe of the tropical zone. The canopy turned terrain features into lumps on a green carpet. The hills, in particular, had a look characteristic of Indochina.

They were perfect, conical mounds, separated by little valleys. Crockett thought they looked like the breasts of nubile maidens.

Butler stepped to Crockett's side. "It's beautiful."

"Beautiful enough to kill you."

Crockett took out his map and compass. Butler shaded the lenses on his binoculars, glassed the valley.

The village squatted on the eastern extremity of the plain. It was no more than a dozen houses and a lodge. The lodge consisted of three closely-spaced buildings. Lodging for staff, lodging for VIPs, and a hall for dining and events. The lodge had been built for mine officials. Abandoned since the mine was shut down, reactivated and refurbished for the meeting.

The railroad terminus sat three hundred yards west of the lodge. Railroad tracks extended north-by-east and snaked between the hills.

An engine was parked at the end of the line. Attached were two coaches, separated by a flatcar. The flatcar was heavily sandbagged, with twenty-millimeter anti-aircraft cannon at either end. Heavy caliber machine guns—Dushkas—were set on tripod mounts. They were sandbagged in the center of the flatcar and at the ends of each passenger coach.

"The guests have arrived," Butler observes.

"Yes. VIPs in the first coach, troops in the last."

There were hills behind the lodge. So close it looked like the buildings had been crushed against them. On the other side of the valley were two low hills and a small mountain. All the mountains in the vicinity seemed small. The mountain Crockett was standing on was three thousand feet. The one he was looking at was less than a thousand. That mountain was connected by a saddle to a low hill to the west.

Crockett's charts were plastic-covered ten-by-ten grids, cut from 1:50,000 and 1:25,000 maps. The features were identified by their elevations. The mountain he was standing on was identified as Hill 868. It stood at the southern side of the valley. From north to south, the two hills and the mountain on the west side were Hills 34, 48, and 180. Their heights in meters.

There was no number assigned to the saddle attached to Hill 180. It was lower than Hill 48, higher than Hill 34.

The hill wasn't on any of his maps. The cartographers had considered it part of the ridge that stretched south from Hill 180. Careless. In his mind, Crockett designated it Hill 40.

"That hill isn't supposed to be there," Crockett said.

"You mean it's supposed to be on the map and isn't."

Crockett shrugged. "Don't think it matters. Best shot is from Hill 34. We'll have a clear line of fire."

"Don't you get the creepy-crawlies?"

Crockett looked at Butler sideways. "You got them, too?"

"Damn straight."

Appleyard stepped from the jungle, joined the two men at the lookout. Crockett saw a tall soldier, dressed in unmarked olive drab fatigues and a floppy hat. The sniper was weighed down by a Dragunov rifle and twenty magazines of rifle ammunition. A Swedish K submachine gun and a further thirty mags of submachine gun ammo. A dozen lemonka hand grenades. Two canteens and a Tokarev pistol were hooked to his web belt. The belt was hung with a further three canteen pouches, each crammed with rifle magazines.

"What's wrong?" Appleyard had heard them talking.

Butler gestured with his binoculars. Swept the tableau. "What don't you see?"

The sniper quartered the ground. "No PLA."

Crockett frowned. The valley had to be under the protection of the People's Liberation Army. The team had climbed Hill 868 with extreme caution because they expected it to be occupied. Every one of the hills surrounding the valley should have had a PLA overwatch.

"There's PLA on the train," Butler observed. "Those twenty mike-mike cannon and Dushkas can rip these hills to shit."

"It *is* a secret meeting." Crockett was unconvinced. "They might be overconfident, but we can't afford to be careless."

Appleyard pointed to a black gash in the face of Hill 180. "What's that?"

"That," Crockett informed him, "is the exit from the copper mine."

"Exit?" Butler looked puzzled.

"Yes. There are two kinds of copper mines. Open-pit and underground. This is underground. The miners would have drilled or blasted shafts from the upper slopes of the mountain. The ore would fall inside, and they would cart it out the front. Through that mouth."

"Kind of back-asswards," Appleyard grunted.

"There is a logic to the process." Crockett took out his own binoculars and scanned the valley. "There are PLA guarding *that* building. See?"

Butler raised his binoculars. Glassed a building at the southern base of Hill 48, close to the mouth of the mine. "Yes. No idea what's in there."

Crockett pointed to a large building below them. It stood at the base of Hill 868, at the south end of the valley. They stared down at its roof. "This could be a barracks for a few hundred men."

"Where are they?" Appleyard asked.

"If they are soldiers," Butler said, "they could be on patrol. Otherwise, it's anybody's guess. What we are seeing is consistent with the satellite imagery. Little or no activity, a sleepy village."

Crockett checked his watch. "The meeting takes place at 0900 hours tomorrow. We need to maneuver to Hill 34."

It was mid-morning on December 20, 1974.

Guillotine was on schedule.

THE TEAM DESCENDED the west slope of Hill 868 and stared at the saddle. The feature was troublesome. It wasn't on the map, and the team had not planned on climbing its steep ridge. At the southern end of the ridge was the hill the cartographers had missed. The one Crockett had designated Hill 40. It had a flat top, looked like a mesa. From there, the ridge sloped gently to the valley floor.

The team had no choice but to climb. They wanted to traverse the reverse slopes of Hills 180 and 48 before climbing Hill 34. The maneuver would bring them to their firing position without risk of detection.

Crockett took point, with his Dragunov slung across his back and Swedish K at the ready. Butler followed in slack, carrying his AK47. Stroud was in third place with his RPD belt-fed machine gun. On his webbing, he carried four one-hundred-round belts in drums, and two more in his ruck. If they ran into trouble, the first three men had enough firepower to stall attackers... long enough for the team to break contact.

Mosby was in fourth place with an AK47 and underbarrel Bonfire grenade launcher. He carried forty magazines of rifle ammunition, fifteen point detonation, and fifteen airburst grenades. Each of the other men carried more grenades to help him spread the load. Spears was in fifth place with an AK47. Appleyard brought up the rear with his Dragunov and a Swedish K.

Crockett advanced with caution. He led them through the jungle at a British slow march. Each man covered his own sector of fire. Every fifteen minutes, Crockett would signal the team to stop. They would drop to a crouch, freeze, and listen.

In the jungle, they had learned to trust their ears and noses more than their eyes.

When you can't see your hand in front of your face, you can smell the sweat of a killer, or the sweat of prey. You learn the difference. Fear-sweat stinks. Your ears could detect the presence of the enemy. The birds and insects fall silent at his approach. The absence of natural jungle noise sounds an alert.

Crockett climbed the saddle. When he got to the top of the ridge, he waited for the team to gather. The canopy was thinner. They could look north to the top of Hill 180, and south to Hill 40 at the end of the saddle. From where they stood, the two hills looked flatter than before. The vegetation was actually depressed at the hilltops.

The features noted, Crockett started down the other side. At the foot of the reverse slope, he turned right and made his way north. The canopy was thick and blocked the sky. The jungle was so gloomy he walked into the supply depot before he realized what it was.

Thousands of sacks of cement had been stacked in the middle of the jungle. Crockett put his hand on one as though to convince himself it was real. The fingers of his gloves had been cut off to protect his palms while affording him a measure of dexterity. He felt the thick brown paper under his fingertips. Gritty, gray cement dust had collected in the seams.

There was no need for camouflage netting. The dense canopy concealed the depot from aerial observation and satellite photography. Crockett was sure access roads were also hidden.

Butler crept to Crockett's side. Crockett hand-signaled him to silence. They had blundered into a supply installation. Where there were supplies, there were bound to be sentries.

Crockett and Butler backed away, gathered the team, and initiated a course correction.

The team diverted a hundred yards east, back onto the reverse slope of the saddle. They had to work harder on the slope, but they bypassed sentries. Crockett worried about Chinese patrols, but all he could do was exercise caution.

They reached the top of Hill 34 without incident. Stared down at the lodge. The thirty yards Dung would cross from the living quarters to the events building. Crockett and Appleyard unslung their Dragunovs and built their firing position. Spears took out his spotter scope and took up station at their six o'clock.

Butler, the 1-1, took charge of security and area defense. He set up Claymores to cover arcs around the team. Positioned himself, Mosby and Stroud to cover the north, south and west approaches.

Darkness fell and the team froze in place. The rule was, no movement after dark.

Not a sound.

Once down, you stayed down.

They sniffed the air, listened to the night.

Waited for dawn.

UNDER NORMAL CONDITIONS, spotters and snipers reverse positions every hour. The exchange of roles relieves the sniper's tension. In this case, the team expected Dung to show himself at 0900 hours. There was no reason to switch. Crockett and Appleyard would put two bullets in him the moment he showed his face.

"Where is he?" Appleyard whispered.

It was 0930 hours. The lodge was quiet. Unarmed staff moved between the servants' quarters and the conference building. PLA troops manned the crew-served weapons on the flatcar.

The team had been in firing position for an hour.

"Switch out with Spears for half an hour," Crockett instructed Appleyard. "After that, you and I switch."

They had to sustain their vigil. At least one of Crockett or Appleyard had to be available as primary shooter.

Appleyard left his Dragunov and traded places with Spears.

Butler crawled to Crockett's side. "What's going on?" he asked.

Crockett refused to take his eye from the Dragunov's scope. "They're late."

"Son of a bitch."

"We adapt. This could be over in five minutes or five hours. No big deal."

Crockett focused his attention on the lodge. Swept the reticle over the second-floor windows, the front door, the side door. Nothing moved.

From his left, an explosion. A Claymore.

The team was in contact.

THE TEAM WENT to work like a machine. PLA attacking from the north were the first to fire. The Claymore had *not* been tripped by a tiger. Bullets snapped past Crockett's ears. Stroud raked the bush with his RPD. "Contact left," he yelled.

Another Claymore exploded, this time to the west. Mosby cut loose with his AK47. "Contact rear!"

Firing, the first Chinese threw themselves at Butler and Stroud. The Americans cut them down, but more PLA swarmed behind them.

Stroud and Butler flung grenades at the Chinese.

The PLA flung them back. Stroud caught one and hurled

it toward the enemy. They were playing catch with lemonkas. The grenade exploded among the PLA—a brief orange flash and a puff of black smoke. Cut to pieces by fragmentation, men screamed.

Another grenade landed near Butler. If it exploded, it would kill both him *and* Stroud. Butler picked up a dead Chinese and threw him on top of the lemonka. Flung himself onto the corpse. The grenade exploded. The blast shredded the body and blew Butler onto his back. Shrapnel buried itself in the corpse, stitched Butler's leg.

Mosby fired contact detonation grenades from his Bonfire.

Crockett and Appleyard slung their Dragunovs and reached for their Swedish Ks. Crockett found Butler and grabbed him by his webbing. "How many?"

"Lots," Butler grunted. His left pants leg was shredded. He was covered with blood and shreds of meat.

The 1-1 used "lots" to mean at least a hundred.

In Laos or Vietnam, the Black Sheep could have defended the high ground and called for air support. Twenty-five miles inside China, that was out of the question. "Withdraw right," Crockett snapped.

Mosby fell back on them, changing out his AK47 mag. Appleyard raised his Swedish K. Fired into the bush.

Limping, Butler started down the south slope of Hill 34. They had no choice but to give up the high ground. Spears, Crockett and Appleyard followed. Mosby and Stroud brought up the rear. Stroud laid down a blistering volume of fire with his RPD, and Mosby hammered the PLA with grenades.

Chinese spilled from the troop coach. The Dushkas came alive and the twenty-millimeter anti-aircraft cannon spat fire.

Around the team, foliage shredded. Green tracers streamed from the heavy machine guns. Bullets smacked into tree trunks and ricocheted. Twenty-millimeter cannon shells exploded, showering the team with shrapnel. Appleyard jerked. Fell against Crockett. The two men tumbled down the hill.

At the bottom, Crockett hauled Appleyard to his feet. A piece of shrapnel had smashed Appleyard's left shoulder blade and buried itself in his back. He was in agony, but clung to his weapon.

Behind them, Spears, Mosby and Stroud crashed through the bush. The vegetation offered a measure of concealment. The crew-served weapons on the train fell silent... The PLA were afraid of hitting their own men.

The sight of Mosby and Stroud shocked Crockett. Mosby had been hit at least twice, once in the shoulder, and again in his side. Stroud appeared to move normally, but his fatigue shirt was wet with blood.

"We need a strong point," Butler gasped.

Crockett's eyes swept the battlefield. Two hundred yards away, at the base of Hill 180, the mouth of the mine beckoned. The team could use the building at the base of Hill 48 for cover.

"You good?" Crockett asked Stroud.

"I'm good."

"The mine," Crockett snapped. "Strong point. Stroud and I will cover."

Butler and Appleyard led the way, concealed by the bush. Spears and Mosby followed. When they reached the building, they sprinted across the open ground. Butler cut down the PLA guards.

The anti-aircraft cannons on the flatcar traversed left.

Mosby dropped to a kneeling position in the open, braced his rifle, and cut loose with the Bonfire. The grenade sailed into the sky in a high arc. Fell on the flatcar and exploded. There was an orange flash from behind the sandbags and black smoke shot skyward. One of the anti-aircraft cannons fell silent.

A bullet hit Mosby as he fired the Bonfire a second time. Mosby was a big man, but the bullet spun him. The grenade fell behind the troop coach and exploded harmlessly.

Crockett saw the second twenty-millimeter cannon traverse left. Lifted Mosby by his webbing. Stroud joined him. Together they dragged Mosby behind the building.

Men were shouting in Chinese. PLA had followed them down Hill 34 and were charging across open ground. Stroud changed out a drum. Opened the RPD's top cover, positioned the belt, slapped the plate shut.

Crockett and Spears dumped their magazines into the charging Chinese. Dropped the mags and changed out. Stroud racked the open bolt and let fly with the RPD. One-handed, Mosby fired the Bonfire. Half a dozen Chinese went down in the blast.

The wall of the building splintered. Screams and shrieks of terror echoed from inside. Something hit Crockett's head and knocked him down. Dazed, he struggled to one knee. Blinked blood out of his eyes and stared at the chaos.

He could see right into the building. It was a kind of barracks or hospital ward. Rows of beds were draped with white mosquito nets. He was sure he saw several men and women in white uniforms. The Chinese gunners knew the Americans were using the building for cover. They fired their cannon and Dushkas right through the structure.

Crockett stared through holes blown in the wall by cannon shells. Saw men roll out of bed, shot to pieces by machine gun fire. They were running this way and that, hurling themselves at the walls in a frenzy. Some tore at the shell holes with their bare hands. Ripped their fingers to tatters trying to escape. The men and women in white uniforms threw themselves on the floor.

One man, foaming at the mouth, stared at Crockett. A cannon shell decapitated him. The body crumpled, the neck a dirty stump. The opposite wall splintered. Light streamed through hundreds of bullet holes.

The mine was twenty yards away, a cavernous black maw. Butler was firing from inside. Spears and Appleyard straggled toward him. A bullet hit Appleyard in the back, another drilled Spears through the outside of his thigh. Appleyard fell and dropped his Swedish K. Spears dragged him to the safety of the mine.

"Go," Crockett urged Mosby.

Mosby struggled to the entrance of the mine and threw himself down. He'd been hit twice. His hip, legs, and back were bleeding from twenty-millimeter shrapnel wounds. Cursing, spittle flying from his lips, he held the AK47 between his knees. Changed mags one-handed, reloaded the Bonfire.

Crockett tore his eyes away from the mania inside the building.

Stroud's ammunition drum was empty. Crockett pushed him toward the mine. They ran together as the others fired over their heads at pursuing Chinese. Mosby fired the Bonfire again. The grenade flew through the air in a flat trajectory, hit one of the Dushkas, and exploded. Shrapnel blew the gunner's face off. Twisted, the weapon fell off the train.

The team huddled together at the mouth of the mine. The PLA swarmed forward, occupied the shattered building. More PLA infantry arrived from the hill. Stroud changed out his drums, opened fire. The RPD cut the Chinese down like a scythe.

Explosions burst around the cave mouth. The Chinese plastered them with twenty-millimeter cannon fire. Limestone shattered. Stroud cried out, let go of the RPD, and clutched his head. Flying rock had opened his scalp.

Crockett changed out the mag in his Swedish K. Racked the bolt. His watch read 0950 hours. The battle had lasted less than twenty minutes. The mission was compromised, and his entire team was wounded.

They were trapped.

I DRAIN my coffee and order a refill from the waitress. She tops up Crockett and Heth's cups while she's at it. When the girl has left, I turn to Crockett.

"What do you think it was?" I ask. "War crimes? The PLA shot up a hospital and slaughtered innocent patients to get to your team."

"That's an obvious guess," Crockett says, "but it's off the mark. Not up to your standard, Breed."

"Why is it off the mark?"

"I wouldn't call the slaughter a war crime. China wasn't at war. At worst, those killings were an internal human rights violation. Honestly... do you think the Chinese would bother to murder witnesses fifty years later?"

Crockett enjoys playing cat and mouse, and he's pissing me off. Unfortunately, he's right. The Chinese have a terrible record on human rights. They don't even try to hide it.

"So what is it, Sam?"

"The mine was abandoned." Crockett sips his coffee. "Why would they hide thousands of tons of construction material in the jungle?"

"They were building something."

## 18

## CATHEDRAL AND CHAPEL

**Yunnan, December 21, 1974**

"They were building something," I breathe.

"They were *going* to build something," Crockett corrects me. "They'd barely started. We stumbled into their supply depot. I think the big building at the base of Hill 868 was a barracks for workers, not soldiers."

"You didn't see any construction workers."

"No. I think they were kept inside to avoid detection by spy satellites. It isn't difficult to time the orbits of those platforms. The only way to get 24/7 coverage is to task a bird in geo-stationary orbit. We hadn't done that. The Chinese moved material and workers when the birds were out of sight."

"What were they building?"

"Let me finish my story."

CROCKETT TOOK stock of the team.

Appleyard was worst off. His left shoulder blade had been

shattered and he could barely move his left arm. Worse, he had been shot in the back, and the AK47 round had exited through his belly. Stroud, a trained medic, was binding the wound as best he could.

Mosby bore bullet wounds in his shoulder and side. Butler stuffed combat dressings into the entry and exit wounds. Shrapnel had shredded the big man's back and legs. Splinters in his hip were grinding bone.

A bullet had plowed a furrow in Spears's thigh. Missed the femoral artery. He applied a tourniquet. Shrapnel had torn up Butler and Stroud. Blood streamed from a gash in Crockett's temple. He took off his neckerchief, bound the wound.

"They're going to rush us," Butler said.

The twenty-millimeter cannon on the flatcar was silent. PLA gunners were stacking magazines, preparing to attack. Chinese infantry gathered behind the hospital and barracks buildings.

Crockett turned to Mosby. "Can you take out the twenty mike-mike with a grenade?"

Mosby shook his head. "Not one-handed. Someone better take the weapon."

Crockett nodded. "Spears. Swap with Mosby."

Spears handed Mosby his AK47 and took the Bonfire. Mosby handed him the bandolier of grenades.

Butler grunted. "You know we can't break out."

"We're not going out the front," Crockett said.

"Found a back door, have you?"

"We'll find one. Remember, the miners sank shafts all over the place."

His face white, Appleyard stared at Crockett. "I can't make it out."

"We'll carry you."

Appleyard shook his head. "I won't make it. You go, I'll hold as long as I can."

The two men stared at each other. Crockett nodded. "Okay. We'll leave right away. Spears, you're rear guard. Take out that twenty mike-mike with a grenade before you follow. That'll take heat off Appleyard."

Spears braced the Bonfire and took aim.

Crockett took out his flashlight. "Have yours ready," he told the team. "But conserve batteries. Let's go."

The mouth of the tunnel was fifteen feet wide and twenty feet high. There were narrow-gauge railroad tracks leading into the blackness. There was granite in the walls, but most of the rock was limestone. Crockett's eyes adjusted to the gloom. He could make out the shadows of rusty ore carts. Crockett took a breath, switched his flashlight on, and plunged into the mine.

Cold. The jungle outside had been hot, well into the nineties. Inside the mine, the air was blessedly cool. The humidity wicked from shiny stone walls. Crockett swung his flashlight around, played it on the floor so he would not trip on the railroad ties.

He pushed deeper.

From the mouth of the cave, he heard an explosion. The drumbeat of AK47 fire. Then—two more explosions. More gunfire. Spears must have silenced the anti-aircraft cannon.

Appleyard could not hold for long.

The team was closely bunched behind Crockett. They did not fear ambush inside the mine, and they wanted to stay close to the comfort of his flashlight. They followed the shadowy outlines of the men in front of them. Crockett's light glistened off wet blue and green stones. Behind was nothing but darkness and the sound of gunfire.

Crockett gagged. A foul smell saturated the cold air. The

sharp odor of ammonia struck him like a physical blow. He staggered.

"Fuck."

"What is that stink?" Butler gasped.

There was no holding his nose. Crockett tried to breathe through his mouth, pressed on. Thirty more feet and the tunnel opened into a vast space. The flashlight was barely strong enough to reach across the gulf.

The cave was a vast cathedral, its ceiling a limestone dome. The floor was sixty yards in diameter, the vault a hundred meters high. Far from smooth, the limestone walls were craggy with sharp, jagged ridges. Black hollows.

The walls rippled and the floor shifted. Crockett brushed the back of his hand across his eyes. At first, he thought the stench and his injury were making him dizzy. No, the floor *was* alive. Wet with bat urine, guano, and a paste of crumbling bones. Beetles and cockroaches as big as mice scurried away from the light. Snakes slithered between rocks. It was impossible to distinguish predator from prey.

Above, Crockett heard the sound of rustling paper, the rippling of thin leather wings. Tens of thousands of bats hung from roosts in the dome. Their clawed toes were locked onto stone ridges. Densely packed, they swayed against each other as Crockett played the light over them. Red, resentful eyes glared at him. The flashlight beam reflected from retinal blood vessels. Crockett's limbic brain told him he was in the presence of evil.

The railroad tracks crossed the open space.

"This is the gullet of the mine," he announced to no one in particular. "We're under Hill 180. The miners sank shafts from the surface wherever they found copper veins. Ore was cut from the shafts and shoved into this space. Loaded into carts and rolled out."

"What about the bats?" Mosby seemed to have forgotten his pain.

"When the mine was abandoned, they must have sought shelter in here." Crockett played the light over the floor. "That stink... it's guano. Batshit and piss. It's a god-awful pool of poisons and nutrients. If a bat falls, or a snake wanders in, those beetles will strip it to bones in a minute."

"Can we get out?"

"We'd have to climb over bats to find a shaft. They aren't likely to attack us, but I wouldn't want to piss them off."

Butler turned on his own flashlight. "Look at that."

A pallet of brown paper bricks sat on the floor, close to one wall.

"Wait here," Crockett instructed Mosby. Stroud and Spears had caught up.

They played their flashlight beams about the dome of the cathedral. The leather bats hung in their roosts. Males shrouded females in their wings, fucked them upside-down. It was a scene from a medieval triptych, a vision of hell. Crockett watched Stroud's features twist with revulsion. For a moment, the 1-0 feared Stroud would lose it, start blasting away.

Spears saw it too, put his hand on Stroud's shoulder. The machine gunner jerked. "Easy, brother."

Crockett and Butler stepped to the pallet. The thought of the creatures crushed under their boots made Crockett's skin crawl. Worse than the leeches that infested the jungle above.

He picked up one of the bricks. To his surprise, it was heavy and flexible. It felt like children's modeling clay wrapped in wax paper.

The substance was sweating. The corners of the paper were dark with a greasy film.

"C-4," Butler said.

"Close enough." Butler put the brick back on the pile. "It's

Chinese plastic explosive. Higher velocity and more powerful than C-4, but much less stable."

"What's it doing here?"

Crockett looked around the dome. "I think our friends are planning to build something in here. It might have something to do with that supply depot we bumped into yesterday. Interesting, but it doesn't help us now."

Crockett played the light over the opposite wall. He saw another tunnel. Smaller than the one they had come through. Wide enough and high enough for a man to walk erect. "There," he said, and crossed the chamber. His boots crunched on bones and insects.

The echoes of gunfire died away. The Chinese must have overrun Appleyard.

A quick check told Crockett the others were still with him. He turned around and flashed his light on the wall of the tunnel. Butler followed. A grimly determined Mosby was in third, dragging his leg. Stroud was next, RPD ready, eyes darting. Spears brought up the rear.

The narrow-gauge railroad continued for another hundred yards. Crockett noticed the rails and spikes were shiny, the sleepers brand new. The tracks came to an abrupt stop. More rails, sleepers, and spikes were stacked neatly against the tunnel wall. Iron tools used to carry them lay on the floor.

Crockett raised his fist, signaled the others to stop. They froze and listened. Waited for their hearts to stop pounding in their ears. The Chinese were on their trail.

Straining his eyes, Crockett could not see into the blackness. It was the complete absence of light. He heard no voices, saw no lights. The Chinese were too far back to detect. He turned his light back on.

They had left the bats behind in the cathedral. There was no good reason for the bats to roost in *this* tunnel. No more than they had to roost in the tunnel that led to the mouth of the mine. But no matter how far he hurried down the tunnel, Crockett could not escape the stench of guano and ammonia. The odor soaked the rocks.

He took out his compass. He did not know if there were any iron deposits in the surrounding rock, but he doubted it. The railroad tracks were a hundred yards behind him.

Crockett was leading the team south. They must have been traveling under the long saddle that did not appear on their map. Two hundred yards gone. Another hundred, and they would be under the unmarked Hill 40. The mesa with the flat top.

The PLA were still chasing them. Crockett practically ran down the tunnel.

Was it his imagination, or was the darkness lightening ahead?

Crockett burst into another large, empty space. A smaller limestone dome. Less than half the size of the last. A chapel, not a cathedral. But the top of this dome had fallen in. The lips were jagged and festooned with vegetation. He could not see the sky. The canopy of the jungle blocked the light.

It was a sinkhole. That was why the unmarked hill looked flat from the outside. Hill 180 looked the same. While this dome was intact, it must have been weakened by shafts dug into the mountain. Then it collapsed. In time, the soft limestone of the cathedral would also give way.

The colony of bats occupying the space did not appreciate the intrusion. There was a thunder of wings and a hundred thousand bats burst from the walls. The animals squealed with anger and beat their wings fifteen times a second. Crockett raised his arms to protect his eyes as hundreds flew past him through the tunnel. They swarmed past Butler, then Mosby and the others.

Crockett swung his light around. He expected the toxic

stew of guano, beetles, and animal skeletons that littered the floor. He didn't expect the sacks of cement neatly stacked six feet high. Piles of steel rebar. He glanced at Butler. They were thinking the same thing.

The bats were also fleeing in the opposite direction. They were flying down a smaller tunnel. That tunnel was low. A man couldn't crouch in it. Crockett didn't stop to think. He knew they couldn't climb out of the sinkhole, and they weren't going back to the cathedral. He dropped on all fours and crawled.

He moved fast. There were places his rucksack brushed the ceiling. Bats flew past him, racing to their destination. Fought for space. The tunnel was a passage, not a roost. At one point he got stuck. The passage was too narrow to traverse with his ruck on his back.

For a moment, Crockett was overcome by claustrophobic terror. Then he saw the way through. He lay flat, shrugged off his ruck, and ran a strap from the ruck to his belt. Fastened it with a snap clip. Snipers crossing exposed areas wanted to look like hollow suits of clothes. They dragged equipment behind them to reduce their profiles. Butler and the others got the idea, followed suit.

Crockett crawled along the tunnel floor, dragging his ruck. If it narrowed further, they would be fucked. To his relief, the tunnel widened. Before long, he could get back onto his hands and knees. They were still heading south.

Another hundred yards and the tunnel bifurcated. One branch went straight, another angled left. Crockett stopped and sniffed. The stench was so bad he couldn't discern a difference between the two paths.

A small bat flew past him. Six inches from Crockett's nose, it alighted on the tunnel floor. He found himself staring at a pointed face, pug nose, and intelligent eyes. The animal's ears were long and elfin. Crockett told himself those eyes could see in the dark more effectively than a nightscope. The ears were sensitive enough to hear the beating hearts of animals a hundred yards away. That nose could smell… food.

The little bat sniffed, deemed Crockett of no interest. Turned, took two steps down the tunnel. Beat its wings and took flight.

Crockett blinked blood and sweat out of his eyes. Followed the bat.

Time after time, the tunnel forked. Sometimes two or three times in the space of thirty yards. Each time they came to a fork, Crockett waited for tiny bats to guide him. Each time he made a decision, he took out his SOG knife and gouged a mark on the ceiling. In a spot the Chinese wouldn't think to look, but the team could find if they had to backtrack.

Hours later, they emerged into a smaller chamber. It was more irregular in shape, more like a cave. Above was another sinkhole, much smaller than the first, completely obscured by vegetation. The opening was twenty feet above the floor. Crockett shrugged on his rucksack, slung his weapons, and climbed.

When he reached the lip of the sinkhole, Crockett stretched his arms and gripped rock with both hands. He pushed off, allowed himself to dangle. Like a bat, he thought. He felt his sinews tense under the weight of his body and pack. Then he raised himself and threw a leg over. Rolled onto the jungle floor.

He waited for his breathing to normalize. Listened for sounds of pursuit. There were none. The team had made its way over a mile from Hill 180. He was sure the Chinese were familiar with the larger tunnels. He doubted they could follow the team through the mile-long maze he had navigated.

Crockett flashed Butler a thumbs-up. They had to get the most lightly wounded to the top. Rig a hoist for Mosby.

They had to make their way to Thailand.

"What were they building?" I ask.

"No idea, Breed. A secret installation, hidden away in an isolated corner of Yunnan Province. In an abandoned copper mine. Under a bat cave. They hadn't even started."

"Did you report it at your debrief?"

"Of course. We made it back into Laos, called for extraction. A mission was launched from Thailand. We filed our after-action reports from Udorn Air Base. Four months later, the Saigon government collapsed. NVA tanks rolled into town and the ambassador was hauled off the embassy roof. *Tons* of after-action reports were burned. They literally shoveled shit into bonfires."

"Is there any chance Appleyard survived?"

Crockett sips his coffee. "Why do you ask?"

I'm not giving him any more until he gives me something. "Could he have survived?"

"I don't see how, Breed. The last I saw, his guts were held in by a field dressing and a pistol belt."

"The Chinese could have taken him alive and treated him."

"I'm not a doctor, but I don't think his wounds were survivable."

"But it is possible."

"Breed, none of us would allow ourselves to be taken alive. We always saved the last bullet or grenade for ourselves. I think Appleyard killed so many PLA they shot him out of hand as soon as he was overrun."

Crockett and I stare at each other.

"Okay," he says. "Why all this interest in Appleyard?"

"My contacts at the Company tell me he survived. After the fall of Saigon, he made a career working for the Chinese. Operated for them in Cambodia. Assassinated Vietnamese military and political leaders before the Sino-Vietnamese war of 1979."

Crockett shakes his head. "Appleyard couldn't have survived."

"He killed a man in DC last week."

"Who?"

"Martin Fairchild."

I study Crockett's features for signs of a reaction. He's a gifted poker player.

"Yes," Crockett says. "I remember Fairchild."

"Appleyard was seen at the crime scene with Kang. Appleyard and Kang operated together at least once before."

"Fairchild always operated behind the scenes," Crockett says. "I have no idea why he would be a target today."

"He was convinced Appleyard survived. His death is another data point that ties these murders to Jiang Shi. Do you remember anything else?"

"Breed, that was the last mission of the Black Sheep."

# 19

# LOVE CHILD

**Las Vegas to Pine Bluff**

I stand in the parking lot, watching Crockett and Heth through the Denny's window. They have chosen a table from which they can keep an eye on our unlocked car. I hold the phone to my ear and tell Stein what happened. Summarize Crockett's story.

"We have Kang's photograph and his last cover identity," Stein says. "We'll get him."

Eighteen-wheelers roar past on the highway. I stick my index finger in my left ear, raise my voice. "Any sign of Appleyard?"

"No. We think he's gone to ground, planning his next hit."

I lean back against Crockett's Charger. Cast a glance at the trunk. He must keep his rifle and ammunition in there. The 1911 is bulging in his waistband. Where's the knife? Mine is duct-taped to my right calf, handle down. Concealed by my jeans leg. "Maybe he ran."

"No. These people are professionals. Their reputations are only as good as their last job."

"The Chinese want the Black Sheep dead because they saw a secret installation in Yunnan."

"It's more than that."

"Yes. If the Black Sheep got out, they can get back *in*. But what was the installation?"

"Stay tuned, I'll have answers soon. Meanwhile, keep Crockett alive."

At seventy-two, Crockett is a very heavy dude. I doubt he has trouble taking care of himself. "Stein, tell me what you know before Appleyard knocks you off."

"Breed, your concern is touching. Really, it is."

Stein sounds hurt. To my surprise, I care. "We have to find Stroud."

"I've made progress there." I imagine Stein rubbing her hands together with satisfaction. "Stroud has a son. Jared Twight."

"He didn't take his father's name?"

"It was the seventies, Breed. Twight is the love child of Stroud and Mary-Anne Twight. AKA Sunshine."

"Sunshine? Sounds like a Cocker Spaniel."

"Behave. I have a picture. With that seventies hairstyle, there is some resemblance. Twight owns a marijuana farm in Pine Bluff, Colorado. It's near Denver. He's a licensed producer."

"His father used to run drugs."

"Probably still does. I'll flick this to the FBI. His father can't be far."

"Don't do it, Stein. If the Feds pay Twight a visit, Stroud will be gone forever."

"You think you and Crockett have a better chance?"

"Of course. Stroud knows Crockett."

Stein hesitates. Stroud has played cat-and-mouse with the law for fifty years. He'll disappear at the first whiff of the FBI.

"Where do you think Kang is?" she asks.

"That's a good question, Stein. I don't know. There's no reason he should have more information than we do regarding Stroud's whereabouts. But he is resourceful."

"Alright, Breed. When you find Stroud, bring him in with Crockett."

I disconnect the call, squeeze the phone into my hip pocket. My chest hurts. I take off my jacket, find the cut has stained my white T-shirt. I throw the jacket and shirt onto the back seat. Pull on a fresh T-shirt—black.

The rest stop's come alive. Truckers cast admiring glances at the Charger. I smile. There is something so USA about internal combustion.

Across the highway squats a Wendy's and a tacky strip mall. More truckers and families on holiday. The air is dry. It's Vegas hot and smells of dust. I glance skyward, enjoy the feel of the wind on my face and arms. Stride back to the Denny's.

I throw myself into the booth. Bring Crockett and Heth up to date.

"The Chinese are targeting anyone with knowledge of the mine," I tell them. "The Black Sheep are targets because they can get back in through that maze of tunnels."

"I can't believe Appleyard survived," Crockett says.

"Fairchild was convinced."

"This begs the question, why?" Heth says. "Why now, fifty years later? What were they building inside that mine?"

"Stein says she will have answers soon." I signal the waitress for our check. "Right now, we have to find Stroud."

"He never told me he had a son," Crockett says.

"Stroud might have wanted to keep Twight's existence private. Especially if Twight was also involved in illegal activity."

The Magellan Voyager App on my phone is a marvel. It

integrates GPS data, satellite photography, and a map database in a single package. “There it is,” I say. “Pine Bluff County.”

“That’s an eleven-hour drive,” Heth observes.

I pull a quarter from my pocket and smile. “Call it.”

# 20

## THE FANGS

### Pine Bluff

I lost that toss and drove the next six hours. Heth takes the wheel and drives the last leg to Pine Bluff. We drive through Grand Junction. The terrain changes from flat desert to rolling mountain country. Highway I-70 slopes upward. The higher we climb, the cooler the air. The sky is blue as far as the eye can see. The air is laced with the scent of conifers.

We roll through Denver. Before reaching Limon, we turn off onto state highways and local roads. I stare out the window at fields and hillsides of marijuana plants. Marijuana was legalized for recreational use less than ten years ago. The growth of the industry has been phenomenal.

A sign announces we are entering Pine Bluff County.

"Where do we start?" Heth asks.

Crockett straightens in the back seat.

"Pine Bluff is a small county," I say. "Let's find a watering hole and ask about Stroud."

It's mid-afternoon. We haven't had a break since Vegas,

and a rest stop sounds inviting. "Alright," Heth says. "Let's find a good spot."

"Pine Bluff is the county seat," I say. "We should find something around there."

Heth's eyes flick to the rearview mirror. "Breed, look behind us."

I reach for an old-model chrome joystick and adjust the passenger's rearview mirror.

The highway behind us is choked with Harleys. Two columns of bikers occupying one lane. They stretch back two hundred yards. They're inscrutable behind beards and sunglasses. They wear oily jeans and leather jackets. Cuts—vests made of leather, or by cutting the sleeves off jean jackets. The bikes are cruisers—no windscreens, no frills. Big, throaty dragons.

"Let them pass," I tell Heth.

"I'm not about to race them."

One of the bikers swings into the left-hand lane, pulls even with Heth's window. First, he checks her out, then Crockett. His gaze fixes on me. Silvered shades hide his eyes. His beard is Viking-red, makes him look like a Norse god. I'm sure that's the effect he wants to create.

I raise my hand in greeting, invite him to pass.

The biker nods, pulls ahead.

With mighty roars, the other bikes swarm past. As they pull ahead, I check out their rockers—curved patches on the backs of their cuts.

The convex top rocker bears the club's name: THE FANGS.

The concave bottom rocker indicates the club chapter: DENVER.

The patch smack in the middle is the club's colors. My heart skips a beat.

Fangs bared, it's the face of a snarling vampire bat.

. . .

The bike club is tanking up at a gas station. Lots of big guys. Anywhere from thirty to fifty years old. Most are heavily muscled, a few carry their share of lard. They're all patched, which means they're officially club members. Any nonmember caught wearing their patch might not live to regret it.

Next to the station, sixty feet back of the road, is a diner-bar. In front is a gravel parking lot. A big sign over the door proclaims the establishment to be Kelly's. Another sign, in block capitals says:

COLD BEER — HOT WOMEN

"This looks like a good place to stop," I tell Heth.

"You've got to be kidding."

"My kind of joint."

Heth gives me a dirty look, spins the wheel, and pulls off the road. The Charger lurches to a stop in front of the bar.

Bikers stare at us from the gas station.

I open the door, set a booted foot on gravel, dismount. I stretch, check out the bikers, and tilt the passenger seat forward so Crockett can get out.

Heth slams the driver's door shut. Shoulders her haversack. She isn't about to leave it unguarded again.

The bar is cool and devoid of customers. A fiftyish man with graying hair comes out of the back room and steps behind the bar. "Good afternoon," he says. "This place won't get going for a few more hours."

"That's okay," I tell him. "We could use some beers."

"Alright," the man says. He seems an agreeable sort. "I'll want ID from the young lady."

Heth shows him her driver's license.

"Montana?" The man hands the card back to Heth, draws our beers. "What brings you folks down here?"

"We're looking for an old friend," Crockett tells him. "Don Stroud. He's about my age. Do you know him?"

"Can't say I do." The man sets our beers in front of us. "That'll be eighteen bucks."

I slide a twenty across the bar. The man rings the till, slides two dollar bills back to me.

"What about his son?" I ask. Tip the beer down my throat. The cold drink slides down and I feel ten times more alive. "His name's Jared Twight. Understand he owns farms around here."

The man's eyes narrow. "What business do you have with Jared?"

I shrug. "His father."

Crockett drains his beer. "I haven't seen him in fifteen years. It sure would be good to catch up."

The front screen door creaks open. Half a dozen Fangs file into the bar, led by the red-bearded Viking. "Good afternoon, Amos."

The Viking walks slowly to the bar. Takes off his mirrored shades. His long hair is bound with a bandana. Some of the bikers sit at tables. Others remain standing. More bikers push through the door.

"Good afternoon, Red."

The bikers all wear white diamond patches on their cuts. A white 1% and the white letters ER on a black field with a white border. One of the bikers has 1% ER tattooed on his neck.

Amos clears his throat. "These folks are looking for Jared."

Red stares at me. Lifts an eyebrow. "What's your business with Jared?"

"His father's a friend of ours," I say. "We're hoping Jared can tell us where to find him."

"Sorry, friend." Red shakes his head. "If you want to see

Jared, make an appointment."

I push off the bar. "We're already here. If you tell us where to find him, we'll be on our way."

Red snorts. "You'll be on your way, alright. Back the way you came."

We're facing nine Fangs with more outside. Harley engines rumble. Go quiet. More bikers arriving. I'm conscious Crockett has a 1911 in his waistband. And a SOG knife hidden somewhere on that long, lean body. Spears's killing knife is taped to my right shank.

"Alright," I say. "We'll go. Head east through Pine Bluff."

"You didn't hear me." Red takes me by the arm. "You're leaving the way you came."

I lock Red's wrist and bear him to the floor. Fangs shoot to their feet. One of the bikers reaches under his cut.

Crockett brushes back his shirt. His hand goes to the grip of the 1911.

"Tell them to back off," I tell the Viking, "or I'll break your arm."

"Stay back," the Viking snaps. Then, to me, "Mister, let me up and leave. No hard feelings. You break my arm, it'll heal. These boys *will* kill you."

"Hey, what's going on here?" A young biker steps through the front door. Shoulder-length blond hair, lean and fit. He's wearing the biker uniform. Greasy jeans, white T-shirt, and a black leather cut with a 1% ER diamond. "Mister, you let go of Red. We don't want any trouble."

I release Red's wrist and let him get to his feet.

"These folks are looking for you, Spike."

Spike smiles and steps forward. He winks at Heth, looks me over. His eyes come to rest on the flag tattooed on my shoulder. "Where did you serve, mister?"

"All over," I say. "Afghanistan. Iraq. Other places."

There are memory patches on Spike's cut. One proclaims

him to be an Afghanistan veteran. Another: "In memory of Cpl K. Naughton. Korengal 2007."

"What outfit?"

I hesitate. "First SFOD-D."

Spike laughs. "Red, this man is a one-percenter. I shit thee not."

He approaches and extends his hand. "I was with the 173rd Airborne Brigade," he says. "2007 to 2009."

I shake his hand. "You were in the Korengal."

"You know it."

"I know Kunar."

"What do you want with me, man?"

I nod to Crockett. "This is Sam Crockett. Your father served with him in 'Nam. We sure would like to see him."

Spike bends at the hip and squints at Crockett. "I seen you in pictures," he says. Gives Crockett a sly look. "It wasn't just 'Nam, was it?"

"No," Crockett says. His eyes are wary. "It wasn't."

"My dad founded this club," Spike says proudly. "Like it?"

The young man raises his arms to the sides, shoulder-height. Turns and displays the back of his cut. The bat leers at us.

"Nice." Crockett is not smiling. "Made an impression on your dad."

"He still dreams about them," Spike says. "Fifty years, he can't get them out of his head."

"They stay with you. Will you take us to him?"

Spike strokes his stubble. "I reckon it's alright. Follow me, I'll give you the dime tour." He turns to the Viking. "Red, I'm going to take these folks to see the farm. Meet me there in a couple hours."

He turns to Heth. "Who are you?"

Heth frowns. "Who, me?"

Spike grins. "Who else? I know who I am."

The girl folds her arms, shows Spike her best bitch face. "Heth."

"You can call me Jared. Want a ride?"

Blood colors Heth's cheeks. "No, thanks."

"Suit yourself."

With that, Jared Twight, once of the 173rd Airborne Brigade, leads us out of the bar.

HETH CLIMBS in behind the wheel. We watch Spike mount an eight-hundred-pound Fat Boy Harley. Shiny black paint and gleaming chrome. With a roar, the engine catches. Spike pulls onto the road.

I'm tempted to tease Heth about her new admirer. Think better of it.

"What was all *that* about?" Heth asks. She starts the Charger and pulls out behind Spike.

"I saw the Fangs patch under their rockers," I tell her. "I don't believe in coincidences."

"Since when do you know about bike gangs?"

"They aren't gangs. They're clubs."

"Fine. What's with that diamond patch?"

We follow Spike and his Harley through Pine Bluff. It's a small town. There is a single main street with fifteen buildings on either side. As many houses scattered further away from the road. Before long, the town is behind us and we are driving into the hills. It's a pastoral scene.

"Bike clubs go back to World War Two," I tell her. "Soldiers came home to a changed country. Most of them were fucked up. Watched too many of their buddies get blown in half on the beaches. They were looking for the kind of esprit de corps they had in combat, the rush of doing something exciting. They formed motorcycle clubs.

"One weekend, in the late forties, bike clubs from all over

held a convention at a small town. It was mostly peaceful. The cops got a band to play and entertain the bikers. There were a few fights, a handful of arrests. By Monday, the bikers were gone.

"Some reporter posed a picture of a biker with a mountain of beer cans. He didn't drink them—they collected the empties from inside the bar. The headline was that gangs of bikers had terrorized the town. The American Motorcycle Association published a rebuttal. It claimed 99% of bikers were solid, law-abiding people.

"That implied only 1% of bikers were bad-asses. Since then, only outlaws wear the 1% ER patch. If you wear that patch and run into a true 1% ER, be prepared to fight. They will kick your ass. Or worse."

"Where did you hear all this?"

"Soldiers are natural prospects for bike clubs. A while back, a few of the major clubs recruited vets. There's a natural attraction. Clubs are structured hierarchies. There are rules, policies and procedures. They ride in formation. Like the Army."

# 21

# ICED BULLETS AND WHISKEY

**Pine Bluff**

We follow Spike past acre after acre of planted fields. At the crest of a hill sits a single-story glass structure. It's a greenhouse, a hundred yards long by sixty yards wide. The road continues to a wood-framed building. The complex sprawls over the hilltop. We quickly realize it's not one greenhouse but three, built close together. Inside, plants have been arranged in long rows.

Spike stops in a gravel parking lot, dismounts, and sets his kickstand. There are a handful of cars there, but it is late afternoon, and workers are going home. I park next to Spike's bike.

"We've got twenty acres," Spike tells us. "I own two licenses, ten acres a license. Twenty thousand plants. We run everything ourselves, from genetics to extraction."

"How long have you been at this?" Crockett asks.

"Ten years. Our first operation was small, legal for medicinal use. When the state legalized for recreational, the business took off."

Spike points to the wooden building. "That's our extraction plant. Dad's pride and joy. We have a completely automated industrial process. Biomass is packed into tanks and pumps suck all the air out. We use pure butane as a solvent. The butane you buy for home use has impurities. Providers mix that shit into the gas so you can smell leaks. Taints our product. We use n-butane that's 99.5 percent pure—doesn't smell at all.

"The butane binds with active compounds in the biomass. THC and CBD. The extract goes in a collection tank, from which we separate the goodies."

I get the picture. What impresses me is the scale of the operation. I've seen people grow marijuana plants in a bathtub. This business is staggering. It must cost millions.

"Who pays for all this?" I ask.

Spike looks thoughtful. "We pay for it ourselves, actually."

"Oh yeah?"

Spike looks from me to Crockett and back. "I sold the land to the club for a fuckload of cash, then leased it back. Used the cash to pay for the business. The profits pay for the lease."

I'm tempted to ask Spike how much of the financing arrangement is legal. He anticipates my question. "Don't you worry, we have a city block full of lawyers. We pay good money to make sure our regulatory filings are cool and finances pass muster. Thirty years ago, my old man was a creative entrepreneur. Now our business is one hundred percent legit."

I doubt that. But I believe their intentions are sincere. It's possible they also run unlicensed product and use the legitimate operation as a cover. Buy equipment and supplies for thirty acres, licenses for twenty. The Fangs may smuggle product to states where marijuana is still illegal.

Stroud came home from Vietnam and rode on the wild side. The bats of Jiang Shi haunted his dreams. He ran drugs and formed a motorcycle club. Badass enough to wear the 1% ER diamond. Who knew what The Fangs got into. Stroud and his associates had records, but his son was clean. A good front.

Crockett's eyes quarter the ground. "Where's your Dad?"

"He'll be in the office. Follow me."

Spike leads us over a paved walkway. Between the greenhouses and the extraction plant sits a smaller building. Like the others, this building is a single story. The office and the extraction plant are painted the same white with black trim.

I hang back as Spike opens the door and leads us into the building. We haven't seen a sign of Kang since he killed Spears. There's no reason for him to have known about Twight. Kang hit a dead end the same time we did. Only Stein gave us a clue.

"Dad." Spike knocks on the door of an office. "I've got a surprise for you."

"Come in." The voice is deep, gravelly. Spike opens the door.

Don Stroud rises from a heavy iron desk. He looks fit for his age. Not a tall man. Five-ten, rock-solid. He's wearing boots, jeans, and a white T-shirt. There's a drawing of a leafy marijuana plant on the front. His arms are covered with tattoos and tanned brown by the sun. His skin is leathery, his face lined. A stark contrast to the white handlebar mustache he wears.

My eyes are drawn to the wall behind the desk. Stroud has decorated it with a four-by-four foot poster of The Fangs colors. The bat shrieks over foot-long canines. Stroud works with the colors leering at him.

This is not a kindly grandfather. Apart from the incongruous T-shirt, he's a caricature cut from *Soldier of Fortune* magazine. The kind of retired operator who organizes coups and trains cartels for cash.

I can see this man founding The Fangs.

Stroud breaks into a grin, shakes Crockett's hand. The two men embrace, and Crockett introduces us.

"Why did you name your club The Fangs?" I ask.

The old-timer's eyes slide away. "We ran into bats in Vietnam," he says. "I came back and couldn't get them out of my head. Best cure for anything like that is exposure."

"Like getting back on a horse that threw you?"

"Something like that. Let's go next door," Stroud says. "A reunion's worth a drink."

He leads us from his private office. The next room is a large space, with desks for a dozen staff. Open-plan, half of it is given over to comfortable furniture. Bright orange upholstery, bean-bags on the floor. There's a small kitchen on one side, with a fridge and coffee maker.

Stroud goes to the kitchen and takes half a dozen 1911 magazines from the freezer. Crams them into his hip pockets. Returns with a bottle of Jack Daniels and some glasses.

We pull up chairs and arrange ourselves around a glass coffee table. Stroud sets out five glasses on cork coasters. Places the magazines on the table. He winks at Crockett and chuckles to himself. Picks up a magazine and snicks frozen .45 ACP rounds into the glasses.

"Titanium," Stroud says. He goes around the table until he's dropped five of the iced bullets into each glass. Works his way through four magazines, pours whiskey for us. "Melting ice cubes dilute the flavor."

"Here's to the Black Sheep." Crockett raises his glass.

"To the Black Sheep," Spike says. We all clink glasses.

"I'm glad to see you," Stroud says. "What brings you here after all these years?"

Crockett and I take turns bringing Stroud up to speed. When we've finished, Stroud whistles.

"We don't know what kind of installation they were building," he says.

"The Company has an idea, but they're not ready to tell us. For now we need to stay together and stay alive."

Stroud grunts. "What do you suggest?"

"Come with us," I say. "We'll drive into Denver, find a place to hole up. I'll call Stein and find out where things stand."

"You've probably shaken Kang," Stroud says. "He has no idea where we are."

Stroud gets to his feet, goes into his office.

Have we shaken Kang? I'm not so sure.

Kang found an edge to kill Mosby. Another edge to kill Spears. What would I do if I were in Kang's shoes?

There's a clump of boots. Stroud returns, a boxy submachine gun over his right shoulder. An Ingram M-10 with a Sionics suppressor. Stroud has outfitted the weapon with a one-point sling. He wears a pistol belt, with pouches for three spare magazines on the right side. On the left, a sheath for his seven-inch recon Bowie. I recognize the green micarta handle —A Spears Special.

Over his T-shirt, he wears a black leather Fangs cut with a 1% ER diamond. He picks up his glass and drains the whiskey in one gulp. "I need to start the evening batch," he says. "Then we can go."

I want a handlebar mustache like that.

Stroud leads us out of the office building and toward the extraction plant.

My eyes sweep the parking lot. A handful of cars, including Crockett's Charger. Spike's Fat Boy on its stand. The greenhouses look quiet. I scan the rows of plants. Nothing leaps out.

Assuming he found us, how would he take on four armed men and one badass tomboy?

Stroud comes to the entrance of the extraction facility. Takes out his keys, hesitates at the lock. He turns the knob and pushes the door open. "Harvey must have left it open," he says.

Inside, we find a cavernous room with shiny stainless-steel tanks and pipes. A third of the room is occupied by tall gas cylinders. N-BUTANE has been stenciled on green metal.

Stroud steps to a control panel, examines the settings.

If I were Kang, what would I do?

Kill everyone at the same time.

Stroud reaches for a switch.

"Wait," I say.

"What's wrong?" Stroud asks.

"Does that switch start the automatic process?"

"Yes."

"How does it work?"

"It kicks off a computer program. Harvey packed the biomass tanks this afternoon. The computer starts pumps that evacuate air from the tanks. The n-butane is then added to bind with the cannabinoids."

"Check those butane tanks."

Spike strides to the rows of green cylinders. Examines the valves and hoses.

"Everybody out," Spike says.

"What's wrong?" Stroud asks.

"Get out, Dad. Right now."

We evacuate the building. I leave the door open. Five minutes pass. Spike opens the windows, joins us outside.

"Someone cut the hoses from the tanks. I shut the valves, but the building will take time to air out."

Stroud's tanned features darken. "Had the pumps started..."

"The whole building would have blown up," I finish for him.

"How the hell did Kang find us?" Crockett shakes his head.

"He must have followed us from San Cristos," I say. "If you tried something like this, what would you do?"

"Watch the fireworks."

"He's still here."

A car engine roars to life. There's a late-model Chevy Caprice parked between two other cars.

Kang. He throws the car into reverse. Tires smoking, he backs out of the parking space. The Caprice is a four-door sedan, probably a 6.0-liter engine.

"Son of a bitch," Stroud snarls.

Kang throws the car into gear and pulls onto the road. Stroud opens the Ingram's collapsible stock, raises the weapon to his shoulder.

The M-10 has a high cyclic rate of fire. Over a thousand rounds a minute. Stroud dumps the thirty-round mag in under two seconds. Bullets stitch the Caprice's right side from front to rear. The tires burst and shiny hubcaps are blown off the wheels. Bullets punch through the quarter-panel and doors. The car slews sideways, rocks on its suspension, and stops in a cloud of dust. A lonely hubcap rolls across the road. Tips over and comes to a halt.

I sprint toward the stalled vehicle.

Suppressor smoking, Stroud drops the empty mag. Draws a fresh magazine from his belt, slaps it into the grip, racks the bolt.

The Caprice won't start. Kang throws the door open and gets out. My kick connects before he can get his guard up. The ball of my foot crashes into his sternum. The impact slams him against the car.

Kang fights through the pain. He rebounds from the car

like a wrestler off the ropes. With a sharp *kiai*, he launches a punch at my face. I block it with my left forearm, step in, and drive my right elbow into his solar plexus. The uppercut ruptures his diaphragm and sends shock waves through his heart. The force of the blow lifts him off his feet. He doubles over, and I butt his face with the crown of my head. Kang slams against the car a second time.

The assassin's dazed. I grab him by his right sleeve and the collar of his suit. Drag him over my hip and put him down. My head-butt broke his nose—his face is a bloody mask.

"Breed," Spike calls. "That's enough."

Spike joins me. Together, we stand over Kang.

The assassin spits blood. "I should have killed you," he says.

I say nothing.

Motorcycle engines rumble. One after another, The Fangs ride up the hill. Some pull into the parking lot, others stop on the road.

Red climbs off his Harley Night Train and joins us. He addresses Spike. "When you said to meet you here, you didn't say you'd arrange entertainment."

"This guy tried to blow us up," Spike says. "Gas leak in the extraction plant."

"That so," the Viking rumbles. He looks down at Kang. "Who the fuck do you think you are, Bruce Lee? Guess what? This isn't Bruce Lee Day."

Crockett, Stroud, and Heth have joined us.

Supporting himself on one elbow, Kang looks up at a circle of impassive faces.

Stroud slings the Ingram, draws his knife. "I think this boy needs to learn not to fuck with another man's rice bowl."

"Dad," Spike says, "you guys should go. We got this."

The circle tightens around Kang. I notice the bikers carry chains, pipes and wrenches.

I put my arm around Heth's shoulders, lead her to the Dodge Charger. "I don't think we want to see this," I say.

"Speak for yourself."

Crockett and Stroud get in the back seat and I climb in behind the wheel. Heth gets in next to me. I start the car and pull around the crowd of bikers.

Kang struggles to his feet.

A biker flicks a chain at his face. Kang recoils and the chain misses his nose by an inch. A three-foot long pipe strikes his shoulder. Snaps his collarbone. With a howl, Kang collapses.

Stepping forward, another biker swings a wrench. Shatters Kang's elbow.

"Don't hit him in the head," Red says. "Do his bones."

I drive off the hill. In the rearview mirror, I watch the bikers crowd around Kang. They take turns beating him to a pulp.

"Do you think we're safe now?" Heth asks.

"No," I tell her. "This isn't over."

# 22

## QUESTIONS AND ANSWERS

**Peterson Air Force Base**

I park the Charger in the lot of a McDonald's restaurant. The golden arches gleam in the dusk. Crockett, Stroud and Heth go inside for food. A low guardrail separates the lot from a ditch. I sit on the rail, call Stein.

"We've got Stroud," I tell her.

"Where is he?"

"In a McDonald's with Crockett. Scarfing his dinner."

"Any sign of Kang?"

"He took a run at us. Won't be seeing him again."

"My money was on you."

"I can't take credit. Stroud founded a motorcycle club. Great colors—a vampire bat. Stroud still dreams about the tunnels in Yunnan. While Kang was conscious, the Fangs broke every bone in his body. Several times over."

"Oh." I imagine Stein taking notes with her Montblanc. She stops, processes the image, carries on. "We still don't have a line on Appleyard. He killed Fairchild, and I am in a safe place. All remaining Company targets are under guard. The field has begun to tilt in our favor."

"Love it when that happens. Are you able to tell us more about the Yunnan installation?"

"Yes. I need you to bring Crockett and Stroud to Peterson Air Force Base, Colorado Springs."

"Why?"

"I want to see you."

STEIN'S BEEN one step ahead the whole time. She flew out to Peterson yesterday. Been there ever since she sent us after Stroud. The move makes sense. Appleyard can't touch her on a military installation.

I tell Stein we can be at Peterson in a couple of hours. It's a short drive on I-25 South.

"Send the girl home," she says.

"Can't do that," I tell her. "Appleyard is still out there."

"There's nothing for her to do here," Stein says firmly. "I'm having a tough enough time renewing Crockett and Stroud's clearance. I'll never get hers through."

"She knows what Crockett and I know."

"Only because I *chose* to share that much with you. Now I'm *telling* you she can't be allowed to learn any more."

I need to speak Stein's language. "Let's play this smart, Stein. If she comes with us, we'll know where she is."

Stein hesitates. "You have a point. Alright, but she better get used to twiddling her thumbs. She will not be attending any briefings."

*Briefings.*

Time to get ahead of the curve.

"THERE IT IS," Heth says. "Exit 153."

I peel off the exit and onto the Interquest Parkway. Colorado Springs is growing. Peterson acts as a major hub for NORTHCOM, NORAD, and the 21st Space Wing. The base is spinning off jobs and sparking real estate development.

Heth checks the map on her phone. I could use a GPS, but robotic voices drive me crazy. That, and an experience years ago when my GPS did a hard reset twenty-five thousand feet over the Hindu Kush. Give me a good navigator, a map, and a compass any day.

"Right rudder," Heth commands.

I peel right, just in time. Cut off an SUV. Horns blare.

"Jesus, Breed." Crockett grimaces. "Where did you learn to drive?"

Night has fallen, and Stein gave us special instructions. Heth guides me to the Peterson North Gate. It's normally closed at this hour, but we are to be met by an aide. There are five lanes—two incoming, three outgoing. A tan stone marker announces we have arrived at Peterson Air Force Base.

The mountains are a dark row of shark's teeth to the west. I drive to the gatehouse and take the inbound lane nearest the guards. The way is blocked by a yellow metal barrier, shaped like an inverted right triangle. It is hinged at one end to swing the long pipe fence up and down. I turn my head to greet the guards. Two Air Police, from the Air Force Security Service, step to the door. They wear digital camouflage utilities and carry Beretta M9s in open holsters.

"I'm Breed," I tell them. "We're expected."

There's a blue Caprice parked on the far side of the gatehouse. Behind the three outbound lanes. US AIR FORCE is painted on its side. The door opens and an officer in dress uniform gets out. Joins the Air Police.

"Can we see your IDs please," the first Air Policeman says.

I'd anticipated the request and collected ID from Crockett, Stroud, and Heth. I hand over our Department of Defense cards and Heth's driver's license.

The Air Policeman examines the cards and hands them to the newly arrived officer. The man checks them carefully against a list.

"I'm Captain Brewster," he says. "Please follow my vehicle."

I'm a little surprised the Air Police don't search the Charger. We're carrying a small arsenal in the trunk. Stein must carry a lot of influence.

Brewster gets back into the Caprice. Starts the engine, and pulls in front of the controlled lanes. The second Air Policeman goes into the gatehouse and pushes a button. The yellow barrier rises. His partner snaps to attention and waves us forward with a slashing motion of his left hand.

I follow Brewster into the sprawling base. There are lighted areas, built-up with wide office buildings, barracks, and boulevards. The captain leads us through dark back streets. We drive past shadowy buildings. Motor pools of parked trucks, blue-painted sedans, and Humvees.

Brewster stops at a fenced area. Another gate, a pair of armed Air Police.

There are two chain-link fences, each fifteen feet high, separated by fifty yards of open space. The last three feet of the outer fence bend outward at a forty-five degree angle. Those of the inner fence bend inwards. Those last three feet are strung with razor wire. More Air Police patrol the space between. Two-man dog patrols. Some teams move clockwise, others counterclockwise.

They carry M4 carbines and are accompanied by Belgian Malinois. I've always liked Malinois. A bit smaller than shepherds, loyal and motivated. When the teams pass each other, the dogs bark. Their jaws snap and they strain at their leashes. A bizarre display—the barking is soundless.

Laryngectomized.

Silent killers.

Large signs have been mounted on the fence at hundred-yard intervals. Stroud reads one out loud. "Restricted area," he says. "Use of deadly force has been authorized."

The Air Police check Brewster's ID, then ours. This installation is vast. I can't tell how far the fences extend, how many buildings are enclosed by the perimeter. There appear to be dark airplane hangars at the far end.

Flashlights shine in our faces. The Air Police compare our features to the photographs on the cards.

Satisfied, the guards step back and open the double gate. I follow Brewster through. Peterson is a typical military base. It has an aerospace museum, Base Exchange, and recreational facilities. Different areas of the base are subject to varying levels of security.

This installation looks like a super-secret base *within* a base.

Brewster and I park our cars side by side. We get out, stretch our legs, and he leads us into the big, five-story building.

We're met by a young woman wearing dress uniform and a First Lieutenant's insignia. She ushers us to a bank of elevators and pushes a button.

An elevator door opens and I step toward it. Brewster stops me. "Lieutenant Carmichael will show the young lady to her quarters," he says. "The rest of you will come with me."

"Very well."

Heth and the lieutenant get in the elevator. The door closes and the lights tick off the floors as they rise in the building.

Brewster leans forward and pushes the button again. Another elevator opens and he motions us inside.

The elevator carrying Heth and the lieutenant has stopped on the third floor.

I get in, followed by Crockett, Stroud, and Brewster. Count the floors as we are whisked high in the building.

We get off on the fifth floor. A sterile white corridor with plain numbered offices on either side. The rooms are deserted. Spotless, as though they have been recently cleaned. Wiped of all traces of human occupancy.

"This floor has been cleared for your use," Brewster says. "A number of offices have been converted to temporary quarters. You each have a room. They're not the lap of luxury, but I doubt you'll be here long."

That sounds intriguing.

"The toilets are here," Brewster says. He points to two doors, one marked for men, the other for women. "They are equipped with showers for folks who like to run before work. There aren't any women on this floor now. Feel free to use either."

Six rooms lie at the end of the corridor, three on either side. A door on the right is open. I glance inside as we pass. A duffel rests on a cot. The office's large metal desk has been pushed aside to make room.

We're not alone.

Brewster opens the three doors on the left-hand side. Same arrangement. Small offices, desks pushed into corners. Folding cots, blue-gray blankets, white pillows. I've slept in worse.

"You can bring your things up from the vehicle later. Right now, we are expected in the auditorium."

Brewster leads us back to the elevator. We are whisked to the second floor and the doors suck open. Without hesitation, the captain steps out and turns left. He barely acknowledges an armed Air Policeman standing in front of the elevators. The man carries an M4 and wears body armor—front and back plates.

We stride down a long corridor lined with offices and conference rooms. At the end are a pair of large doors with vertical handles. Two more Air Police armed with rifles and wearing body armor flank the portal.

Brewster walks past the guards, seizes one of the handles, and swings the door open. The cavernous space beyond is dimly lit.

We follow the captain into the room. We are at the front of a large auditorium with amphitheater seating. There is a lectern on one side, a blank rear-projection screen, and a low table in the center. The rows of seats are dimly lit.

Two men are sitting in the front row. They smile and rise to greet us. "Breed."

I recognize them immediately.

Ortega and Takigawa.

Former Delta Force operators. I know them well.

I've worked with both men. Ortega had been a member of my Delta platoon since the early days in Afghanistan. Every chance we got, we went to K2, the Karshi-Khanabad base in Uzbekistan. Practiced parachute jumps on Uncle Sam's dime. He'd been with me the night of my jump with Rahimi. Stein must have sheep-dipped him and flown him to Peterson.

As a consultant, I met Takigawa on a mission to the Hindu Kush. I was impressed by the sniper's sense of humor and coolness under fire. Half-Japanese, Takigawa was six feet tall and barrel-chested. Takigawa left the army shortly after our last mission. Went freelance. Stein knew we'd worked well together.

Ortega, Takigawa, and I exchange handshakes. I introduce them to Crockett and Stroud. The five of us are Green Berets, generations and wars apart.

Brewster takes an envelope from his jacket. Inside are five sheets of paper. He hands one to each of us.

"What are these?" I ask.

I know the answer before the captain hands me a ballpoint pen. "Non-Disclosure Agreements," he says. "Before you are told any more, you must sign them."

None of us are strangers to NDAs. We sign on the dotted lines.

Satisfied, Brewster folds the documents back into the envelope. Stuffs it into his breast pocket. "Make yourselves comfortable," he says.

Without another word, the captain leaves the auditorium.

I plant my hands on my hips. Lock eyes with Ortega and Takigawa.

"Don't you love this cloak and dagger shit," Takigawa says.

"Goes with the territory."

The door opens and a familiar figure steps into the room. Long, straight brown hair. Beautiful, cold features, and skin as pale as ivory. A black pantsuit and white blouse.

"Gentlemen," Stein says. "I believe you know each other."

# 23

# THE MONSTER

**Peterson Air Force Base**

Stein walks toward us.

"Three murders," I say. "A killer at large."

"That's not the worst." Stein surveys our little group. "You have questions, I am here to answer them. Please, gentlemen. Be seated."

I find a seat in the front row. "Tell us about the installation in Yunnan."

"Alright. We had knowledge of it when I last saw you in DC. The situation has progressed, and it is bad."

"How bad?"

"More terrifying than your worst nightmare."

Crockett and Takigawa sit on either side of me. Stroud and Ortega occupy the wings. Stein steps to the front of the auditorium, takes a remote control from the lectern.

"I've been seconded to the Company's China Committee," Stein says. "We oversee the China Desk."

Stein touches a button on the remote control. Behind her, the rear-projection screen lights up. It extends wall-to-wall, floor-to-ceiling. "At issue are developments in China's biological warfare program."

*Click.*

A map of China appears on the screen.

"China has had an active program since 1950," Stein says. "First, remember China was the victim of Japanese biological warfare. Between 1933 and 1945, Japanese biological weapons killed 270,000 Chinese. More appalling, the Japanese used civilians for experiments. This experience remains an open wound in the Chinese psyche.

"Second, China adopted the Soviet Union's warfighting doctrine. The Soviets maintained an extensive stockpile of biological weapons. Pursued an aggressive development program.

"China denies having a program and weapons stockpiles. This is a lie. We know they have a program, yet the world accepts the fiction."

Stein pauses, wrinkles her forehead, carefully chooses her next words.

"The Nixon rapprochement in 1972 drove a wedge between China and the Soviets. The Soviets were an existential threat, so we promoted China's progress. Long after the disintegration of the Soviet bloc. We failed to recalibrate policy, though China was becoming our number-one competitor."

*Click.*

Bright blue dots sprinkle the map. Stein looks at the screen. "These are Chinese stockpiles. Anthrax, botulinus, tularemia. Their problem is—everybody has these. Nothing special."

*Click.*

The blue dots disappear. The map is peppered by black dots, and a single red dot.

"The biosafety scale ranks laboratories from Level 1 to

Level 4. Level 4 requires the most stringent measures, reserved for the most dangerous pathogens. The black dots represent China's Level 3 labs. The red dot, in Wuhan, represents the Wuhan Institute of Virology. It is China's only publicly acknowledged Level 4 lab. The lab works on Severe Acute Respiratory Syndrome—SARS."

*Click.*

A large red star appears on the screen at the lower edge of the country. Close to the Vietnamese border.

"Jiang Shi?" I lean forward.

"Yes. Mr Crockett and Mr Stroud know the valley well. It is an undisclosed Level 4 laboratory in south Yunnan province. Twenty-five miles inside the China-Vietnam border."

"Undisclosed?"

"The Chinese kept it secret for fifty years," Stein says. "We learned about it when our mole, codename Phoenix, was promoted. He became privy to Jiang Shi."

Crockett leans back in his chair, steeples his fingers.

Stein continues her story. "The Jiang Shi installation was built in 1974. The Chinese constructed it underground, in an abandoned copper mine. The valley is isolated. Access is by railroad, once used to transport copper ore from the mine. The Chinese put their best scientists to work at Jiang Shi. Their families live in major cities and want for nothing."

"How did we miss the movement of these scientists?" I ask.

Stein squints at me. "*That* is a question for our Deputy Director of Human Intel. He might not be in the role much longer."

I watch her pace back and forth. "Wuhan is under civilian management," Stein says. "Jiang Shi is run by the PLA—the People's Liberation Army. It started off working on the usual suspects, plus one or two interesting specialties. Rabies and bubonic plague."

"Fuck," Takigawa grunts. "What kind of people mess with plague?"

"We maintain regular contact with Phoenix through a concealed Virtual Private Network. He provided a comprehensive report—the contents were horrifying." Stein fishes a mobile phone from the pocket of her suit jacket. Punches a speed dial. "Brewster, send in Doctor Drye."

The door opens and a middle-aged woman enters. She's plain and sturdy, wears glasses and a print dress.

With a gesture, Stein introduces the woman. "This is Doctor Anne Drye. She works at the US Army Medical Research Institute of Infectious Disease—USAMRIID. Her team evaluated the report."

Stein hands the woman the remote control. Yields the floor.

*Click.*

The wall is filled by an image of a green sphere studded with spikes. Photographed against a dark background, the spikes sparkle with highlights. Tipped with little knobs, they look like a hundred golf tees stuck into a volleyball. The sphere itself wears a shiny silver coat.

"I'll try to be brief," the woman says. "This is a coronavirus. It lives in bats without making them sick. In its natural state, it does not infect humans. From time to time, viruses jump from one species to another. In 2003, a virus like this jumped from bats to humans—The SARS outbreak.

"How a virus learns to jump from a bat to a human is not known. Since 2003, work has focused on zoonosis—the animal origin of human viruses.

"The technology required to sequence the genetic material in these viruses is mature. Labs conduct studies to determine how a bat coronavirus learns to infect humans. Those spikes on the surface are made of proteins. They stick to human cells and allow the virus particle to penetrate. Once inside, the virus seizes control of the host's resources. The virus multiplies, killing the human cell in the process. Any questions?"

Drye pauses, looks around the room. She has our undivided attention.

"Let's park that," Drye says. "Look at this baby."

*Click.*

The image of the sphere is replaced by the image of a baby sausage. The sausage has been photographed against a black background. Its center is dark, but it sports a shiny coat of translucent material. The surface is covered with spikes. These are shorter, and more hair-like than the ones on the coronavirus.

"Pretty, isn't it," Drye says.

I don't think the sausage is pretty at all. The image makes my skin crawl.

Drye continues, her pace deliberate. "This is a lyssavirus," she says. "It's a group of viruses, like coronaviruses. This is a micrograph of rabies."

Pausing for effect, Drye steps aside to show off the virus.

"We've all heard of rabies. If you are bitten by a dog, get vaccinated. The virus attacks the nervous system, so symptoms are neurological. Paranoia, hallucinations and hydrophobia. The victim sinks into a coma. Once symptoms appear, the infection is one hundred percent fatal."

*Click.*

The image of a bat leers from the wall. A long, narrow skull. Jaws, lined with rows of sharp teeth. A red pug snout. Leathery ears with ribs of cartilage at the tips, and sensitive red flesh sinking into the canals. The animal's eyes are malev olent marbles. I feel nothing but revulsion.

"What do coronavirus and rabies have in common?" Drye asks. "Bats. Bats serve as hosts for both rabies and coronavirus. The viruses coexist in the bat's system without making the animal sick."

I lean back, glance at Stroud. As though hypnotized, he stares at the screen. His face has gone as white as his handlebar mustache.

"The Jiang Shi facility has been built inside an abandoned copper mine," Drye continues. "The mine and associated caverns are home to millions of bats. Rabies and coronaviruses have coexisted in these bats for hundreds of years."

*Click.*

The image on the wall snaps into a split-screen. The sausage is shown on the left, the sphere on the right.

"Imagine," Drye says, half to herself. "Rabies and coronavirus circulating for years in the bloodstreams of bats. Bouncing off each other. Getting friendly.

"Yet—rabies and coronavirus infect humans differently. Coronavirus is inhaled, or transferred by touch from one's fingers to a mucous membrane. Rabies is passed through a bite. In the saliva of an infected animal. Aerosol transmission of rabies occurs, but it is rare.

"One can speculate why it is more difficult for rabies to infect humans than coronavirus. One thing is for certain—the spike proteins have a lot to do with it."

"The spikes?" Ortega's eyes dart from one image to the other. The rabies spikes are little hairs. The coronavirus spikes look like golf tees.

"Their proteins are different." Drye turns to face us. "To increase human infectivity, genetic engineering modifies the spikes. It makes them more sticky, facilitates entrance into the host."

"Did the Chinese modify the rabies virus?" I ask.

"Yes." Drye folds her arms. I swear the woman shivered. "Phoenix sent us the genetic sequence of weaponized rabies.

It contains the spike proteins of the SARS coronavirus. More perverse, it also contains the gp41 and gp120 protein sequences from the HIV virus. These give AIDS the ability to overcome the human immune response.

"Inserting sequences from different virus families has not been possible—until now. HIV, coronavirus, and rabies are not related. The Jiang Shi lab inserted SARS spike proteins, HIV gp41, and HIV gp120 into rabies.

"Let me be clear. This is a technological breakthrough. The envelope and spikes of weaponized rabies will look very different from the image you see. It will have the bullet-shaped corpus of rabies, and the knobby spikes of coronavirus.

"The Chinese have created a monster."

Stein clears her throat. "Doctor, please tell the group what this virus can do."

Drye faces us. "Weaponized rabies infects humans by aerosol. It is airborne. Symptoms appear within five days. The alien SARS and HIV proteins increase infectivity. Once the spikes bind to human cells, it's game over."

"You sure about this?" Crockett asks.

"Yes," Drye tells him. "The sequence exhibits 95 percent homology with SARS spike proteins. 98 percent homology with HIV proteins. That cannot happen by accident. The Chinese deliberately inserted those sequences into the lyssavirus genome."

The room falls silent as we digest Drye's statement.

"Following construction of the Wuhan lab," Stein says, "all research on coronavirus, dengue, and influenza was moved to the new facility. Jiang Shi henceforth focused exclu sively on lyssavirus research—rabies."

Like a stern schoolmarm, the doctor stares at us. "Humans have no immunity to this virus. Existing rabies vaccines will not be effective because of the altered spike proteins. Aerosol transmission guarantees an unprecedented degree of virulence. Once symptoms appear, death is inevitable."

"It's a lousy weapon if you can't protect your own troops," Crockett observes.

"The Chinese are not fools," Drye concedes. "They are working on a vaccine. They know the exact structure of the viral envelope and spike proteins. I know why they concentrated the work in Jiang Shi."

"Why?" Takigawa asks.

"Viruses aren't bombs or bullets. They die. Let's say you load your little beasties into a warhead and fly it from Peterson in Colorado to Ramstein in Germany. When you land, you find your weapon dead on arrival. Every weapons designer is faced with the same problem. How do I keep the little beasts alive?"

I'd never thought about that. A simple fact, with enormous consequences. "Tell us more about that issue."

"Alright. The Soviets maintained a stockpile of twenty tons of smallpox. The stockpile had a half-life. That means half the viruses would die in a certain period. Over time, *all* the viruses would die. So they had to continuously manufacture smallpox to top up.

"The Soviets manufactured smallpox by inoculating chicken eggs on an assembly line. They literally ran the eggs on a conveyor belt. Slow and inefficient. With mechanical bioreactors, the Soviets produced 100 tons of smallpox a year. Still not fast enough. They directed all their efforts to enhancing yield.

"Guinea pigs were used as *living* bioreactors. Experiments were conducted with a different virus—Marburg. Fifty guinea pigs produced enough Marburg to kill a million people. The result was a brilliant proof of concept."

The loathsome strategy sickens me.

Drye sees the revulsion on my face. "To effectively manufacture weaponized rabies, the Chinese need *efficient* bioreactors. I think they want to create a virus reservoir in the Jiang Shi bat population."

"That's insane," Stroud whispers.

"No, bats are marvels of evolution," Drye continues. "A bat's metabolic rate increases fourteen times in flight. Its body temperature reaches forty-one degrees Celsius—enough to fry a human brain. Bat DNA is continuously damaged by heat, then repaired. Bats have immune systems uniquely adapted to make them resilient hosts.

"An animal bioreactor either dies, or is sacrificed. Its tissues are ground up to recover active virus. Alternatively, if the animal is a living host, the virus can be recovered from its blood. It survives to produce more. Bats are ideal for this technology."

Stein stares at the doctor. "What happens if there is a lab accident—what happens if this virus escapes?"

Drye shrugs. "The monster will wipe out the human race."

# 24

## SLAYING DRAGONS

**Peterson Air Force Base**

"The monster will wipe out the human race."

Stein steps to Drye's side. "Thank you, Doctor. You've rendered some complex science accessible. Please stay."

The woman nods.

I swallow. "Alright, Stein. I'm scared."

"You should be. The Chinese have created a doomsday weapon. In the twentieth century, we feared nuclear war would destroy the world. The twenty-first century reality is that viruses can do what the bomb has not."

Stein takes the remote control from Drye and touches a button. The wall is filled with a photograph of a lush, green valley surrounded by hills.

"This is Jiang Shi," Stein says. "The PLA selected the abandoned mine as a laboratory site due to the proximity of the bat caves. The animals acted as reservoirs for both rabies and coronaviruses. As far back as 1974, the Chinese were interested in rabies as a biological weapon.

"By coincidence, in December 1974, a Special Forces team was sent to Jiang Shi on an unrelated mission. Operation Guillotine. Mr Crockett and Mr Stroud are intimately familiar with the particulars."

Stein smiles, then addresses Crockett and Stroud. "Your team was detected by the Chinese. A firefight ensued, and you escaped through the mine. One man, Appleyard, was so badly wounded he was left behind. The rest of you escaped through the tunnels. Appleyard later went freelance, worked for the Chinese."

"Appleyard couldn't have survived," Crockett says.

Stein shakes her head. "He did. Your control, Martin Fairchild, confirmed it."

"If he did, he would never work for the Chinese."

"It would have been easy for Appleyard to rationalize. Consider the ambiguity of his work for China. He operated against the Vietnamese, our old enemy. Far from seeking retribution, we might have given him a medal. Sweetened with a pecuniary incentive, the temptation must have been irresistible."

"Alright," I say, "let's focus on the virus."

Stein shrugs. "The rest of the team escaped. The key point is—Mr Crockett and Mr Stroud can find their way through that maze of tunnels back to the lab."

"What does the lab in Jiang Shi look like?" I ask.

Stein turns to Doctor Drye.

"Space is limited in those caves," the woman says. "The lab would be concrete, built under the cave floor. Three levels. One for administration, another for the lab, and a third for machinery space."

"What kind of machinery?" I ask.

"At a minimum, pumps for filtered ventilation, and to create negative pressure. There will be a facility for sterilizing air flow. The machinery will become more complex as the lab expands from development to production."

"How will they build the bioreactors?"

Drye folds her arms. "They aren't there yet. First they have to find a vaccine. Then they will want to manufacture the vaccine and the virus."

"Humor me, Doctor. How will they build the bioreactors?"

"They would use different technologies to produce the virus and the vaccine. To control the *in vivo* reservoir, they would construct concrete caps over large openings. Concrete plugs in the mine shafts and tunnels. Create a massive negative pressure environment. Sterilize the air leaving the lab. Allow access through an airlock at the cave mouth."

"Do you think they can create a viable weapon?"

"Everything depends on developing a vaccine. By holding the vaccine, they hold the enemy to ransom."

I shake my head. "That's fiendish."

"Why do you think they selected rabies?"

"I don't know."

"Researchers have created a strain of bird flu highly transmissible to humans," Drye says. "Sixty percent fatal. But—survivors reduce control over outcomes. Rabies is one hundred percent fatal. This simplifies the calculations. Suppose the Chinese shorten the incubation period to three days. They can predict how far the disease will spread before it burns itself out."

"Or before a vaccine burns it out."

"Exactly."

The doctor fusses with the remote control. An enormous map of the world fills the wall.

"This is a Mercator projection," Drye says. The screen displays the map in bright blue lines drawn over a black background. Jiang Shi is a familiar red star in southern

China. “Watch this simulation of how rapidly the virus will spread if it escapes Jiang Shi.”

Red dots multiply and spread throughout China. London, Paris, and New York bloom. The clusters widen until the entire map is covered in red.

“My God.” I suck a breath. “How long?”

“With this reproduction number, weeks.”

“How can it be stopped?”

“Upon detection of the accident, the Chinese should drop a nuclear bomb on Jiang Shi. That would sterilize the valley.”

“Why a nuclear bomb?” I ask. “Why not napalm or fuel-air munitions?”

Drye studies me. “That’s a fair question. Neither napalm nor fuel-air can be guaranteed to sterilize the valley. Napalm burns at twelve hundred degrees Celsius. Fuel-air burns at seventeen hundred degrees Celsius. A nuclear explosion generates between fifty and one hundred million degrees Celsius. No living organism would survive.”

“If a major pandemic occurs,” Stein says, “politicians will be indecisive. They’ll waffle and dither until it’s too late.”

Drye stares at the map on the wall. “China will not destroy a weapon they worked hard to develop. The Chinese have fallen in love with their monster.”

# 25

# FAIRCHILD

**Langley, 2 Weeks Ago**

"The Chinese have fallen in love with their monster."

Stein releases the subdued group to return to their quarters. Admonishes them to say nothing to Heth. She hangs back and touches my arm.

"Breed, we need to speak. Alone."

Stein ushers me into an elevator. A sensor pad has been mounted on the control panel beneath a column of buttons. She taps her ID card against the pad and presses B.

"What is this place?" I ask. "Area 51?"

Stein doesn't crack a smile. "It's more secure than you imagine Area 51 to be."

"I don't see any black airplanes or buildings."

"You won't. Apart from the security fence, everything in this area is designed to look normal. Ninety percent of the security is invisible."

"Very Doctor Strangelove," I say.

"Hardly. This building was pressed into service on short notice. Offices have been vacated and converted to temporary quarters for our team. Uncomfortable, but they'll do."

We step from the elevator into an open-plan office. The room is sixty feet wide by a hundred feet long. Rows of long desks, monitors and laptops. Twenty of the men and women sitting at the desks sport crisp uniforms. Half a dozen wear civilian clothes.

Stein leads me past the desks. There is a narrow corridor on one side of the room. Two hundred feet long, it leads past a number of other offices and conference rooms. Some are glassed-in. Others are hidden behind cream-colored walls and wooden doors.

One such inscrutable doorway is labeled B27. Stein waves her card and lets us in. The door swings open to reveal a large office. A wide desk and a telephone. On the desk, a laptop and a leather-bound notebook. Open, with a gold Montblanc laid across its pages.

"I'm using this office. Make yourself comfortable."

Stein steps behind the desk, settles into a recliner. I lower myself into one of the easy chairs across from her. Take a load off.

"What is it, Stein?"

Stein stares at me. Puffs her cheeks. The dark crescents under her eyes are impossible to miss. "I want to share things with you that weren't appropriate for that briefing."

"Tell me."

"I'm taking the team into Jiang Shi," Stein says. "I'm under no illusions. You're the only man I can think to lead it."

*What balls.*

"You're crazy," I say.

"No." Stein takes a slip of paper from her jacket pocket and hands it to me. I suck a breath and she smiles. "Not enough zeroes?"

"You *are* crazy."

"The highest authority wants this problem to go away. Money is not an object."

"What about the others?"

"Takigawa said he needed a good mission."

"That sounds like Takigawa."

"Ortega was still in the Army when I approached him, but he didn't take any convincing."

"You are a charmer, Stein."

"Somehow the country always finds men like you guys. When it counts."

"What about Crockett and Stroud?"

"Crockett's a piece of work, isn't he? He's arrogant enough to do it for fun."

"That's a fair take, but Crockett's no fool. Bring your wallet."

Stein sniffs. "Stroud is a wild card, but I'll get him. If money doesn't do it, I'll have the IRS and FBI shake down the Fangs."

I pocket the piece of paper. "What do *you* get out of it?"

"I don't want the world to end because some idiot in Jiang Shi drops a test tube."

"They could move it out of Jiang Shi."

"You heard Doctor Drye. The Chinese located the lab there for a reason. They want to use the Jiang Shi colony as a reservoir for weaponized rabies."

"What if the bats get loose? The Chinese can't seal every exit."

"With netting and powerful enough negative pressure?" Stein shrugs. "It's an engineering problem. They obviously think they can. This is the right thing to do, Breed. But it may be a one-way ticket."

"Don't worry," I tell her. "I plan to cash this check."

Stein smiles. "There's more. I was put on that committee

because my Deputy Director doesn't want to touch this with a barge pole. The China Desk and Doctor Drye briefed us on China and Jiang Shi. They told me to look into it, come up with options."

"Isn't that always the way?"

"I told them to drop a bomb on the place. They laughed."

"You went off to do research."

"Yes. Fairchild was our China Hand. He ran operations in Saigon when our first advisers arrived in 1958. He organized the missions into Laos and Cambodia. Quarterbacked Guillotine.

"I needed the names of the men in Crockett's team. After the meeting, I went to Fairchild."

THE CHINA COMMITTEE meeting broke up, each man lost in thought. Charles Poole, the Deputy Director of Plans; Warren Thiel, the Deputy Director of Proliferation; Jacob Fischer, the Deputy General Counsel. Stein couldn't tell if they were struggling to digest the information or completely numb. She hurried to catch Fairchild in the corridor.

"Anya." Fairchild was an amiable acquaintance. He walked on spindly legs. Stiff and wobbly at the same time, the gait of an eighty-year-old man.

"Martin, I need to speak with you. Have you time for a coffee?"

Fairchild stopped and turned to face her. "We certainly haven't had many opportunities to get to know one another."

"No, we haven't."

"Let's go to my office." Fairchild smiled. "I suspect you want to speak of things best kept private."

Fairchild's office was deep in the bowels of the headquarters. It was small, cluttered, dusty. A laptop lay open on the desk. The rest of the space was occupied by bookshelves and filing cabinets. Stacks of file folders covered every flat surface.

Stein wondered how long it had been since Fairchild had opened the filing cabinets.

They set their coffee cups on the desk. Fairchild lowered himself into a wooden recliner with squeaky springs. Offered Stein a chair.

"I daresay Poole found himself out of his depth," Fairchild said.

"You're not afraid of what the Chinese can do with weaponized rabies?"

"I'm terrified. But let's be honest. If it is not weaponized rabies that ends the world, it will be some freak mutation of bird flu, or Ebola."

"Are you that pessimistic?"

"I am. Look around the world. No government or national health care system is prepared for such a pandemic. National leaderships are not up to the task. They will be more concerned with their political fortunes than stopping a plague. Faced with an agent as lethal as weaponized rabies, the human race won't have a chance."

Stein swallowed. Deep down, she knew the old man was right. But she had come for information.

"Tell me about the Special Forces mission that went into Jiang Shi," Stein said.

"It was a long time ago." Fairchild clasped his hands behind his head and leaned back. "The mission failed."

He told her about Guillotine.

Stein sipped her coffee. "Who were on the team?"

"Crockett was the 1-0. A resourceful man. Apart from Appleyard, I don't remember any of the others."

Stein thought the old man was lying. He had followed Appleyard for fifty years. He knew damn well who the other men were.

"I need their names," Stein told him. "I need to know where to find them."

"I believe Appleyard retired somewhere in Thailand. Isn't it funny how men of action retire? I am not a man of action, yet I need to remain active. The Company seems to find me useful, so they allow me this little space."

Stein pressed harder. "You must have their names in your files."

"I don't know that I do." Fairchild waved at the filing cabinets, the dusty stacks. "This was fifty years ago. The after-action reports were top secret. They were destroyed during the fall of Saigon.

"Everything I have from that period is on paper. We didn't have computer storage back then. Those were punch card days, don't you remember? I followed Appleyard's career because he was active. The others may be in those files, and they may not. They may be alive—and they may not."

Stein wanted to wring Fairchild's scrawny neck. "Martin, I need those names. We have to find those men."

"Why?"

"A copper mine. Those tunnels are a maze. The Black Sheep are the only ones who can lead a team to the lab."

"Thinking ahead, are you?"

"Someone has to."

"I'll see if I can find anything."

Fairchild sipped his coffee. He was in no hurry to dive into the dusty stacks.

"The Army personnel office must have their records."

"Yes, while they were serving. But—they resigned. Remember, they left the Army and were re-employed by shadow companies. They were meant to be untraceable."

Stein's frustration was approaching boiling point.

"Thanks, Martin." Stein stood to leave. "I have to go. Please look for those names."

"Of course, Anya." Fairchild shook her hand. "I'll call as soon as I have anything."

Stein strode to her own office and picked up the phone. Called Lee Lessop, her lead analyst. "We need to find six men," she said. "Ex-Special Forces. Resigned circa 1971 or 1972 following the dissolution of MACV-SOG. Subsequently employed by the Company as Black Sheep. Last operation was an incursion into China, December 1974. Their Company control was Martin Fairchild. Are you getting all this?"

Lessop said he was.

"The team leader's name was Crockett. Another man was named Appleyard. Go to Army personnel. Pull the records of every Green Beret with those names who served in Vietnam between 1969 and 1975. Cross-reference with Company files.

"Appleyard worked freelance for the Chinese. Call the China Desk, tell them I need all they have on Appleyard, the Black Sheep, and a place called Jiang Shi."

"Lots of hooks," Lessop said. "We'll pull it together."

"Put everyone on this. I want updates every six hours."

Stein disconnected the call.

I DO MENTAL ARITHMETIC. Check my recollection of dates.

"This happened before we met for lunch at Gilbert's," I say. "You were traveling with bodyguards. What happened in between?"

"You don't miss a trick, do you?" Stein shakes her head. "The China Desk advised us Phoenix had missed his regular check-in.

"The desk contacted another asset, Fox Orange. Fox Orange informed us Phoenix had disappeared and had been replaced by his deputy."

"Did he fuck up when he sent you the Jiang Shi material?"

"Unlikely. Phoenix was careful. There is a more likely possibility."

"You have a double agent inside the Company."

# 26

## DEATH HOUSE

### Chevy Chase, 1 Week Ago

"You have a double agent inside the Company."

Stein looks miserable. "We had Phoenix. The Chinese have their mole."

"Why didn't they move on Phoenix before?"

"Agents are constantly evaluating what is worth sharing and what isn't. Jiang Shi is massive. The Chinese mole *had* to report its exposure. That blew Phoenix."

Stein picks up her Montblanc. Taps the ballpoint on the desktop.

"Think about it," she says. "In 1974, *we* didn't care about what Crockett saw. We didn't know *what* he saw. Construction materials at an abandoned mine? We were too wrapped up in the fall of Saigon and our retreat from Vietnam. If *we* didn't give a shit, why should *they*?

"The Chinese left Crockett and his team alone for fifty years. They had Appleyard, he would have given them chapter and verse. The Chinese lost track of the team, like we did—no one cared. Only Fairchild kept track, because it was his mission, and he was a China nerd."

"Makes sense." I say. "It was an assassination attempt that failed. Had they gone after the team in 1974, it would have called unnecessary attention to Jiang Shi."

"When they discovered we'd learned their secret, the Chinese panicked. Eliminated Phoenix. Sent Kang and Appleyard to clean house."

"They couldn't hope to silence everyone," I say. "Poole chairs the committee. He will have reported to the Director of the CIA. This has gone to the National Security Advisor and the president."

"Of course. All the Chinese can do now is tighten security. Eliminate the individuals who might be able to find their way back into the facility."

"The Company's worried about your safety."

"We didn't know how the Chinese would react. Everyone involved was assigned protection."

I look around the room. The dim ceiling lights, the plain white walls, the desktop with Stein's laptop and notebook. "The mole is someone who attended that meeting."

Stein's brow furrows. "It wasn't Fairchild."

"How do you know?"

"I saw what Appleyard did to him."

MANICURED LAWNS, big expensive houses. Stein's driver navigated Chevy Chase searching for Martin Fairchild's address. Stein was oblivious to the wealth that surrounded the vehicle. Her attention was focused on the stack of brown files on her lap. Dossiers detailing the lives of seven MACV-SOG operators. Breed's father, Sam Crockett, and the five other men sent on Operation Guillotine. She wanted to grill

Fairchild. Wring from the old man everything he knew that *wasn't* in the files.

"Looks like trouble," Stein's driver said.

Stein looked up. Her eyes swept the neighborhood. Big houses, four-car garages, cherry trees. The place hadn't changed in seventy years.

The image was marred by fire trucks and police vehicles parked on the street. Fire hoses snaked toward a sprawling two-story mansion. Police officers had strung yellow police tape to screen the house from passersby.

Blackened and smoking, much of the house's flank was a charred skeleton. The front looked intact.

"Pull over," Stein commanded.

A white ambulance van stood parked across the street. EMTs stood next to it, waiting to take bodies away.

Stein stepped from the Suburban onto the Chevy Chase sidewalk. Strode up the lawn with one of her bodyguards in tow.

"Fire department all done?" She flashed her ID at a policeman.

"Not quite." The man examined the ID. "The arson investigator is inside, and so are the bodies. You don't want to go in there."

Stein turned to her bodyguard. "Wait here."

She reached into a pocket, took out a pair of latex gloves, and pulled them on. Went to the front door and stepped inside. The smell almost knocked her flat. The horrific stench of fuel and burned flesh.

Charred and soaked, the living room retained its upscale character. Expensive furniture, paintings, bookshelves, all burned. Two bodies, not so upscale. One on the floor, another on the sofa.

The corpse on the floor looked like a ruined turkey

dinner. Clothing had been burned from the body. The belly had burst from expanding gas and bubbling fat. Displayed flesh that was a mix of brown grease and black char. The blaze had melted the limbs. The legs had burned past the knees, leaving several inches of bare femur. Fire had left the arms stumps below the elbows, twisted in grotesque paralysis.

Stein had joined operators on missions. She had never seen or smelled death like this.

A gravelly voice came from behind Stein. "This guy was stabbed."

Stein turned. The fireman was middle-aged, with two days stubble. Heavy fire-retardant jacket, distinctive fire helmet. He carried a small digital camera in one hand. "I'm Cernovich," he said. "Arson investigation."

"How do you know he was stabbed?"

Cernovich took a BIC ballpoint from his pocket and squatted next to the burned turkey. With the pointed pen cap, he poked at the chest. "You can tell there's a blade stuck between his ribs. One of those wide hunting or utility blades. Probably with serrations. It got stuck when the killer tried to pull it out."

"You can tell all that?"

"Not hard, you got eyes to see. Killing with a knife? Not so clean."

Stein looked at a lump of metal on the floor. "Browning Hi Power."

"You know your guns. The killer fought hand-to-hand with this guy. Disarmed him, killed him with the knife." Cernovich pointed at another charred turkey on the couch. "That guy got shot in the face."

Together, they stepped around the second corpse. Like the first, there was not much left of the arms and legs. Only the torso, a charred basket of burned flesh and melted fat. The head was a black ball tipped back on the neck.

"Don't touch," Cernovich advised. "It'll fall right off."

Stein fought the urge to vomit. The eye sockets were empty holes. The nose had burned away. She could see an entry wound in the cheek, right next to where the nose should have been. The lips were gone, the mouth a black hole framed by rows of white teeth. The back of the head was charred pulp. The bullet had expanded and shattered the occiput.

"I'd say that was a .45 hollow point," Cernovich observed. "Not my job, but I reckon the cops won't find anyone who heard anything."

"Lab guys should look for pieces of the bullet," Stein said. "They might get lucky."

Stein bent at the waist and squinted. The man's pistol had not been drawn.

"The EMTs will have to be careful with this one," Cernovich grunted. "If they lift him the wrong way, everything inside will spill out."

The image flashed before Stein's eyes. She tried to change the subject. "What caused the fire?"

"Open and shut. The killer took gasoline from the lawn mower in the garden shed. Brought it in, splashed it over the bodies. Two down here, one upstairs. He left a gasoline trail down the stairs to link them all together. Struck a match, left by the kitchen door."

"What's the body upstairs like?"

"That's the main event." Cernovich winked. Produced a pack of Marlboro Reds and lit up. "I'll show you."

"Do you mind?" Stein's nose was parsing olfactory stimuli. For some reason, she was able to distinguish all the different smells from each other. Each was having a different effect on her stomach.

Cernovich took a drag and puffed over the corpse's head. "Why? *He* doesn't give a shit."

The grizzled veteran led Stein first to the kitchen, then did a switchback to the staircase. They climbed the charred steps together. Stein could see a blackened track in the middle of the stairs.

"Don't worry," Cernovich said. "They'll support your weight. Walk on the edges of the risers."

When they reached the landing, Cernovich showed Stein the hall. He reminded her of a real estate agent showing off a property.

"Bedrooms are down that way," Cernovich said. "Den and library this way. You can see the gasoline trail and the fire. Leads straight to the den. The bedrooms weren't touched. The killer didn't have enough gasoline to torch the whole house, so he torched the bodies. The fire spread, but the neighbors called us in time. We saved most of the structure."

The investigator led Stein to the den. The two bodies on the ground floor had prepared her, but this was bad. She knew Fairchild, and that made it worse. Her eyes took in the burned corpse bound to the straight-backed chair. She shut them, covered her mouth with her hand.

Cernovich took a drag. Tapped cigarette ash on the floor.

Stein took her hand away and sucked great gulps of foul air through her mouth. Composed herself.

"You knew him," Cernovich observed.

Stein nodded.

"It makes a difference."

Fairchild's thin frame had been reduced to a charred scarecrow. His hands had been bound with duct tape behind the back of the chair. His ankles had been similarly taped to the front chair legs. His thighs and calves were stumps with protruding bones. The arms were melted to his shoulders. The hands and wrists, still taped, had fallen to the floor. A grotesque V-shape. There were no fingers.

The face was the stuff of nightmares. Fairchild's mouth

had been sealed with duct tape. The skin of his face had been roasted off, but the fire could not conceal the deep parallel cuts in the meat of his cheeks. He'd been cut to the bone, deep enough to expose his mandible.

Like the corpse on the sofa, Fairchild's nose had burned off. There was a bullet hole in his face. Stein did not bother to examine the back of his head.

"You see things like this in mob hits," Cernovich observed. "Never seen it in this kind of neighborhood."

"Thanks. I've seen enough."

Stein turned and walked back to the stairs.

Cernovich contemplated Fairchild's remains and puffed.

"THAT WAS A MILITARY HIT," I tell Stein. "Marred by bad luck."

"How so?"

"Appleyard's good. He bypassed the bodyguard outside the house. Waited for him to pass, then breached the kitchen door. The bodyguard in the living room didn't hear him. Appleyard climbed the stairs, surprised Fairchild, choked him out.

"When Fairchild came to, he was duct-taped to a chair. Gagged. He probably tried to scream, but his cries were so muffled, no one heard. Appleyard proceeded to interrogate him. It's a method used in the Middle East and Asia. Flaying. He asked Fairchild a question and said he would take the gag off if he would answer. When Fairchild didn't answer, he cut his face with the knife. Grabbed the dermis with a pair of pliers and peeled. Fairchild would have broken his arms and legs trying to get free."

"Jesus Christ."

"Fairchild held out for a while, but he talked. They always do. Appleyard isn't a sadist. When he had what he wanted, he put Fairchild out of his misery with a bullet in the face. A suppressed .45. Inherently subsonic.

"Appleyard went downstairs and shot the bodyguard on the sofa before the man could draw his gun. Then he got unlucky."

"The second bodyguard came inside."

"Yes. Maybe he was thirsty, maybe the bodyguards were swapping assignments. He surprised Appleyard. They fought at close quarters, and both their handguns were taken out of play. Appleyard pulled his knife and stabbed the bodyguard. It was messy, as these things often are. When Appleyard tried to draw the knife from the man's chest, it caught on his ribs and the blade broke.

"Appleyard wasn't going to waste time digging around for a broken blade. He pocketed the haft and his gun. Went to the garden shed and grabbed as much gasoline as he could. There would be spare fuel for the lawn mower. He came back inside, soaked the bodies, linked them with a fuel trail, started the fire."

"And Kang?"

"Kang acted as lookout. Probably in a car out front. Is that where the witness saw him? Appleyard and Kang left separately once the house was alight."

"Two scary men."

"Appleyard's older than Kang. More experienced."

Stein slides open a desk drawer. Reaches in, takes out a piece of metal. Lays it on the desk.

A broken blade.

I turn the steel over in my hand. Seven inches long, a SOG recon Bowie. A beautiful, Parkerized finish.

"Matters escalated with the killing of Fairchild," Stein says. "I was instructed to present my options to the committee."

"By this time, they're not hard to guess."

"The president always has three options." Stein ticks them off. "Option One, diplomacy. Phone up the Chinese and ask them to stop what they are doing."

"Like that's going to work."

"Option two is what I proposed originally. War."

"They thought you were joking."

"I wasn't." Stein holds up a third finger. "The third option. *Tertia optio.*"

"Covert action."

# 27

## THE FIST OF GOD

### Peterson Air Force Base

The folding cot in my room was a luxury, a shower more so. I dry off and change my clothes. Rap on Takigawa's door.

"Come," he calls.

I step inside, find Takigawa and Ortega talking.

"Pieces coming together, man." A cigarette dangles from Takigawa's lips. He's working on five days of stubble. I think Toshiro Mifune in *Yojimbo*. Smile to myself.

"You worked with this chick before?" Ortega asks.

Takigawa offers me a cigarette. I shake my head. "Yes. She's uptight, but she's got balls."

"What about the old-timers?" Takigawa takes a drag.

I shrug. "I've known Crockett all my life. Stroud is an unknown quantity. Use your judgment."

Ortega looks at his watch. "We're supposed to meet them at the elevators in five minutes."

Takigawa crushes his cigarette on a US Air Force saucer.

I jerk open the door. Crockett and Stroud wait at the end of the hall.

STEIN LEADS us to the amphitheater. Brewster stands with armed Air Police, waiting for us like a bizarre butler. She walks past them, seizes one of the handles, and swings the door open. The cavernous space beyond is dark.

We follow Stein into the room. The same auditorium as yesterday. Only the lighting is different. The space is a black cavern—the rows of seats aren't lit. Instead, the ceiling spotlights are focused on the front table.

Sitting on the table is a cylindrical canvas pack. Twenty-four inches high and eighteen inches in diameter. It has been rigged with a carrying harness and shoulder straps. A rucksack configuration. The canvas is olive drab. Military.

The hairs stand on my arms. The air is cold, but it is the object on the table that makes me shiver.

No wisecracks from Takigawa. Crockett, Stroud, and Ortega are stone-faced. I don't think they're breathing.

I stand in the presence of a power larger than myself. The pack is spotlit like a sacred relic on an altar. An icon from God to remind men of their insignificance.

"Alright, Stein." My voice is hoarse. "What is it?"

Stein stands ramrod straight, still as a statue.

"*That,*" she says, "is a backpack nuclear bomb."

THE CAPTAIN STEPS to the front of the auditorium. Forty years old and fit, he wears clean digital fatigues. Bike clubs have their colors, we have ours. He's wearing Sapper, Special Forces, Ranger, and Airborne tabs.

One more tab than I've got.

All those tabs on his shoulder announce Captain William

Vogel is a badass. He may have started out as an engineering sergeant and gone to Officer Candidate School. Or he went in as an officer, day one. No matter. This guy is as serious as a heart attack.

The captain stands easy, hands clasped behind his back. "I'm Captain Vogel," he says. "I am here to instruct you in the use of these backpack nuclear weapons. My team is here to assemble the weapons, maintain them, and ensure they are functional in all respects."

Two other men stand behind the captain. Civilians, they are dressed in khaki trousers, Oxford shirts, and thigh-length lab coats. One man is in his late fifties, balding and bespectacled. The other is younger, with unruly dark hair.

Vogel gestures to the older man. "Doctor Bauer has worked at Sandia National Laboratories for the last forty years. His specialty is the miniaturization of nuclear weapons. In the early nineties, he participated in mothballing these devices. In the last few days, we have called upon his expertise to reassemble them. Tom Kramer has worked with Doctor Bauer for the last three years. We will accompany these weapons until you are inserted on your mission."

Military instructors all sound the same. Perhaps it is the repetitive nature of their training function that does it. Their presentations invariably sound like recordings. It is as though they deliver content directly from the training manual. The captain is no different.

Vogel puts one hand on the green canvas case. "This," he says, "is the B54 Special Atomic Demolitions Munition, Mod Two. The SADM. In its present configuration, it will generate an explosive yield of one kiloton. That is one thousand tons of TNT. The device is eighteen inches long and twelve inches in diameter. It weighs fifty-eight pounds. It has been designed to be deployed by one man."

Kramer steps forward to assist the captain. He unzips the case, reaches in, and hauls out a heavy metal drum. Sets the drum on its side with its circular face toward us. He nods to the captain and steps back into the shadows.

"The B54," Captain Vogel continues, "consists of two sections. A front case and a rear case. The rear case is facing you. The circular cover is secured in place with a combination lock. This is to prevent unauthorized access to the arming panel."

Vogel stoops, twirls the dial, and lifts off the cover. Sets it on the table. Inside, switches and dials are arranged like a clock face. The simplicity of the arrangement astonishes me. The arming panel might have been built in a high school shop class.

"The B54 was designed to allow combat engineers or Special Forces to use fractional kiloton nuclear explosives in the field. Traditional doctrine requires *two* men be present to arm and fire a nuclear weapon. This doctrine was deliberately modified when designing the B54 and its operational procedures. *One* man can arm and fire the B54."

A ballpoint pen appears in Vogel's hand. He uses it as a pointer. "Gather around, please. I don't think you can see from where you are sitting."

I get up and step close. The others form a semicircle around Vogel and the bomb.

"The control face can be divided into two sections," Vogel continues. "The upper two-thirds is the fusing assembly. The bottom third is the timer assembly."

The captain points with the tip of his pen to a concave recess at the eleven o'clock position of the clock face. The recess is occupied by a small metal and plastic block with an ovoid cross-section. "This is the Safe Well," he says. "Inside the Safe Well is the Plane Wave Explosive Generator. It is a shaped charge of conventional explosive. Think of it as a primer."

Vogel points with the pen to an egg-shaped recess at the three o'clock position of the clock face. "This," he announces, "is the Arm Well. Above and to the right is an electric detonator. Immediately to the left is an electric transducer. To arm the device, the operator removes the primer from the Safe Well and plugs it into the Arm Well."

The captain turns his attention to the bottom third of the control face. The line between the two sections is marked by a warning printed in bold capitals:

DO NOT TURN PAST 27 HOURS

The warning refers to a row of analogue windows labeled in hours and minutes. It is plain the bomb was built long before digital technology. Immediately below the timer indicators are a switch and a knob. A black plastic knob at the six o'clock position and a silver dog-leg switch at the seven o'clock position. The dog-leg switch is set so it is pointing to the word SAFE. The word ARM is stenciled above it.

"The timer," Vogel says, "is straightforward. The operator turns this black knob until the timer displays the amount of delay desired. The Mod One bomb timer can be set from five minutes to twelve hours. The Mod Two timer can be set as long as twenty-four hours.

"The operator arms the bomb by removing the primer from the Safe Well and inserting it into the Arm Well. Finally, the operator moves the Arming Switch from the SAFE position to the ARM position. This releases the black timer knob and the countdown begins. When the countdown reaches zero, the electric detonator fires the primer. The shaped charge sets off the bomb."

"How do you disarm it?" I ask.

"Disarming the bomb is simple." Vogel points at the dog-leg switch with his pen. "Simply turn the Arming Switch from ARM to SAFE."

He then points to a small metal screw nestled at the eight o'clock position. "Alternatively," he says, "the operator can turn the Safe Screw to disarm the bomb. This requires a small Phillips head screwdriver."

Vogel looks up at us. "This device is live. We have two such on the premises. You are welcome to practice with it so long as one of my team is present. As you can see, arming and disarming the device is simple.

"Additional training will be given in the deployment of the B54 by parachutist. The bomb will be packed in a slightly larger container with shock-absorbent padding. The parachutist jumps with the bomb attached to his person. Before landing, he lowers the device on a seventeen-foot cable to reduce the impact shock. The operator then removes the bomb from the shock-absorbent case. He ensures it has not been damaged and continues with the mission.

"Are there any questions?"

"What's it going to do?" I ask.

"What do you mean?"

"Give me an idea of scale. Orders of magnitude, something to compare it to."

Vogel nods. "That's a fair question. My team has been briefed on the geological structure of your target. I will ask Doctor Bauer to answer."

Bauer steps forward and clears his throat. "This bomb will create a crater with a diameter of at least one mile. It is an underground explosion, but make no mistake. Blast effect will destroy everything to a diameter of two miles. Everything underneath the blast will be vaporized to a depth of a quarter of a mile. The crater, however, will only be a few hundred feet deep. Material not turned to dust will fall straight down."

"What if both bombs are detonated?"

"Excellent question." Bauer warms to the topic. "If both bombs are set with the same time delay, it is unlikely both will produce a nuclear explosion. The timing devices are coarse, and one bomb will go off fractions of a second before the other. In that case, the bomb that explodes first will destroy the other bomb. There may be a detonation of the second bomb's primer, but the nuclear material will not detonate. This is because of the nature of the internal construction, which is classified."

Vogel contemplates the bomb. "The second device's radioactive material will scatter, adding to local contamination."

"Thank you," I say. "That answers my question."

"Any other questions?" Vogel looks around the room.

There are none.

"Thank you," Vogel says. "I will meet you at sixteen hundred hours. You will learn to rig the device for parachute deployment."

With those words, the captain and his team leave the auditorium. I stare at the nuke. The device will obliterate everything for a mile around.

The fist of God.

# 28

## THE PLAN

**Peterson Air Force Base**

Nothing ever goes according to plan.

Why then do we spend so much time planning? Combat is a business of chaos, where control is an illusion. Soldiers have a sweating need to control what they can. The plan is a reference point for orientation. A common basis for change.

The tables in the conference room have been arranged in the shape of a horseshoe. Stein and I sit at the front. On our left are Crockett and Stroud. Ortega and Takigawa sit to our right.

Stein's notebook is open on the table in front of her. Next to it are her gold Montblanc and a remote control for the rear-projection screen.

"You've all signed NDAs," Stein says. "I have outlined the problem. Today we are going to make a plan. I will bring subject matter experts into the discussion as required. For the moment, let us confine the exercise to those in this room."

Stein turns to Crockett. "Mr Crockett, I would appreciate

your honest answers to three questions. I require a simple yes or no. Your answers will determine the feasibility of the mission."

Crockett fixes Stein with a level stare. "Shoot."

"First, can you find the sinkhole from which your team escaped?"

"Yes."

"Second, can you lead this team back through the tunnels to the Jiang Shi chapel and cathedral?"

"Yes."

"Finally." Stein takes a deep breath. "Can you haul a drum eighteen inches long by twelve inches in diameter, weighing fifty-eight pounds, through those tunnels?"

"Yes."

We all let out a breath.

"Alright," Stein says. "Our basic requirements have been met. Let me propose a straw man for discussion.

"Jiang Shi is twenty-five miles inside the China-Vietnam border. We will fly in an Air Force plane out of Kadena Air Force Base in Okinawa. Our flight path will take us over Vietnam and Laos. Our transponder will spoof a commercial flight. The six of us will jump at 35,000 feet, and navigate under canopy twenty miles across the border. Our destination will be one of three drop zones inside China. All three will be within hiking distance of Jiang Shi."

Stein looks around the room. "Challenge?"

Crockett fixes Stein with a steely gaze. "Have you ever jumped?"

"No." Stein responds without hesitation, stares Crockett down. "Breed and Ortega are tandem-qualified. I will ride with one of them as passenger."

I clear my throat.

"Sam is current. I jumped with him last week." I look at Stroud. "When was the last time *you* jumped?"

"It's been years," Stroud says. "But I have jumped the new wings. I'm confident I can navigate."

I nod. "If we have time, a few practice jumps will go a long way."

What I want is an opportunity to evaluate Stroud. Determine whether his confidence is mere bravado.

"We will jump with two devices," Stein says.

"Two bombs," Takigawa says. "We'll be able to carry less ammo."

"Understood," Stein says firmly. "But—the mission depends on having at least one functional bomb. If we get both into Jiang Shi, we will set one in the chapel and one in the cathedral. If we only get one through, we will make the determination opportunistically."

Ortega raises his hand. "I don't know about you guys, but I've never jumped into jungle. Landing in trees sucks. This is all going to be about drop zones, wind and weather."

"And the moon," Takigawa says. "We want a new moon."

"Less than a week away," Stein says. "Crockett, you and Stroud have both HALO jumped in southeast Asia."

"Yes, we have." Crockett leans back in his chair, stretches his long legs. "Ortega is right. The weather is unpredictable and the terrain is a bitch. If we land in the trees, we'll have to rappel down. Ideally, we'll find clear drop zones. I'll need maps and photographs of the whole area. Have you guys operated in the jungle before?"

Crockett looks from Takigawa to Ortega and settles his gaze on me. There is a challenge in his eye.

"We've all had jungle training," I tell him. "Hawaii and Panama. But that wasn't our war. We don't pretend to be at home in the jungle like you are."

Crockett is my friend, but I sense an arrogance in him. The same arrogance he showed when I suggested he waited too long to open his parachute. We're all competitive, or we wouldn't be here. But there is something reckless about Crockett's attitude.

"You can't move in the jungle the way you move over other terrain," Crockett says.

"I think you should select a drop zone and two alternates," I tell him. "Plot them on a map along with the position of the sinkhole. We'll discuss their suitability as a group."

"Let's talk about weapons," Stein says.

Crockett smiles. "The toolbox."

"We need to use weapons that can't be directly traced to the United States." Stein picks up her pen, writes a heading on a page of her notebook. "Back in the day, trade was restricted between the communist bloc and the West. Nowadays, weapons are sold everywhere. The AR15 and AK47 platforms are ubiquitous. Having said that, we shouldn't go overboard. Breed, what do you suggest?"

"Chinese and Russian weapons are easy to get," I say. "Our standard rifle should be the Chinese AK47. One Bonfire grenade launcher. One Russian RPD with hundred-round drums. Chop down the barrel. Our sidearms should be North Korean Tokarevs. Lemonka hand grenades."

Stein scribbles in her notebook. A shopping list.

"Dragunovs?" Takigawa asks.

"I don't think so, dude." I shake my head. "We won't be doing any sniping this trip. We need firepower.

"There are well-known companies that make parachutes for tandem and tethered bundle jumps. Everybody uses them the world over. You'll find Russian, Chinese, and American jumpers using the same gear. Take a look at the Vector SOV3.

"Unmarked uniforms made in Asia. Ditto ammunition, but make sure it's quality. Nothing wrong for one guy to carry a Swiss compass if another guy carries one made in Taiwan. Our GPS come from Hong Kong. Personal gear, whatever you're comfortable with. No ID, no personal photos, no phones."

"Once in the jungle," Crockett says, "I should take point. I'll carry an AK47. Stroud is lethal with an RPD—he'll take slack. Whoever carries the Bonfire should be number three. I don't know how you want to fill the other positions, but I suggest the lady occupy number five."

All reasonable proposals. I would have suggested them myself. Once again, I get the sense Crockett is bullying me.

I tilt my head toward Stein. "I have a couple of special requests."

"Whatever you need."

"The Chinese made a pistol with an integrated suppressor. The Type 64. I want one."

"Why?"

"Once we're through the tunnels, we're certain to run into sentries. My first preference is to bypass them, plant the nukes, and sneak out. If we can't bypass them, I want to neutralize them with a suppressed pistol. The Type 64 is 7.65mm, inherently subsonic."

"Where will I find this jewel?"

"Go to the armorers at the Company and tell them what I want. They'll find one for you."

Stein makes a note. "What's your second special request?"

"An 84mm Carl Gustav recoilless rifle and a dozen rounds of dual-purpose ammunition. Go to the black market. Some corrupt trooper in Burkina Faso will sell you one."

Takigawa whistles.

The Carl Gustav is a three-foot-long rifled tube. It's not a rocket launcher—It fires portable artillery shells. Vents the recoil through the breech. A Venturi damper built into the breech reduces the pressure of the backblast. With the Carl, an infantry unit can engage tanks, bunkers, and infantry with one weapon.

Crockett grunts. "Planning on taking on the whole PLA, Breed?"

"You ran into Dushkas and automatic cannon in Jiang Shi," I tell him. "This time we'll be ready for anything."

Stein makes a note in her careful, New England prep-school script.

"This afternoon," she says, "we'll receive our first briefing on parachuting with the SADM."

"Where do I get maps and photographs?" Crockett asks.

"I will have Captain Brewster bring them to this room. You can return to your quarters. He will call when they are ready."

The group breaks and shuffles out of the room. I hang back with Stein. "We've been talking about the caves—chapel and cathedral. What does the actual facility look like? What kind of structure did the Chinese build in that mine?"

"We have no photographs, but Phoenix gave us a description. What he *heard* it looked like. It is consistent with Drye's concept. They blasted a deep pit in the floor of the cathedral and built a concrete structure with three levels. An administrative floor, a Biosafety Level 4 floor, and a machinery space. Covered it over with concrete and rebar. There's access through the administrative floor. Vents to support negative pressure labs."

"Let's get an artist to draw our best guess of what it looks like. I want to consider the PLA security measures and where we plant our B54s."

"Our intel is thin, isn't it."

"Let's beef it up. Get artists to sit with Crockett and Stroud. I want drawings of the chapel and the cathedral. Scale maps of the tunnel system. Have them do it independently."

"Don't you trust anybody?"

"Memories are flawed, especially after fifty years. Discrepancies may be informative." I look out the window at the blue sky over Peterson. "Can you arrange practice jumps for Stroud?"

"Yes. I'll do it right now."

"I want at least four jumps," I say. "A static jump, a free fall, a HALO, and a night free fall."

"Worried he might hurt himself?"

"I'd rather he killed himself here than in China."

Stein smiles. "I think he'll look rather dashing, jumping out of a plane—with that handlebar mustache."

"Is that the key to your cold, black heart?"

"Wouldn't you like to know."

# 29

## THE PRIMER

**Peterson Air Force Base**

Infantry should be an Olympic event. You wake up in the morning and work out. Go about your day, work out again before sleep. It's been days since I ran, so I ask Brewster for Air Force gym sweats and running shoes.

It's dark. I jog slowly to the front gate, turn, and make my way along the perimeter fence. I warm up at seven minutes a mile. For fun, I'll estimate the dimensions of the compound.

The size of the installation amazes me. One side is two miles long. I round a corner and find another double gate. It's huge. I'm running across a tarmac—an access road that leads from a group of airplane hangars to the main runways.

I find my rhythm. Air floods my lungs, perfuses my blood with oxygen. Oxygen to burn with sugar. Fuel for my laboring muscles.

Behind me, the tap-tap-tap of running shoes. Light footsteps.

Stein pulls even, then passes me without a word.

*Shit.*

Her tight little rump, in Air Force blue, drives me crazy. I pick up the pace, catch her. She's doing six-and-a-half minutes a mile. I can cut it.

Stein glances at me, smiles sweetly, and—*sprints.*

She's fifteen yards ahead before I respond. Gear up, pump my arms, catch her.

A hundred yards more, and she slows back down to six-and-a-half minutes a mile.

We pass an Air Police patrol. They're walking the dead space between the fences. The Malinois spots us, throws itself against the interior perimeter fence. The dog's handler hauls on the leash, forces the animal to heel.

The dog hadn't made a sound.

Stein sprints again, and again I catch her.

When she slows down after a hundred yards, we are both drenched in sweat.

Five more times, Stein surges. Five more times, I go with her.

When she surges for the eighth time, I give up. She's lighter, built like a runner. I watch her lope away at six minutes a mile.

*Try that with sixty pounds on your back.*

The compound is two square miles. More than half of it is devoted to mysterious hangars. Having covered five miles of the perimeter, I jog to a stop. Hands on my hips, I walk to catch my breath.

Stein intrigues me. She acts cold and witchy, but her heart is in the right place. Good-looking, born with a silver spoon in her mouth. She's worked her cute little ass off. Didn't have to. Does that make her stupid or twisted?

Twisted, I think. That beautiful woman has been damaged.

Wouldn't be the first time.

I start jogging. Three more miles, a shower, then bed.

The growl of an engine startles me. I look back. No sirens. An over-powered Caprice, of the Air Force Security Service, roars past. The vehicle's light bars flash blue and red.

I strain to see what's going on. More vehicles are converging on a spot half a mile ahead. Their headlights bathe the perimeter fence in a dazzling glare. These are Humvees. Air Police with rifles are piling out.

There are no coincidences. I run harder.

I reach the cordon in minutes. An Air Police with an M4 at port arms bars my way. "Stand back, Sir."

Two dog patrols stand in the kill zone between the interior and exterior fences. One Malinois is sitting by its handler's side. The other is visibly upset, straining at its leash. Its handler holds it back, commands it to heel.

The dog's muzzle and cheeks are red with blood. Streams have poured down its chest and matted its fur. The animal's paws and wrists are soaked.

A man lies crumpled inside a hole cut in the fence. His face is ghastly white in the glare of the headlights. His throat has been torn open. The edges of the wound are ragged. His trachea and arterial plumbing are ugly hoses lying half-in and half-out of the corpse. While he was still alive, the arteries spurted his life onto the dog and the gravel. Now, their copious flow has been reduced to a dribble.

Stein rushes to me. "What's going on?"

We're two hundred yards from our quarters. Black crescents soak the front and back of her sweatshirt.

"Something's wrong," I tell her. "This guy tried to break *out*, not *in*."

The Officer of the Guard is speaking into a walkie-talkie.

The dead man's sightless eyes glisten. Youthful features, an unruly shock of dark hair. He looks familiar.

Stein clutches my arm. "That's..."

The penny drops. "Tom Kramer," I say.

One of Vogel's engineers.

I turn and dash for the building. "Find Vogel and Bauer," I yell. "Get them to meet us at the auditorium. Go!"

Heart pounding. Not from exertion—from fear.

Bang through the front door. Run over Captain Brewster on the way to the elevator. Grab him by the collar and drag him along.

"What's happening?" Brewster stammers.

Into the elevator. Punch the second floor. The door sucks open and I go straight to the Air Police guard in the corridor. "Was Kramer just here?"

The guard blinks. "No, Sir. I mean... he was here almost an hour ago."

Sprint to the butterfly doors. The armed Air Police recognize us, stand aside. I burst into the auditorium.

Darkness visible.

The B54 sits where we left it. On the table, spot lit, caught in powerful beams that lance it from the ceiling.

Kramer has removed the security cover and placed it on the lectern.

*Tick. Tick. Tick.*

"Is it live?" Brewster asks.

I squat in front of the bomb to bring my face level with the arming panel.

The timer is counting down the minutes to a one-kiloton nuclear explosion. Fifteen of them, to be exact.

I study the arming panel. It looks different. Small open holes stare at me from the metal plate. Holes where the Timer Knob and Arming Switch used to be mounted over rotating posts. Sixties technology, the bomb looks like it was assembled in someone's garage. The holes in the plate were made with a Black & Decker drill.

*Tick. Tick. Tick.*

Stein races into the auditorium. Takes in the situation at a glance. "Can you disarm it?"

"I don't know. We need Vogel and Bauer."

The Safe Screw is missing. Again, all that remains is an empty hole. I turn to Brewster. "Call base security, evacuate this compound. Clear the base for a mile in every direction. *Do it.*"

There's only one way I can think to disarm the bomb.

*It's not briefed.*

Vogel and Bauer race into the auditorium. Bauer goes white. "Oh my God."

Brewster rushes to evacuate the compound.

"Kramer's wrecked the Timer Knob, the Arming Switch, and the Safe Screw." I look up at the engineers. "We have ten minutes. Can we remove the plate and disarm it?"

Vogel shakes his head. "Under normal circumstances, yes. But—he may have booby-trapped the device."

"How?"

"Any number of ways. A filament attached to the back of the plate."

"The primer has to explode to set off the device," I say. "Can I disarm the bomb by removing the primer from the Arm Well?"

"Yes, but the Arm Well might be booby-trapped."

"But—if the primer explodes as I remove it, will the device go off?"

"No," Bauer says firmly. "The primer would annihilate this room. Radioactive material would be scattered everywhere, but the device itself would not explode."

*Tick. Tick. Tick.*

"That settles it," I say. "Clear the building. You have five minutes."

"Breed," Stein says.

Eight minutes to go. "You're wasting time," I tell her.

They leave me alone with the bomb.

I reach forward, hold the primer between my thumb and first two fingers. Feel for any play. There is none—it is firmly seated. Under the spotlights, the metal detonator and transducer sparkle.

*Tick. Tick. Tick.*

Two minutes remaining, plenty of time. I contemplate the primer.

This is the dumbest thing I've ever done.

If the bomb goes off, the mission is toast.

If the primer goes off, *I'm* toast.

I suppose it'll particularly suck if I'm around when both the primer *and* the bomb go off.

Maybe I should have evacuated with the others. We could all live with a bit of a tan.

But then, the Chinese would win.

I take a deep breath.

Pull the primer.

THE COLORADO NIGHT chills me to the bone. I step forward, meet Stein, Vogel, and Bauer at the fence. I toss Vogel the primer. He catches it and hands it to Bauer.

"You guys can go in," I tell them. "The timer counted down to zero and nothing happened."

Vogel and Bauer enter the building.

"Call off the emergency," I say. "Where's the team?"

Stein takes her phone from her pocket. "Brewster took them to the other side of the base. I'll get him to bring them back."

"Who knows how close we came?"

"Our team. The base commander. No one else."

"Base security?"

"They only know there was a breach. They do not know the details. Kramer needs to be cleaned up."

"He's a mess," I agree. "Where's the Officer of the Guard?"

Stein nods toward the fence. The Air Police are drifting back to the vehicles that surround Kramer's corpse.

A first lieutenant in digital fatigues walks toward us. "Anya Stein?" he asks.

"Yes."

"I'm Officer of the Guard. I have been instructed to speak with you."

"What happened at the fence, Lieutenant?"

"It started earlier this evening, Ma'am. Thomas Kramer tried to make a phone call out of the base. He was informed no calls were permitted from the compound without your authorization."

"Who did he want to call?"

"The call wasn't connected. It was an area code in Albuquerque."

"We'll trace it," Stein says. "Go on."

"Two hours later, he tried to leave through the front gate and was turned back by our men. Per your instructions... no one is allowed in, no one is allowed out."

"So he cut the fence." Stein shakes her head. "By then he was desperate to get out."

"Dumb move," the lieutenant says. "A dog detected him, and the handler let the animal off the leash."

Stein thanks the lieutenant and we walk to the building.

"The Chinese have their hooks in all our labs," Stein says. "Academic labs, government labs, you name it. It's always money. Grants, scholarships, the works. We'll find Kramer got a scholarship from some China relations non-profit. Because he used his social media accounts to promote goodwill."

"Don't joke."

"I'm not joking. It will be that, or something equally absurd. Of course, it would be wrong to deny such a bright spark a top security clearance. We need people like him at our major weapons labs. We still don't know how they managed to pirate the design of our latest stealth fighter."

"You know what the number-one question is, don't you?"

"Yes." Stein frowns. "The Chinese do not know about our mission. Under my instructions, Captain Vogel isolated both Kramer and Bauer. They were stripped of their phones and flown here with the nukes."

"Vogel said his team was briefed on the target."

"We had no choice," Stein says. "We needed them to determine the yield required to do the job."

"The idiot tried to call out," I say. "On a base phone. He must have been desperate."

"I'd say the Chinese have been buying data from him from ever since he joined Sandia. When we check, I bet we'll find he was living well beyond his means. A nice gig, but if he didn't warn them about the bombs, they would not forgive him."

I find it hard to feel sorry for Kramer. "Young guy, bright future."

"Twenty-eight years old." We reach the door and Stein swings it open.

"Smart enough to build a bomb, dumb enough to take on a laryngectomized Malinois."

"Apparently so."

I shake my head. "What is it with kids these days?"

# 30

## THE CHICKEN SWITCH

**Peterson Air Force Base**

The C-130 Hercules squats in the middle of the cavernous hangar and broods. Stein and I stand in its shadow. There are other aircraft in the hangar, other men and women working at the far end. Their voices and footsteps echo as though from miles away.

"Are you sure you want to jump with me?" I ask her.

"Yes. You have more jumps than anyone on the team. If I'm tying these bones to anyone on this mission, it's you."

"Cranky today?"

"It's bad enough I have to worry about traitors like Kramer. Now the idiots in management have their fingers on the goddamn chicken switch."

"How's that?"

"Poole's debating whether we want to be the first ones to use a nuclear weapon since 1945. Whether the Chinese will invade Taiwan, sink one of our carriers, or turn their nuclear keys. He'll go on debating until somebody in Jiang Shi drops a beaker and ends the world."

"Care to tell me about it?"

"Why not? It's office politics, that's all."

Stein tells me how she obtained approval for our mission.

THE CHINA COMMITTEE met in Poole's office. Large, comfortable, lots of mahogany. Deep leather chairs in a mini sitting room. At one end of the room, by the window, squatted a conference table large enough for eight.

Stein didn't like Poole. She didn't like any of the senior management at the Company. Fair enough, they didn't like *her*. Their tolerance was based on mutual utility.

"We asked you to present realistic options, not fantasies," Poole said.

"There is only one realistic option," Stein retorted. "The president will not ask China to pretty please destroy their weaponized rabies. They'll say they don't have any."

"We're not going to recommend World War III."

"I didn't think so." Stein searched the eyes of the committee members. "What does that leave?"

"How does Fairchild's death change things?" Poole looked uneasy.

Fairchild was in pieces. When the EMTs tried to separate his charred body from the chair, it came apart. His head fell off, rolled on the floor. His arms came away at the shoulders, and his torso broke in half. When the EMTs finished vomiting, they scraped the contents into a plastic bucket. Delivered everything to the morgue.

Among the committee members, the grisly details were whispered.

*Did he really... fall apart?*

*Stein saw it.*

*Stein was there.*

*Think she lost her lunch?*

*I'd love to have seen that.*

*Stein's a robot.*

*Bitch ate a Snickers bar not two feet from the corpse.*

*I'd like her to eat something else.*

Stein stared at Poole through cold eyes. "Fairchild's death changes everything."

"Answer the question, then." Poole was losing patience.

"Isn't it obvious? After the Chinese disappeared Phoenix, we thought they might be panicking. Fairchild's murder confirms this. They tortured Fairchild to find out all he knew about the whereabouts of the Black Sheep. The Black Sheep, and everyone in this room, are in danger."

Warren Thiel was one of the more rational men on the committee. "How do we know Fairchild gave them anything?"

"Appleyard shot him to put him out of his misery. Obviously, Appleyard got what he wanted."

Thiel steepled his fingers. "Where are these Black Sheep?"

"We're searching Fairchild's files now," Stein assured him. "We will find them and bring them in. They are the only ones who can find their way through that warren of tunnels."

"Your third option," Poole sneered.

"Yes," Stein spat. "Our only *practical* option."

"Who's to say the Chinese haven't moved the damn bug out of Jiang Shi already?" Poole protested.

"Doctor Drye," Stein snapped. "The Chinese have centralized their biowar brain trust in Jiang Shi. They want to develop the Jiang Shi bat colony into a living reservoir of bioreactors."

"Do we have any backpack nukes left?" Thiel asked. "The B54 was decommissioned upon the fall of the Soviet Union. The bombs were dismantled."

"True." Stein had time for Thiel, because she had time for rational men. "What has been dismantled can be reassembled. We have all the parts mothballed. The devices can be made ready in short order."

"This is a suicide mission," Thiel said. "Who will go?"

"I'll go." Stein's voice was flat. "I'll need a Black Sheep to lead me through that maze of tunnels. The rest, leave to me."

Silent, the men stared at her.

"What's the difference between dropping a bomb and carrying one in?" Poole wasn't playing devil's advocate. He was not a fan.

"I should think that's obvious," Stein said. "The footprint of an underground SADM explosion is tiny compared to a surface blast."

"You think the Chinese are going to lie down and do nothing?"

Stein met Poole's stare. "Yes. They can't win a nuclear exchange. What are they going to do? Bitch to the UN? They know we have evidence they've developed a doomsday bug."

"We can wait to see how the situation develops," Poole said.

"Yes." Stein's voice dripped sarcasm. "Let us watch and wait while the Chinese develop a vaccine. Let us allow them to develop a bat species to host the weapon. Let us watch while they productionize the weapon in the caves of Jiang Shi. By all means."

"The committee cannot make this decision," Poole said.

"The president," Stein snapped, "has Title 50 authority."

Poole whirled on Jacob Fischer, Deputy General Counsel. "What's your opinion?"

Fischer squirmed. "Technically, Stein is correct. This would be the first test of the president's Title 50 authority in a nuclear context. We could craft a presidential Finding in a matter of hours."

"Fine." Stein turned to Poole. "I suggest you allow the president to determine who should be involved."

Warren Thiel gazed at her. "You have a point," he said. "Have you considered what will happen if you fail?"

"Yes. The president will be provided maximum deniability."

Thiel turned his head. Lost in thought, he stared out the window.

"You're nuts." Poole waved his hand in dismissal. "I will not be part of this."

"We are *all* part of this," Stein told him. "This is the China committee."

"This is a nightmare." Poole stared at her. "I will *not* advocate for your proposal."

Stein refused to blink. "Then I will."

Poole's face turned purple.

Thiel returned from his daydream. "This is a matter for the president," he said. "I suggest Stein prepare a proposal."

The committee would permit Stein to make the presentation.

OUTSIDE POOLE'S OFFICE, Thiel walked Stein to the elevator.

"Thank you for your support, Warren."

"I think your assessment of our options is spot on," Thiel said.

"Would you like to come to the White House tomorrow?"

"I'd like to, but the Iranians are playing with their erector set again. They are actually close to *building* something."

"It never ends, does it? We can't seem to keep the little bastards down."

Thiel chuckled. "When you finish Jiang Shi, we might have more work for you."

"I'm always available to help."

The elevator door opened. Stein and Thiel got in, pushed the buttons for their floors.

"You'll get some good exposure out of this," Thiel told her. "As usual, Poole has maneuvered himself into an indefensible position."

"I want to solve the problem."

Thiel contemplated her. "Yes. Well, by the time this is over, I suspect we will be looking for a new Deputy Director of Human Intelligence. You will be considered."

"I appreciate your confidence, but it's not my strong suit."

"No, it isn't." The door sucked open at Thiel's floor. He stepped out, held the door while he finished his thought. "Remember—you are here for greater things."

Thiel winked and allowed the door to slide shut.

Stein shut her eyes.

*If I survive*, she thought.

THE NEXT DAY, Poole and Stein spent an hour with the president and the National Security Advisor. Stein briefly described Jiang Shi. Stressed Drye's conclusions and the threat of weaponized rabies. The president approved her plan. Ordered counsel to draft a Presidential Finding.

Stein and Poole stepped outside. The mission was on. Her heart would not stop pounding. She clenched her fist and strode toward the exit.

The long corridor of the West Wing ran from the Oval Office to the Chief of Staff's office. Unable to contain himself, Poole stopped halfway, turned to Stein.

"You've miscalculated," he said.

Her back to the wall, Stein faced him down. "The president doesn't think so."

"The Chinese will not stand by and let us walk a nuclear weapon across the border to blow up their lab."

"We've been through this."

"They will respond in kind. They will attack Taiwan with

conventional forces. Take out one of our carriers. Launch a nuclear strike of their own."

"Those options have been considered in our threat assessment. With our Japanese and Australian allies, we can hold Taiwan. Aegis systems protect our carriers. The Chinese will not launch a nuclear strike. If they did, we would win."

"What makes you so goddamn sure? Who died and made you God?"

"God gave me a brain to think for myself. I will not leave the Chinese with the ability to end the world. Either intentionally, or by the most colossal fuckup to end human history."

A pretty staffer walked past. Stein and Poole studied the floor until she had gone.

Poole lowered his voice. "I believe there is a material risk the Chinese will launch on us. I will continue to advocate against this mission. You will monitor comms for an abort command."

Stein smiled. "I misjudged you, Poole. I respect your conviction. I thought you were just another retarded bureaucrat."

Poole snorted. "I'm a Deputy Director, Stein. Last I looked, you were an Assistant Deputy Director. I'll get that abort command. By all that's holy—when I do, I will fuck your bony ass till your eyes bleed."

Stein watched the Deputy Director of Plans storm out of the West Wing.

"POOLE'S MANEUVERING to have us cancelled?" I ask.

"Yes. I came from the comms office. He was testing our protocol to ensure I would receive the abort command."

"Think he'll get it?"

"Who knows? He's lobbying the Director and the General

Counsel. We have the Memorandum of Notification, but they are testing the Title 50 powers. If they determine the president's authority is unclear, they may convince him to abort."

Hands on my hips, I turn to stare at the C-130. "Stein, once we jump out of the plane, they must not abort."

"Breed, once we are in China, I will stop listening for the abort command."

Stein means what she says.

I'm wearing jungle fatigues and a tandem harness. For the first time since I've known her, Stein is out of uniform. She's wearing light-blue colored jeans, sneakers, and a white T-shirt. Over the T-shirt, she wears a black suit jacket. The jeans have been pressed. The creases are knife-sharp.

"Take your coat off."

Stein shrugs off her jacket. Folds it over one arm, looks for a place to set it down. She lays it on the back of a chair. It's next to a table stacked with parachute equipment. On her belt, she wears her SIG.

"The president didn't buy Poole's warnings about Chinese retaliation. So Poole argued the use of a nuclear weapon was immoral."

"Morality is a good defense," I say. "Always nice to be on the side of the righteous."

"The Japanese used Chinese civilians for biological warfare experiments. Autopsied while the patients were still alive. So the organs would be *fresh*. Was *that* moral? General MacArthur cut a deal with the Japanese doctors. They gave us their data. Not *one* was prosecuted for war crimes. Was *that* moral? Now the Chinese are ready to shove weaponized rabies up our ass. I'm sure *that's* moral."

I've never seen Stein so wound up. I take her by the shoulders. "Stein."

Stein realizes she was ranting. Embarrassed, she stares at me.

"Relax," I tell her. "It'll happen. Here, put this on."

I hand her a passenger's tandem harness.

Stein exhales through puffed cheeks. Shrugs on the harness. She's under pressure. I'm focused on the mission, what's going on within the fences of our secure installation. Stein is worrying about the mission, office politics, and Appleyard.

"Alright," I say. "Your harness is cinched tight. Don't worry about the D-rings and fasteners in front. Stand straight."

Stein takes a deep breath and stands with her feet together, arms at her sides. I step behind her, very close. She's trembling.

"You're the passenger," I tell her. "All you have to do... is nothing."

"Nothing," Stein breathes.

"Nothing. Your role in this evolution is completely passive. You hook to me at four points. Four connectors on your harness that clip to D-rings on mine. Two at the shoulders."

I take the quick connectors at her shoulders and snap them to the D-rings on my harness. Push the locking pins home. "These connection points are rated to five thousand pounds each," I tell her. "I've locked them shut. Two more will join us at the hips. I'm connecting them now."

Stein and I are standing so close I can feel the flutter of her heart. She's calming down. Existing in the moment.

"Now we're one person," I tell her. "When we leave the airplane, you should be inert. Cross your wrists over your chest like you're going to sleep."

I take her hands and fold them for her. Lay my right hand on her brow and tip her head back. She closes her eyes. "Arch yourself," I say, "and rest your head against my shoulder. That's all you have to do. I'll stick my arms out and do the flying."

Her hair is soft. I smell the faint scent of her shampoo.

"You'll do everything," Stein says.

"That's right. I'll do everything."

Stroud and Heth walk into the hangar.

"Tandem is the best introduction you'll get to jumping," Stroud tells Stein. "Doing it at night should spice things up."

I put my arms down. Stroud is hauling his parachute. Heth scowls at the way Stein and I are hitched to each other. If looks could kill, we'd both be dead.

"One jump left to do," Stroud says. "Too easy, Breed."

"I figured you could run the program in less than a day." I pull the locking pins from the connector snaps, unhook myself from Stein.

"Why did you ask for a static jump?" Stroud laughs. "All you do is put your feet together and act like you're going into a car accident. There's nothing to do."

Stroud's bravado annoys me. It's like he's trying to prove he's still a badass. All the Black Sheep have that quality. Crockett, deploying his parachute at the last minute. Appleyard, working as an assassin when anyone else would have retired.

I introduce Stein and Heth. The two women shake hands, race to see who can drop the other's first. They look each other up and down. The air thickens with hostility.

*Oh shit.*

"You good?" I ask Stein.

"Yes. I'll see you at the briefing." Stein lifts her jacket from the chair and pulls it on. "Remember. Nothing about the mission."

Stein marches out of the hangar.

Heth stares at Stein's retreating back. "That's the witch queen who doesn't want me around?"

I shrug. "People are getting killed. What you don't know won't hurt you."

"I've still got it," Stroud grins. "Not just another pretty face."

"Is your jump tonight all arranged?"

"Yes. Don't worry, I'll nail it."

"You'll miss the briefing," I tell him. "Don't worry, I'll bring you up to speed after."

Heth fumes. "What am *I* supposed to do?"

"You can be Stroud's ground man," I suggest. "Pack his chute."

Heth treats me to a dirty look. "Breed, I'm going to put some bad medicine on that witch."

## 31

## TREE JUMPING

### Peterson Air Force Base

The fist of God rests on the table.

One thousand tons of TNT—in a sixty-pound drum. Mute, the B54 reminds us of the gravity of our mission.

Vogel and Bauer stripped down the device and reassembled it. The bomb is fully functional. Last night's close call reinforces our appreciation that the device is not a toy.

Crockett steps to the front of the auditorium.

The wall behind Crockett is split into three rear-projection screens. On the left is an artist's sketch of the Jiang Shi cave complex. In the middle is a black-and-white satellite photograph of the village. The third is a map of northern Vietnam and Yunnan province.

"Is there anyone here who is *not* qualified to rappel?" Crockett asks.

He's staring at Stein. Stroud is in a C-130 seven thousand feet above ground level—twelve thousand above sea level. Preparing to jump into the dark.

Stroud, Ortega, Takigawa and I can rappel in our sleep. Stein is the question. She qualified in the FBI, says nothing.

Absent a response, Crockett carries on.

"Jumping into the jungle is like nothing you've ever tried," he says. "In triple canopy jungle, the trees are a hundred and thirty feet high. Each of us, with the exception of Stein, will carry a one-hundred-and-fifty-foot rope. Should we get hung up in the trees, we will lower the bombs and rappel to the jungle floor. Stein is Breed's passenger. She will descend using his rope, and he will follow."

"Is this likely to be necessary?" Ortega asks.

"We hope not," Crockett says. "It's called tree-jumping. The British SAS developed the method in Malaysia. If we hit our drop zones, we won't have to rappel. Let's look at this map."

He takes a laser pointer and highlights a region on the map. "All the rivers in this region originate on the Tibetan Plateau. The Yangtze runs east to the Pacific Ocean. Another two run south-by-east toward Vietnam and the Gulf of Tonkin. These are the Red River to the east and the Mekong to the west.

"Here's the point. In this area, the border between China and Vietnam lies close to the Red River. Villages and commerce spring up around rivers. When we inserted by land in 1974, we found heavy population around the border. We successfully evaded detection. We travelled by night, we waited long periods to cross highways, we covered as much ground as we could in the jungle. In fifty years, the population has increased. More area is devoted to paddies. There are better roads."

None of that sounds good. Stein sits, impassive.

"Jiang Shi is an unusual village," Crockett continues. "It didn't depend on agriculture. It sprang up because of the mine. When the copper mine closed, the village withered.

That's why Jiang Shi is isolated. There's nothing but jungle around it."

"Where do we land?" asks Takigawa.

"I'm sure none of us wants to HAHO into the jungle. Red River tributaries serve agriculture in southern Yunnan. It's beautiful country. Paddies, villages and roads occupy the valleys. Red roads wind among paddies and green hills. Foothills slope up toward the mountains. On the lower slopes, farmers have cut terraces. After that, it's all jungle, with very few clearings.

"I have selected three drop zones. The primary is three hours from the sinkhole. The other two are within five. The drop zones are on flat clearings outside small villages. The landing won't be easy. There's bamboo and high elephant grass. But it's better than landing in the trees."

Ortega frowns. "What if we're seen?"

"I'll take that," Stein says. "We are operating under unlimited rules of engagement. If anyone sees you, kill them."

Takigawa looks skeptical. "Anyone?"

"Anyone." Stein is firm. "If you let anyone see you, you have signed their death warrant. That must be one hundred percent clear."

Crockett smiles. "That's how we operated fifty years ago. You're sheep-dipped. There is no Uniform Code of Military Justice to hold you back."

"We will land in the dark," I say. "Discovery is unlikely. Once off the drop zone, Crockett takes point with an AK47. Stroud is slack with an RPD and one nuke, Ortega will be Number Three with a Bonfire and the second nuke. I'll be Number Four, with an AK47, and the Carl G with four rounds of ammunition. Stein will be Number Five with an AK47 and the radio. Takigawa will be rear guard with an AK47. Each of you will carry an extra round of Carl G ammunition, except for Stein, who will carry two. That's a total of ten rounds."

Crockett nods. "There is no reason for us to expect ambushes, but the PLA have ramped up security around Jiang Shi. We expect increased patrol activity."

"We expect land mines," I say. "The Chinese will use them for area control. Reduce the need for patrols."

"Watch for traps and contact," Crockett says. "I will take everything in front of me, one hundred and eighty degrees, eye level and below. Stroud will take the left overhead and ninety degrees right. Ortega will take the right overhead and ninety degrees left. Breed, you will take both overheads. I assume Stein has not received patrol training. Takigawa will take the rear and, if necessary, cover our tracks."

Perfect patrol discipline. Corrected for Stein as an unreliable Number Five.

"Alright," I say. "Everyone has a briefing pack. Crockett, what are we looking for?"

*Click.*

The image on the far left displays an artist's charcoal sketch of a limestone outcrop, covered with vegetation.

"Not much to look at, is it?" Crockett shakes his head. "You'll find granite, limestone, and sandstone in the area. The sinkholes are limestone. Soft, crumbly, easily weathered. This sketch is my recollection from fifty years ago. A limestone outcrop. It could look different today. There will be overgrowth of vegetation. But—the vegetation may appear flattened as it curls around the lip of the hole. You could fall in."

"If we arrive toward daybreak," Stein says, "we may see bats flying toward the hole. If we arrive toward sundown, we may be lucky enough to see bats leaving."

I hadn't thought of that.

"Show us the caverns," I tell Crockett.

*Click.*

We turn back to the artist's conception of the caves. A long web of spider holes extends over a mile under the saddle. Small tunnels and sinkholes, among them the one from which the team escaped.

The ridge extends from the sinkhole and rises north to the hills of the Jiang Shi mine.

Hill 40 conceals the chapel. This is the smaller cave, with a collapsed dome open to a sinkhole.

Hill 180 conceals the cathedral, with its massive limestone dome. The gullet of the mine. The large tunnel, used to cart ore from the mine, runs from the cathedral to the base of Hill 180. There, the mouth of the mine opens to the Jiang Shi valley.

The two hills are joined by a saddle. The saddle covers the smaller tunnel that joins the chapel and cathedral.

"It's pretty much as I described it," Crockett says. "This drawing also captures the surface features. The railroad, the village, the lodge, the hospital, and the barracks."

Stein gets up, extends her hand. Crockett gives her the laser pointer.

"We think the scientists live in what used to be the hospital building," Stein says. "It once served the mine. When the mine closed, it was used to treat people from the area. When the valley became depopulated, they maintained a small clinic. Used the rest of the space for quarters."

*Click.*

Stein displays an aerial photograph of Jiang Shi on the third screen. The first screen displays the artist's planimetric sketch of the surface terrain.

"No sign of life around the hospital," I observe.

"You can see people around the lodge and the barracks," Stein says. "Those are soldiers and administrative personnel. The scientists are moved from their quarters in the hospital to the lab every morning. They return in the evening. Transfers are timed to occur during periods our satellites are not overhead.

"China's top scientists have been centralized in Jiang Shi. Their Level 3 labs have no names of significance. Token capability resides at Wuhan. Destroy Jiang Shi and we decapitate their biological warfare establishment."

"Heavy weapons?"

*Click.*

The screen displays another aerial image of Jiang Shi. It looks like a black-and-white negative.

Stein points to light-colored patches on the screen. "I had a U-2 spy plane out of Osan tasked to cover the village after dusk. Metal cools at a slower rate than the jungle. These bright spots are metal vehicles. Some are parked under vegetation. Look at these in the village. They are sitting inside houses."

"They converted houses to garages for camouflage," I say. "Those are armored personnel carriers, mobile SAMs, or mobile anti-aircraft artillery."

"I count eight heavy vehicles," Takigawa says. "That's a lot of armor."

I lean back. "This is good intel. With luck, we won't have to tangle with armor. We can place the nukes and disappear without engaging anyone. Show us what you think the lab looks like."

*Click.*

An artist's cutaway sketch of Hill 180, the sinkhole on Hill 40, the chapel, and the cathedral. Sunken beneath the floor of the caves are underground structures. Three levels deep.

"This," Stein says, "is our best guess. Based on what Phoenix provided. In 1974, the first structure to be constructed was in the cathedral. It's the largest space, completely shielded by the dome. They blasted a depression in the floor, built the lab, and covered it up. The floor of the cathedral is certainly concrete now, covered with the usual bat shit. There will be an entrance of some sort to the administrative level.

"Over the years, they probably wanted to expand. It would be difficult to dig deeper. We think they blasted a similar depression in the floor of the chapel. Repeated the process. There will be an underground passageway between the two structures."

"Concrete and rebar?" I ask.

"Yes. We've briefed Captain Vogel and his team on the mission. He will present on the best placement of the B54s. Detonation of a single device will be enough to vaporize the lab and collapse the caves. Everything within a half mile radius of ground zero will be sterilized. Blast effects will level the surface within a mile radius."

"Jiang Shi?"

"Jiang Shi will cease to exist. Of course, a surface detonation would imply a larger radius of destruction. This will be an underground blast, hence a much smaller radius."

The room is silent.

"To exfil," I say, "we need to be a mile away."

"At *least* a mile," Stein says, "and downwind of the fallout. Remember, the blast will throw tons of limestone, concrete, and vegetation into the atmosphere."

Takigawa laughs nervously. Says what we are all thinking. "Lady, this is insane."

# 32

## COORDINATES

**Peterson Air Force Base**

I hate what I am about to do.

My heart pounds. The issue has to be faced.

The team files out of the auditorium. I hang back and call out, "Sam, can we speak for a minute?"

"Sure." Crockett walks back to where I am standing at the table. The doors swing shut, leaving us alone.

"Tell me again how you got these six-digit coordinates for the sinkhole."

Crockett shrugs. "I figured we had a bit of time after we climbed out. We were all wounded, but I was in better shape than the others. I did a standard triangulation."

I lay a map on the table, next to the B54. Underline Crockett's coordinates with a fine-point pencil.

"What features did you use?"

"We were at the base of the ridge, modestly elevated. I had a clear line of sight to Hill 180 and Hill 868. Those two sightings were enough to give me a location. I took a third sighting on a peak ten clicks south and confirmed it."

"These six-digit coordinates are good to a hundred meters," I tell him. "In thick bush, we could pass the hole inside half that and not know it."

Crockett stiffens. "Ninety percent of the time, 1:50,000 maps are accurate to fifty meters. You know that."

"You could have gone to eight."

"Six is more conservative."

"The last we spoke, you told me you had both 1:50,000 and 1:25,000 maps."

Crockett raises his voice. "What the hell, Breed. The maps were all missing Hill 40, a major fucking terrain feature."

"Sam, you are too good a soldier not to use your tools to maximum effectiveness. You took eight-digit coordinates. Hell, I *know* you took ten."

"What if I did? Given the maps I had, I wouldn't trust them."

I lower my voice. "Let the team be the judge. We all know how to read a map. We'll navigate to the ten-digit coordinates, consider the risk of error."

The contrast with Crockett's truculent tone brings him around. He frowns.

"Sam, if you're wounded or killed, the team needs to know what you know."

Crockett takes the pencil, scribbles numbers on the edge of the map.

Ten-digit coordinates.

The son of a bitch had them memorized.

"Does Stroud know these?"

"All the Black Sheep did. I don't know if they remember them."

I swallow my fury. Withholding information puts the team at risk. Crockett knows this, but he seems to think he and the Black Sheep are a cut above the rest of us. I understand people feel proprietary about knowledge. To engage in power plays. But there is no place for that reticence in a Delta team.

"Anything else you want to know, Breed?"

"Yes. What were the marks you left at the tunnel forks?"

"I looked for flat stones on the tunnel ceilings. Scratched Xs on them."

"On which fork? The one you followed, or the one you passed up?"

"The one we followed," Crockett sneers. "Is that good enough for you?"

"It is… for now."

Crockett turns on his heel and leaves the auditorium.

I stare after my friend. As I grew up, Crockett mentored me. I've spent my life mentoring other soldiers. Capable men of initiative, who learned quickly. There comes a time the student becomes as capable as his teacher. Less experienced, perhaps, but competent.

Crockett cannot accept me as an equal.

THE AUDITORIUM IS DARK. The only light comes from the third rear-projection screen. I've flicked back to the map of Southeast Asia. I slouch in the seat, legs splayed. Steeple my fingers and stare at the image.

"Breed."

The door creaks open and a dagger of light is cast into the auditorium. Stein's shadow stretches across the floor. Reaches for me.

"Yes."

Stein steps inside. Closes the door behind her. She sits next to me, stares up at the map. I shift my legs to give her room.

"I have a present for you." She hands me a package, a small leather box. Heavy. I unsnap the lid. Inside is a gleaming Chinese Type 64 pistol. Integral suppressor. Under the barrel sits a secondary expansion chamber. A slide lock renders the weapon almost completely silent. In the case are two nine-round 7.65mm magazines.

"Thanks. We'll need it."

"What are you thinking about?"

"A bunch of things. Any word on Appleyard?"

"Nothing. His targets have been hardened, he isn't willing to risk an attack. Yet. What's with the maps?"

"Have you given two seconds of thought to how we get out?"

"No. I'm with Takigawa. This is a one-way trip."

"Fuck that." I straighten in my chair. "I'm coming home."

"How do you plan to do that?"

"We have to avoid the fallout. What are the winds like?"

"East, or north-by-east. It depends."

"Anything but straight north or south, and we have a chance."

"Tell me."

"The China-Vietnam border wall blocks us to the south. Any idiot tells you walls don't work, tell him to fuck off. We cannot get out that way.

"If the wind blows south, we're screwed again, because escape to the north leads into the guts of China.

"If the wind blows west, we have a long shot. We'll run east, in the direction of Hong Kong. Find a way into Vietnam, make for the Gulf of Tonkin. Request seaborne rescue."

"That's an awful long shot."

"Yes, but we would have no other choice."

"What if the wind blows north-by-east?"

"Then we have two choices. We can run west and lose ourselves in the jungle. Make for Laos. From there, we call for airborne exfil from Thailand."

"And the second choice?"

"We lose ourselves in the jungle. Head north-by-west to the Tibetan Plateau. From there, make for the Wakhan Corridor and Afghanistan."

"Afghanistan!"

I smile. "We have a few friends there."

"You're crazy."

"You're the one who wants to hump a couple of nukes into China."

"To save the world."

"*This time.*"

"Breed, there's a new moon in three days."

"Sounds like a lot of choices are being made for us."

"Yes. We fly to Kadena tomorrow."

# 33

## BAD MEDICINE

**Peterson Air Force Base**

Heth and I walk the inner perimeter. We pass two Air Police and a Malinois as they patrol the space between the fences.

The dog barks but makes no sound.

"What's wrong with it?" Heth asks.

"Laryngectomized," I tell her. "If those Air Police turn him loose, he'll kill without giving himself away."

Kramer found that out—the hard way.

"My God, what kind of place is this?"

"Peterson is a place of secrets. These guys are serious as a heart attack."

Last night, Heth was evacuated from the compound with the others. No one told her why. No one told her about Kramer's death. She saw the Air Police vehicles at the fence, but not the body. I'm not about to educate her.

"What they did to that dog is wrong." Heth clenches her fist. "Men have to respect animals to work with them."

"I won't argue with you about that." I'm sure the SPCA doesn't know of the practice. If they did, they would file a blizzard of lawsuits.

I've never approved of laryngectomizing guard dogs. We didn't do it in Delta. But then, we used dogs for hunting and tracking, not security. Malinois are intelligent, loving animals. When I settle down, I'll find myself one, another Delta vet.

The laryngectomy procedure always seemed cruel to me. Not because of any physical pain inflicted on the animal. The torture is psychological. I was appalled by the effect it had on the animal's nature. Imagine being pissed off at an intruder. Not being able to express your anger because you can't bark. It's no wonder the guard dogs strike to kill as soon as they're let off the leash.

Heth pushes thoughts of the mutilated animal from her mind. She has more important things to speak about.

"Breed, what are you and Grandfather going to do in China?"

"How do you know we're going to China?"

"I'm not stupid. This is all about Grandfather and that mine."

True enough. But Stein has drawn a line under what we're allowed to share with Heth. "Heth, I can't tell you any more. That's how it has to be."

"This is all wrong." Heth raises her voice. "You're leaving me here with… Lieutenant Carmichael? Why not take me along?"

"The mission is secret."

"Why can't I go home?"

"Because Appleyard is out there killing people. Inside the wire, you're safe."

"Why did you bring me here if you won't involve me?"

"Heth, when all this started, you and I set out to find your grandfather. We didn't know the story. We didn't know why Kang tried to kill him. We didn't know Appleyard was in play."

"You and Grandfather are the two most important people in my life—next to Tall Deer." Heth faces me, arms folded. "I don't know where you're going, but I know you might not come back."

"There's a chance," I tell her. "But I always plan to make it home."

"And Grandfather?"

"Sam's hard to kill."

"You don't *have* to go. That woman's making you go."

"Stein can't make me do anything I don't want to do."

Heth grabs my shoulders. Her fingers dig deep. "Then *don't* go. This whole business is bad medicine."

"Whoa. What's all this about bad medicine?"

"I'm dreaming death, Breed. I'm dreaming evil."

I take Heth's hands and put my arm around her shoulders. Walk slowly. "Tell me about it."

"There's nothing to tell. I wake up and feel evil in the air. Like a blizzard of wings in the dark. I can't see them, but they're so thick I can't breathe. And I *know* there will be death."

I shiver. *It can't be.*

"Everybody gets bad dreams."

Heth looks miserable. "Breed, I'm not just anybody."

She has no idea how bizarre that sounds.

"Tall Deer works strong medicine for the Salish," Heth says. "We're not supposed to talk about it. He's my grandfather, and I'm his blood. I have his talent. He's been training me since I was four years old."

Tall Deer is revered as an elder of the Salish. Active on the tribal council. But I know him as a hunter and a guide.

I shake my head. "You mean Tall Deer is a medicine man?"

"Yes. And I will be, too. Talk about secrets. You're not supposed to know this."

"My lips are sealed. What's this got to do with bad dreams?"

"Powerful spirits come to us in dreams. A medicine-worker is sensitive. The worst dreams are those without an image. I couldn't see wings, but I felt them. I felt the evil, and I knew it was after you and Grandfather."

Heth throws her arms around my neck and hugs me. "Don't go."

She's in tears. What am I supposed to do?

I hold her close, my hand on her back. Stroke her gently. "Heth, it's too late. We have to go."

That was the wrong thing to say. Heth's body shakes with sobs. I think of her as a badass tomboy. The problem is, at twenty-four, she's very much a child.

I'm not trained for this.

Inspiration strikes.

"Make medicine *for* us, Heth. Can you do that?"

Slowly, Heth stops shaking. She sniffs.

"I'll try," she says at last. "But I don't know if I can protect you. I see and feel things, but I'm not strong enough to make things happen. I wish we could speak with Tall Deer."

Crazy thing is, I believe her. Once, my team was being airlifted out of a combat zone. I crouched next to a Black Hawk, waiting for the others to climb aboard. I heard a voice in my head say, *Drop*. Without a second thought, I threw myself to the ground. A Dragunov round drilled the side of the helicopter right where my head had been.

There was no one else there. I climbed in, and the chopper lifted off. There was no explanation for the voice. Only that it was not my day to die.

I hug Heth tight. This time, I'm the one who needs contact.

Jiang Shi is evil.

We'll need all the help we can get.

# 34

## NAVIGATION

### Over the Pacific

Travel in cargo planes is awesome. If there's cargo, I throw an inflatable mattress on top of a crate, pull a cargo strap over myself, and go to sleep. It's like a time machine. The crew wakes me up, and I'm there.

If there isn't cargo, I lay my shit on the floor and spread out.

Any way you look at it, travel in a C-17 Globemaster is great.

This flight is particularly comfortable because there are only a dozen passengers. The six in the assault team. Captain Vogel and Bauer to babysit the nukes. Four others from Stein's intel unit.

We left Heth with Lieutenant Carmichael. She took me aside. "Come back," she said. Then, staring at Stein, "Leave *her* wherever it is you're going."

I hope Heth works strong medicine. She wanted to call Tall Deer. I explained we weren't allowed to phone off the base. Wondered what Stein would say if I told her we wanted to ask a Salish medicine man for help. Work a spell to keep us safe.

The cargo bay has been divided by a bulkhead two-thirds of the way forward of the ramp. A warning has been painted on the bulkhead. The red block capitals stand a foot high:

RESTRICTED AREA NO ADMITTANCE

Stein's team carried laptops and other equipment onto the plane. Cloistered themselves behind that bulkhead. A door opens, and Stein steps into the cargo bay. She looks around, fixes her gaze on me.

"What have you got in there, Stein? I'm guessing encryption for comms."

"You guess right. We are in constant contact with Washington."

I sit, cross-legged, on my inflatable mattress. Motion Stein to join me. We're all dressed in unmarked jungle fatigues and jungle boots. I'm cleaning the Type 64. It's a beautiful Chinese pistol, designed specifically for special operations. NVA Special Forces used them for assassinations during the Vietnam war. Later in the seventies, Chinese Special Forces used them against the NVA.

What goes around comes around. I've outfitted the weapon with Tritium sights to help me register targets in the dark. Once inside the chapel and cathedral, I will use it to neutralize sentries.

"You're worried about the abort command."

Stein takes a knee. Watches me oil the weapon.

"Yes. Poole hauled the General Counsel and Jacob Fischer into the Oval Office again. Argued that Title 50 did not give the president authority to covertly deploy a tactical nuke."

"We haven't turned around, so it didn't work."

Stein smiles. "The president asked counsel if Title 50

*prohibited* him from issuing a Memorandum of Notification in a nuclear context. They said no. He sent them back to the drawing board."

"Sounds like the highest authority doesn't want to leave the Chinese with a doomsday bug either."

"I'd hate to be Jacob Fischer. When he went into the Oval Office the first time, he said the president had the authority to do this. Poole twisted his arm into going in again and saying the president's authority isn't clear. He will be sacrificed."

"How do you know all this?"

"Let's say I have allies," Stein says. "Conditional on success."

"Warren Thiel?"

"He's maneuvering against Poole."

"I don't know why you put up with it."

"Because that's what it takes for me to make a difference."

Stein gets up. Walks to where Vogel and Bauer are sitting with their backs to the cabin wall. In front of them, lashed to a sturdy pallet, are two bombs in olive drab rucks. When we reach Kadena, they will be configured and packed for parachute insertion.

Vogel looks calm and composed. Bauer is slowly recovering from the near-disaster Kramer inflicted on us. After I yanked the primer, the two professionals called a bomb disposal team. X-rayed the B54's case. Made certain Kramer did not wire conventional explosives to the front plate.

When they were certain the bomb was not booby-trapped, Vogel and Bauer stripped the device down to its last screw. Put it back together again.

Satisfied, Stein gets up and walks to the security bulkhead. Opens the door and disappears into her top-secret enclave.

I holster the Type 64 and join Ortega. He occupies one of the folding seats that line the sides of the cargo bay. He's spread maps, compasses, GPS, and other navigation equipment on one of our equipment crates. He made sure the crate was strapped down before we took off.

"What do you think?" I put down the seat next to him and collapse into it.

"It's straightforward, man. Flight time from Kadena to our jump-off point is two hours. We'll start pre-breathing in-flight an hour before we jump. Depressurize the cargo bay, and off we go."

"I'm counting on you to navigate us to the drop zone."

"It's all good. GPS is set for the DZ and two alternates."

"Remember what happened to me when I jumped with Rahimi."

Ortega laughs. "Fuck, dude. That was Murphy's Law. Here."

He reaches into a haversack and produces another GPS unit.

"Outstanding," I tell him. "We like redundancy."

"Stein's prettier than Rahimi," Ortega says.

"She's an ice cube."

"Nah." Ortega leans back and rests his head against the fuselage. "She likes you, man."

"You're dreaming."

I've wondered why Stein keeps showing up at my door. I'm happy for the work, but am I *that* good? There are *lots* of operators with my skills. Of course, I *have* demonstrated the one talent that matters. I win, and I'm alive.

"Ask us Latinos, baby—we know. That woman's eyes are for you."

Stein is a bundle of mixed messages. Girls like Tracy, at Gilbert's, are easy. They're either up for it, or they're not. Every now and then, Stein lifts the cover enough for a peek. Then she slams it shut and screws the lid on.

I get to my feet. "Hard work, dude," I tell him. "I like to keep things simple."

Ortega shrugs. "Suit yourself, bro. Just saying."

Can two wrongs make a right? I wonder if Stein is as fucked up as I am. How many ugly thoughts does she wall up like rats in the back of her skull?

Force the thought from my mind. "I'll program my navigation board. We'll have double redundancy."

"There's a plan."

"Watch the old-timers."

"Anything specific?"

I shake my head. "Just be careful."

Ortega cackles. "Don't worry, man. That ice cube will *melt*."

# 35

## INSERTION

### 35,000 Feet over Vietnam

I meet Stein's eyes across the cargo bay of the Globemaster. I see anxiety, not panic. That's okay, it's expected. The six of us sit in two rows of three each. The plane has a wide ramp, and we'll jump in pairs, close together. Ortega and Takigawa. Crockett and Stroud. Stein and myself, in tandem.

To spoof a commercial flight, we fly a jet transport. We'll slow down to jump. Hopefully, no curious flight controller will notice the brief change in airspeed.

The Air Force has assigned us three jumpmasters. Two to assist me and Stein. The third stands with the loadmaster at the head of the ramp. The cargo bay has been depressurized, and we are all breathing aviator-grade oxygen. The jumpmasters and I watched Stein through the pre-breathing exercise. She was an ice cube.

*Six minutes.*

I can't hear the jumpmaster. He holds up six fingers, all I need to see. The traffic light glows red.

Stein casts her eyes toward the front of the plane. I smile to myself. She is more afraid of an abort command than she is of falling thirty-five thousand feet.

What if Poole issues the command with the team half-out of the plane? Stein and I agreed. If the nukes leave the plane, *we* leave the plane.

Arms extended sideways, palms up, the jumpmaster gestures for us to stand.

The two jumpmasters with Stein go to work. Body straight, arms at her sides, she stands in front of me. Her harness is clipped to mine, the safe pins pushed into place. Not so straightforward. We each carry our personal weapons. Our rucks and HF ManPack radio are clipped to D-rings on the front of Stein's harness.

I watch Ortega and Takigawa waddle to the ramp, nukes and rucks between their legs. Crockett and Stroud carry the Carl G and its ammunition. The Carl's three-foot-long firing tube has been strapped horizontally across Crockett's chest. I didn't trust the nukes to the old-timers.

One of the jumpmasters slaps my back. Flashes me a thumbs-up.

The other jumpmaster steps back from Stein. Flashes her a thumbs-up. Like she's done this hundreds of times, they bump fists.

*Three minutes.*

The ramp is open. We stare at the black sky of a moonless night. Below us lies a thick carpet of cloud. I feel Stein's heart hammering in her chest. I reach up, pull down my NODs. The night vision devices restrict my peripheral vision. Wearing them over jump goggles is like looking through a pair of drinking straws.

*Thirty seconds.*

Like athletes before the gun, Ortega and Takigawa shake their arms loose.

Stein's left hand brushes mine. She grasps my index finger and squeezes. My heart jumps.

The traffic light flashes green.

Ortega and Takigawa dive into space.

Stroud follows.

Crockett pirouettes and jumps out backwards.

*Showboat.*

We're at the edge of the ramp. Stein crosses her hands over her chest. Tips her head back against my shoulder. Like I showed her.

Jump.

We fall into space. The drogue catches and swings us belly-to-earth. I spread my arms, flat and stable. We're perfectly aligned.

*One-thousand-one. One-thousand-two.*

Five seconds pass. I pull the main. The blast of air rushing past makes it impossible to hear anything. I sense rather than hear the nylon of the canopy deploying from its tray. The parachute lines draw out the risers.

I clutch Stein to my chest and brace for the shock. Air rushes into the cells and the wing opens with a crack that's audible over the wind. Stein's legs, held tightly together, snap skyward and bang into our rucks. The canopy's deployment is uneven. First we are thrown to the left, then we are bounced to the right. My helmet slams into the risers.

We dangle thirty-five thousand feet over the Vietnamese jungle. Through our NODs, we stare at the clouds beneath our feet. The chaos of the jump and parachute deployment are over.

I key my mike. "This is Five-One Actual. Check in."

"Five-One Bravo," Ortega says.

"Five-One Oscar." It's Takigawa.

"Five-One Kilo." Crockett.

"Five-One Sierra." Stroud.

Silence.

"Five-One India," I say. "This is Actual. Check in."

"Five-One India," Stein acknowledges.

The other canopies glow white, green and black in my night vision. We fly under infrared discipline. Cheap IR scopes are commercially available. You can bet the enemy has them. I view the team's chutes through NODs. The first four are within a hundred yards of each other. Stein and I are sixty yards behind. The jump could not have gone better.

"Team, form up on Five-One Bravo."

Ortega pilots us toward China. Jiang Shi lies there, twenty-five miles away. We don't know how thick the cloud layer will be. It could mask torrential rain.

Ortega carries a homing device. Because he is the most likely to hit the drop zone, it enables the rest of us to converge on him. As alternate pilot, I carry a homer, but will not activate it unless Ortega is incapacitated. While meant for use on the ground, we can also use the devices in the air.

The homing devices are a last resort. Our best bet is to maintain Ortega's bearing as we enter the cloud bank. We should emerge within sight of each other.

"Five-One Bravo," I say. "This is Actual. What do you think of those clouds?"

"Nimbostratus, six or seven thousand feet," Ortega says. "Covering the drop zone."

"Do you want to try for an alternate?"

"Negative, Actual. They're all wet."

The problem with rain clouds is turbulence. Harsh winds can scatter a drop over the whole of creation. These nimbostratus are low. With luck, we won't have too rough a ride.

On and on, we glide. With each passing minute, we lose altitude. The drop zone and the clouds get closer. I watch for flashes of lightning. Sparks within the clouds that promise trouble. I can't see any. Fifteen minutes gone, and the worst to come.

"Bravo," I say. "Turn your homer on. Team, let's tighten it up before we enter the clouds."

Of course, there's the risk of a mid-air collision. What worries me more, a mid-air or a scattered team? A scattered team. A lost nuke is not in my game plan.

Gravity drags us into the clouds. I check my altimeter and GPS. We're on course, won't be in the clouds long. Three or four minutes, then we'll maneuver to land. I sense tension in Stein's limbs. She knows the clouds don't mean anything good. Nothing she says or does will contribute—she's smart enough to remain silent.

The first drops of rain splash my NODs and goggles. Not a lot of wind. Tropical rain often falls straight down. Before long, we're gliding through a car wash.

My head is on a swivel. I check the airspace around me for other canopies. Check my altimeter, check my GPS. A shadow passes dangerously close on my right. A wing glares in my night vision, a black body underneath. I can't tell who it is.

I'm soaked. The NODs are useless. Flying through these clouds, I see nothing. I'm a pilot on instruments. Check my watch. Another minute or so and we should be through.

Stein tries to rub water from the lenses of her NODs. It's hopeless.

"Five-One Bravo," I say. "This is Actual. Sitrep."

"On course, Actual. We'll be clear in a minute."

At six thousand feet, we break through the clouds. I'm shocked by the glare in my NODs. We're across the border, flying over China. The Red River valley is clear, lined by thousands of lights. Unlike the Hindu Kush, Yunnan Province is electrified. The Chinese have built dams all along the rivers. The lights are blinding in my NODs. A swathe of darkness lies to the north. Those are the hills and mountains that conceal Jiang Shi.

I look for the team. Four canopies close by. Ortega and Takigawa fly in close formation. Behind them, another parachute. Stroud or Crockett. Two hundred yards behind, a fifth chute emerges from the clouds.

"This is Actual. Who's the straggler?"

"This is Five-One Sierra," Stroud says. "Sorry, Actual. I got separated in the clouds."

Damn. If he tries to catch up, he'll lose altitude and land short.

"No rush," I tell him. "Watch us land, maneuver in your own good time."

Ortega and I have jumped together so often we can read each other's mind. He judges the wind, dips his wing, and eases himself into a two hundred and seventy degree left turn. We're under a thousand feet. I see the lights of a village a mile to the east. Paddies, a clear field.

We stack ourselves for landing. Give each other room so as not to crowd the approach. I watch Ortega release the first B54. The nuke slides to the bottom of its seventeen-foot suspension cable. It touches down, tumbles. Ortega flared before the bomb hit, minimized the impact. He joins it on the ground.

Takigawa lowers the second B54. His landing is equally well executed. He lands on his feet, but disappears from view. I blink as I stare through my NODs. The field, which looked smooth from above, is overgrown with shoulder-high elephant grass.

Crockett executes a perfect landing.

I undo my oxygen mask, allow it to dangle. I bend to Stein's ear. "Legs together," I tell her. "When I tell you, bend your legs at the knees and touch the rucks. I'll take the impact."

The ground rushes up to meet us. I pull hard on the rear risers and flare. "Now," I say. "*Lift.*"

Stein lifts her knees. I've flared as much as I can, but we're nose-heavy. There's a rush as we barrel through the elephant grass. My legs take the impact—not hard. I lean back, find myself on my ass. Stein and the rucks lie on top of me. She tears off her mask.

I unclip our tandem harness and free our weapons. Roll over, get to one knee, and search the sky for Stroud. Rain streams down my face. I blink it out of my eyes, spit.

There he is. A black figure under a dark wing. In the green glow of my NODs, the cloud cover is a bright background. I had feared Stroud would land short. He's about to make a perfect landing. In seconds, he lands fifty yards to my right.

I pass my arms through the straps of my ruck. Help Stein shoulder her pack and the radio. I gather the chute, head for the spot where I saw Ortega land. We're soaked, and the elephant grass is wet. The ground is muddy and slick.

The team assembles within fifteen minutes, and we distribute weapons and equipment. Ortega and Takigawa check the B54s. Both nukes are undamaged. We lift them from their foam-lined parachute cases. Stroud and Ortega carry them in ruck configuration.

Stroud's face runs with rain or sweat. I can't tell which. Probably both. His handlebar mustache hasn't drooped in the slightest.

We bury our parachutes and helmets inside the tree line. The rain is miserable, but no farmers will be outdoors to catch sight of us. Without helmets, we mount our NODs on lightweight plastic skeleton frames. Secure them with canvas chinstraps and Velcro. Wear them under floppy jungle hats.

The jungle has taken twenty years off Crockett's age. AK47 at low ready, he turns to me. I nod my head, and he takes point.

It's up to Crockett to lead us to Jiang Shi.

# 36

## TRACKING

### Yunnan

Every generation has its war. Mine was in the desert of Iraq and the mountains of the Hindu Kush. Crockett and Stroud love the jungle. We move slowly, scan our designated surveillance zones.

This is hell. The further into the jungle we go, the denser the vegetation. Maneuvering at night, with NODs, is terrible. My field of view is restricted to thirty degrees. It takes forever to cover my designated overheads. Crockett isn't having a better time of it. But then, they didn't have NODs fifty years ago. They went to ground at night and maneuvered during the day.

The soft green glow of the NODs against our eyes is a security risk. We agreed it was a low risk, worth taking.

The mosquitoes are insufferable. In the dark, they swarm in thick, choking clouds. They clot your nostrils and lips until you unroll the protective mosquito net Velcroed to the inner brim of your hat. The fine mesh stretches over your NODs, further restricting your vision.

But it's leeches I worry about. In the dark, we can neither see, nor feel them. I imagine myself covered, come daylight. Picture the slugs bloated with my blood.

Crockett cleaves the brush like the prow of a ship through water. Streamlined and smooth, the vegetation closes behind him. He doesn't leave a trace.

I carry the Carl G and four rounds strapped together in tubes. The rest of my loadout is a two-quart camelback and magazines of AK47 ammunition. The recoilless rifle itself is strapped vertically against the left side of my ruck. Two rounds are on the right side, and the other two are strapped vertically across the bottom. Like the others, I carry a loop of rappel rope over my shoulder.

I push myself to adapt.

Before jumping, I took 1:50,000 and 1:25,000 maps. Cut out ten-by-ten squares of the key areas of operations, covered them in plastic. My maps cover the drop zones. Movement from each drop zone to the sinkhole we plan to enter. Jiang Shi and the surrounding hills.

I marked the most pronounced terrain features. The biggest problem is visualizing the terrain. A hilltop that *should* be visible according to a map might be completely obscured by triple-canopy jungle.

Every step of the way, I practice land nav. Check my GPS, my compass. Deliberately, I shadow Crockett and check his route. I have always been good in the field. I can read a map and visualize the terrain ahead of me as clearly as any virtual reality game.

My confidence grows. I see where Crockett is going. He avoids the trails. For area control, the PLA are likely to mine certain trails. Their patrols will be aware of which ones. We aren't, so we move in the bush.

Crockett isn't a superman. Back in the day, he and Dad didn't maneuver at night. They didn't have NODs, and you can't see shit without them. That makes it impossible to read an azimuth. Never mind that. How do you take a bearing when the furthest you can see is five feet ahead? In the deepest jungle, you can't do land nav by map and compass. During the day it's a pain in the ass. At night it's impossible.

The old-timer uses GPS, and that's fine. But he is *not* a superman.

The principles of maneuver and warfare are the same. The terrain is different.

We struggle through the triple canopy jungle. The rain drums on the vegetation, runs off, pours on our heads.

Stein covers the ground without complaint. Any apprehension she might have felt in the air is gone. She's a machine. Of course, she carries the lightest load, about forty-five pounds. Her AK47, the ManPack radio, and two Carl G rounds. Her ruck is stuffed with spare mags, water, and two Meals Ready-to-Eat.

The rest of us carry a hundred and twenty pounds each. Crockett and Stroud are tough birds. They look good now, but wait till this hike is over. They'll be wrecked for a month.

Or we'll all be dead.

THE VEGETATION IS SO thick I can't see further than the bomb on Ortega's back. If I turn, I see Stein, two yards behind me.

A rustle of leaves, and a hand gently touches my shoulder.

Stein?

I turn slowly. It's Takigawa. Jungle hat, mosquito netting, NODs. Looks like an alien creature. He's slipped past Stein to talk to me. Pulls me close, whispers in my ear. "We have a shadow."

"How far," I ask. "How long?"

"A hundred yards. Fifteen minutes."

If Takigawa says we have a shadow, I believe him. We were right to be cautious. If the Chinese are patrolling in the bush, the trails must be mined. One of their units spotted signs of our passage.

"Execute Cobra," I whisper.

"Roger that."

Takigawa slips back without another word. Allows Stein to pass and resume her place. I stop and let her pass. She looks at me, but I cannot read her eyes through our NODs. Instead, I take Takigawa's place as tail-gunner, the rear guard.

I look back the way we have come.

The jungle has swallowed him up.

Takigawa and I had discussed this scenario on the plane. Crockett never thought an enemy patrol would come upon us from behind.

My agreement with Takigawa was simple. Should the Chinese approach from the rear, he would separate from our patrol and lead them away. It was a subtle trick. If properly executed, they would follow his trail and never know the difference. He would shake them later, and meet us at Jiang Shi.

Of course, he might *not* shake them. In that case he would be killed.

In the worst case, our pursuers would find themselves faced with two trails. Not certain which to follow, they would split their force. We would have to contend with half as many.

I stop, close my eyes, strain my ears. Struggle to discriminate between the different jungle sounds. The cries of birds, the crash of monkeys, the whine of mosquitoes. Catalogue the sounds coming from different sectors of the jungle in front of me. One-third left, one-third center, one-third right.

There is a soft rustle. Stealthier and more deliberate than natural jungle noise. Maneuvering left-to-right at a thirty-degree angle. Slowly, I step backwards, AK47 ready.

More movement. I'm not sure I hear it. This is a ripple in the ether. I sense it the way a shark detects pressure waves. The natural jungle sounds go silent as the alien movement progresses. Left, center, right. A definite progression.

Cobra is working. The Chinese patrol is following Takigawa. His deviation from our bearing was so slight, they did not notice.

I listen. Step back, listen some more. When I am sure we have lost our shadow, I turn and catch up to Stein. Takigawa will not reach the sinkhole by dawn. Maybe he's the lucky one. He could be miles away when the bomb goes off.

Our little band has been reduced to five.

# 37

## THE TUNNELS

### Jiang Shi

Crockett is leading us to a stream. I study the map. The stream runs past the limestone outcrop that conceals the sinkhole. Fifty years ago, he must have used the stream to orient himself after the team escaped. Plotted the location on his map so he could find it again.

We don't need the stream. We have ten-digit coordinates for the sinkhole. Using the stream for a reference will get us there faster, but it's risky. Streams are like trails. Hunters watch them for prey. The enemy does the same. Everything alive needs water. Do the math.

Troubled, I follow the team. The vegetation is thinning. Stein's lithe figure, weighed down by gear, is clearly visible. Beyond her, Ortega pushes through the brush.

A choked cry pierces the air.

*What the fuck.*

I push past Stein and Ortega. Sweat in my eyes, the vegetation close and humid. The jungle opens up, and I come upon the bank of the stream. The vegetation has been beaten back on either side. Above, the sky lightens with the approach of dawn.

Crockett stands with one foot in the water, his arm around a Chinese soldier's head. The man's eyes are crazed with pain. He's sunk his teeth into Crockett's hand as the Green Beret struggles to muffle his cries. Crockett's plunged his knife into the man's right kidney. Severed the renal artery.

*Son of a bitch.*

Stroud raises the RPD to his shoulder, points it at the jungle behind Crockett.

I grab the muzzle of the RPD and force it down. Draw my Type 64 from its holster.

Six feet from Crockett, a second Chinese soldier emerges from the jungle. Raises his rifle.

I hold my suppressed pistol in a two-handed grip, thrust my thumbs toward the PLA. I don't wait to align the sights. My thumbs are pointing at the fucker's face. I pull the trigger. There's a snick as the action reciprocates. The muzzle flash flickers. At seven hundred and fifty feet per second, the subsonic round smacks the PLA in the face. A hole magically appears on the bridge of his nose.

The Chinese crumples as I fire again. The second round drills him in the forehead.

I advance, pistol raised. Cover the jungle behind the crumpled PLA soldier.

Crockett pulls the knife from his victim's back. Wipes the blade on the soldier's jacket. To make sure it's clean, he turns the blade in his hand. A worn SOG seven-inch recon. Crockett smiles to himself and sheathes it, handle down, on the left side of his chest.

"What the fuck happened?" I hiss.

"He was filling his canteen and spotted me. I had to take him out quiet."

"That was real fucking quiet."

Stroud, Ortega and Stein have joined us.

"Where's Takigawa?" Crockett asks.

"Hopefully, a mile away. We picked up a shadow."

Crockett stoops and grabs his victim by the wrists. Drags the corpse into the brush. "Help me get these guys out of sight."

I holster the suppressed Type 64. Stroud drags the man I shot to the edge of the jungle. Lays him next to the other dead body. Shoves them under vegetation.

The Chinese soldier's rifle lies on the bank. I pick it up. Standard Chinese military issue. A bullpup design, like those of the French and Brits, but without the ergonomics. A shit weapon. That's why I outfitted our team with AK47s.

I throw it into the brush.

"Let's get going," Crockett says.

With that, he sets off along the bank of the stream.

Like nothing happened, Stroud follows him.

We're less than two hundred yards from the sinkhole. I say nothing.

Ortega meets my eyes as he passes, shakes his head. "That was not cool, bro."

No, it wasn't. Crockett should never have maneuvered so close to the stream. Ortega resumes his position in the patrol. I allow Stein to pass, then assume tail-gunner position. Stein is sensitive to the vibe, looks worried. She has a thousand questions for me, and no time to ask them.

Like hot lava, I choke down my fury.

Crockett and I need to have things out.

It's a little late.

He's setting a fast pace on the stream bank. I check our rear every few yards. The men we killed had to be part of a larger patrol. They'll be missed. When they are, we can count on a dozen or so PLA to search for them. Those bodies will be found.

I check my GPS. The sinkhole is thirty yards away. Crockett pulls off the trail. I push brush and bamboo to cover signs of our passage. The vegetation is light here. There is less mud, more rock. Ahead, I see the outcrop.

The crackle of rifle fire splits the air. Chinese rifles.

Then… the drumbeat of an AK47.

There's an explosion. The blast of a Claymore.

More rifle fire.

We catch up to Crockett at the outcrop.

"What the hell's that?" Stroud grunts.

"Takigawa." My tone is grim. "The PLA caught up to him."

The gunfire dies away. We are left in silence.

I'm sick to my stomach about Takigawa, but we have to move. We redistribute our load. Stein passes Crockett the Carl G rounds she is carrying. Stroud and Ortega unlimber the straps they will use to tow the bombs as they crawl through the tunnel. The rest of us do the same with our rucks.

Vegetation shrouds the lip. Crockett and Stroud clear a space with their SOG knives. When they have finished, I take a Carl G round from Ortega. Slip it from the carrying tube, load the cannon. I slam the recoilless rifle's breech and lock it shut.

Bat guano stains the vegetation and the limestone. The animals shit as they land and take flight. I strain to hear the rustle of life inside the pit. Nothing. An invisible draft, the ammonia stink of bat piss boils from the pit.

The carrying tube, I lay against the lip of the sinkhole. Take the rappel rope from my shoulder, throw it over the tube, and down the hole. Ortega does the same. We fasten the free ends around nearby tree trunks.

"Go," I say.

Crockett swings himself into space and rappels into the hole. I look down, and he flashes a thumbs-up.

I grab a rope and take a deep breath. Through my gloves, the nylon feels rough. I stand with my feet against the lip, test my weight. Stroud sheaths his knife, takes the other rope. Together, we rappel to the bottom, followed by Stein and Ortega. We agree to leave the ropes in place. At this point, the risk of discovery is outweighed by the need for the ropes to be available for a quick escape.

I switch positions with Stroud. Crockett will lead us into the tunnel, I will follow in second place.

Crockett grins.

Sweat trickles along the cracks in Stroud's weathered face. His handlebar mustache droops.

Stein's expression is a frigid mask.

As though saying goodbye to the world, Ortega raises his eyes to the sinkhole.

Crockett turns and plunges into the tunnel.

Stroud cries out. "Fuck."

I'm startled. My attention has been focused on Crockett's form. Dragging his ruck, he inches forward.

The first bat flutters past. I feel the rush of air from its beating wings. It comes from the direction of the sinkhole, on its way to the chapel.

That's why Stroud was surprised. Above us, in the jungle, dawn has cracked. Bats are returning to their roosts. They fly through sinkholes scattered over several square miles of hills.

More bats stream by. The animals hate being around humans, but we're between them and their home.

Stroud's voice trembles. "Fuckin' things."

"Be quiet," Stein hisses.

Another bat stops, hooks its claws on the rock wall, stares at me. Its eyes are silver dots in the glow of my NODs.

In the claustrophobic darkness, I find the animal's presence comforting.

*Hi, little fella. We're both color-blind, see?*

The tiny thing reads my mind. Squeaks, continues on its way.

I crawl after Crockett. Thirty minutes pass. Forty-five.

He stops, rolls onto his back.

"What's wrong?" I whisper.

"Can't find my mark," he says. "Give me a minute. Look aside."

I turn my head. Crockett flips up his NODs, turns on his flashlight. Squinting, I look past him. The tunnel has bifurcated. Each time we passed this kind of fork, Crockett led us forward. Now he casts about the ceiling of the tunnel.

"Do you see it?"

"No. Didn't expect everything to be the same after fifty years."

Crockett switches off the flashlight, flips down his NODs.

More bats flutter through the air, fill the spaces in the tunnel. I feel their wings beat against my shoulders.

"Crockett," Stroud calls, "get us the fuck out of here."

"Relax," Crockett says. "I got this."

Does he? The stench of ammonia is overpowering. I breathe through my mouth.

Crockett starts moving.

He's following the bats. The same trick that saved him fifty years ago, this time in reverse.

I check my watch. We've been in the maze well over an hour.

There is some importance attached to that figure. It tells me for how long I should set the delay on the nukes.

The plan is to set one nuke in the chapel, the other in the cathedral. The floors below the domes are circular. We will take out the sentries, then conceal the bombs in the shadows. Along the rim, we are sure to find suitable stone alcoves.

We will withdraw before the PLA get wise to our incursion.

After that, our fate will be in the hands of the gods.

# 38

## THE BATTLE

### Jiang Shi

The tunnel widens. Opens to a vestibule.

I crawl forward until I lie next to Crockett. His back to us, a sentry stands not three feet from our noses. PLA camouflage, bullpup rifle, no body armor. The vestibule is not completely black. A red glow suffuses the space, casts black shadows. Dim red lights have been mounted on the ceiling.

Crockett draws his knife.

I shake my head. Suppressed pistol in hand, I rise to my feet. Step to the sentry, push the muzzle against the back of his neck, squeeze the trigger. The hollow point severs his spine and blows his cervical vertebrae out his throat. He crumples. I kick him over and shoot him a second time in the face.

Only his eyes are visible. No night vision devices, he relied on the ambient light. He wears a white mask with filters. No closed oxygen system. Proof against guano dust, but the Chinese are not concerned with aerosol-borne disease.

That's comforting.

We step to the chapel entrance. Flatten ourselves against the walls, look inside. The center of the dome has collapsed. One hundred and twenty feet above us, an open space yawns. Ragged vegetation adorns the lip of the sinkhole.

*God Almighty.*

The roosts make my skin crawl. Leathery creatures hang inverted in long rows. Their eyes stare with malevolence. They sense our presence. The shapes ripple in the dark. Silver in the glow of the NODs, droplets of urine stream to the floor. Saturated with foul odor, the atmosphere in the cave assaults my senses. My head aches.

These are not the cute little bats that guided us through the tunnels. Crockett had described the roosts to us, but I wasn't prepared for the diversity of the colony.

All kinds of bats occupy this circle of hell. Carnivorous animals with snouts pointed like those of wolves. Nectar-licking creatures with delicate jaws and long, flicking tongues. Insectivores drop digested exoskeletal husks into the repulsive soup that covers the floor.

I force myself to focus on the job.

No question, there's a lab underground. The floor isn't natural. Under the stew, it's manmade, concrete-smooth. In the middle is a cement blockhouse. A single door, no windows. Two masked sentries, outfitted like the man I killed. One outside the door, another at the opening to a larger tunnel on the other side. It must lead to the cathedral.

Like the vestibule we occupy, the larger tunnel glows with soft red light.

Why not light the whole dome? Why not white light?

My heart pounds.

*They need the bats.*

Crockett and I nod to each other.

I draw my suppressed pistol. Take careful aim at the sentry outside the blockhouse. Traverse left, shift to the man at the tunnel mouth. At the moment of my natural respiratory pause, I break the shot. The pistol spits. The sentry crumples. I traverse right, shift to the man at the blockhouse. Shoot him in the face.

The men lie still. I walk to them, shoot them both a second time in the head. Slip the empty magazine from the pistol, reload.

Crockett and Stroud join me at the entrance to the large tunnel. I signal Ortega and Stein to plant the first nuke in the vestibule. It will be out of the way. If there is trouble, they will have a measure of cover.

I turn, lead the way to the cathedral.

WOULD THERE BE another sentry at the end of this tunnel? Perhaps the man I killed was meant to cover both ends. I approach the tunnel mouth with the suppressed pistol extended. I'm comfortable with the Type 64. Adjusted its sights and practiced with it before we left Peterson. I know what it can do.

I walk close to the tunnel wall. The tunnels are bathed in red light. The chapel and the cathedral are unlit, for the benefit of the bats.

There is no sentry at the tunnel mouth.

Like the chapel, there is a blockhouse in the center of the cathedral. A large steel door under a dim red light. A masked sentry at the door. Across the floor, another sentry at the entrance to the larger tunnel. The cave that leads to the mouth of the mine.

My eyes sweep the floor. The railroad tracks Crockett told us about are gone. Like the chapel, the floor is smooth concrete, covered by a noxious pool. The surface is pelted by drizzle. Not rain, because the cathedral dome is intact. Urine, from the millions of bats that inhabit the overhead grottoes. Waves of ammonia fumes rise from the surface, drift in the humid atmosphere.

I raise the pistol in both hands. Crockett steps behind me, AK47 ready.

Stroud leans against the tunnel wall. He looks ghastly in the light of my NODs. A pale face, covered with silver beads of sweat. His mustache droops like Doctor Fu Manchu's. RPD slung across his chest, he shrugs off the nuke.

The walls ripple. There are so many bats in the cathedral there isn't enough room for them in the dome. In cracks and ledges, the circumference of the space, they cling by their toes. From floor to ceiling, the cathedral has been wallpapered with the creatures. In overlapping rows, the bats hang from one another. Concealed from view, babies squeal from cradles in the rock.

Stroud wobbles.

The sentry at the far tunnel has partly faced away from me. A forty-five-degree angle. The man at the blockhouse is an easier target. I let out my breath, relax, and fire twice. The first round hits the guard in his left cheek. The second glances off the edge of his helmet and deflects into his temple.

In an effort to support himself, Stroud reaches for the wall. Puts his hand on a dark, leathery wing.

A screech, the beating of wings, and a snap of jaws. Stroud cries out, snatches his hand away from the bat. Too late, the animal's knife-sharp teeth have slashed through his glove, opened it up like a box cutter.

The guard at the tunnel entrance raises his rifle. The dome crackles with automatic fire. Bullets shatter rock, rip into Stroud, knock the B54 onto its side.

Three times, in rapid succession, I squeeze the trigger. The sentry drops his rifle and pitches to the floor.

A tremendous roar fills the air. It's like the ruffling of all the pages in a library of books. Amplified a thousand times. Bats burst from the dome of the cathedral. Swirl like leaves caught in a twister. Flee toward the mouth of the mine, rush down the opposite tunnel toward the chapel. A bat slams into my chest and I ward another from my face. Holster the pistol.

The door of the blockhouse opens. Inside, a rectangle of white light. Three PLA burst into the cathedral, but the light in the blockhouse ruined their night vision. Crockett cuts them down. Behind us, in the chapel, the crackle of Chinese rifles and the drumbeat of AK47s.

Crockett races to the tunnel. He has to hold the mouth of the mine before reinforcements arrive.

I bend to Stroud. Still alive, he coughs blood from shattered lungs. His hands clutch the RPD.

"You miserable son of a bitch," I say. "If you couldn't handle the bats, you should have told us."

"I thought I could," Stroud gasps. "I'll hold the blockhouse."

I grab the B54, open the ruck. Two bullets have hit the rear case, close to the security cover. The dial of the combination lock refuses to turn. Deeply creased, the cover is jammed shut. Don't know if it's leaking radiation. Probably not. The front case, and most of the rear, are intact.

Stroud braces himself with his back to the wall, raises the RPD.

"Cover the door," I tell him. "Remember Crockett and I are in that tunnel."

The dome is filled by a whirling cloud of bats. Gunfire echoes from the chapel and the front of the mine. I grab Stroud's Carl G shell and run toward the mouth. Muzzle flashes flicker from the door of the blockhouse. I pull a lemonka from my webbing, toss it inside.

Cries of panic. Someone inside throws the grenade back out. It rolls in the pool of bat shit.

The lemonka explodes, but I'm well into the tunnel. More crackling of rifles, followed by the hammer of Stroud's RPD. Screams in Chinese.

Chaos. I run through a blizzard of bats, burst into the mine's front cavern. Look left and right. Crockett lies prone, firing his rifle into the valley. He raises himself on one elbow, half-turns to me.

"Breed."

From belly to groin, Crockett's jungle fatigues are soaked in blood. "Sam, what happened?"

"Those twenty mike-mikes throw a lot of shrapnel," he says. "Got hit in the gut."

"Fuck."

"Get down. They're bringing the heat."

I join Crockett at the mouth of the mine. It's daylight. Bats rush past and spiral into the sky, black against the overcast. Behind us, they bounce off the walls. PLA pour from the barracks to our right. The old hospital, now quarters for scientists, looks quiet.

Cannon shells rake the mouth of the cave, burst in the cavern. Shrapnel riddles my rucksack.

Where are they coming from?

Tracked vehicle. Its turret sports a Quad 20mm anti-aircraft array. It's stopped short of the railroad tracks.

"Best get your artillery in gear," Crockett says.

I unlimber the Carl Gustav, throw myself prone, and set the bipod. To avoid the backblast, I lie at an obtuse angle to the firing tube.

Iron sights, all I need at a hundred and fifty yards. I line up the track.

"Firing," I say.

Crockett claps his hands over his ears. Opens his mouth.

The concussion of a Carl Gustav shot is legendary. The backblast is dangerous up to fifty yards from the weapon. Army policy limits the number of rounds fired in training. The blast is so brutal it is known to cause TBI—traumatic brain injury.

*WHAM!*

Flames shoot from the front and back of the recoilless rifle. Roasted by the backblast, bats shriek. My brain explodes inside my skull and squirts from my ears. My guts shake from a body blow. That's what the concussion feels like. Enough exposure to a Carl G will peel the lining from a shooter's lungs.

The 84mm shell lances the front of the Quad 20mm. As if by magic, a black hole appears in the armor. The steel around it glows cherry red.

"Again," Crockett says. He crawls around to my right side, opens the breech. The spent shell casing is discarded with a clang. He pulls another shell from Stroud's carrying tube. Slams it into the Carl G, locks the breech. "Ready."

"Firing," I say.

Crockett covers his ears.

Smoke curls from the mortally wounded Quad 20mm. The driver's hatch opens and a man struggles to climb out.

*WHAM!*

This time, the shell strikes the Quad 20mm between the turret and hull. The ammunition store explodes. The turret is blown into the air, along with the remains of the gun crew. With a clang, it crashes to earth twenty feet away. Lighter human remains rain down as flames blast from the turret ring and driver's hatch.

With that round, my eyes felt like they would pop from their sockets. I hand the Carl G to Crockett. He's left a wide smear of blood on the floor of the cave. It looks like a slug's slime trail, mixed with rock dust. An ugly paste.

"Let me look at that."

"Don't worry about it. Unload more ammo."

Chinese infantry rush from the barracks to the scientists' quarters. Fireflies twinkle from the windows of both buildings. All around us, bullets whine off rock. I shrug off my four carrying tubes and set them on the floor. Open them and free the shells.

Crockett fires his AK47 at PLA infantry. "Wish we had Stroud's RPD."

"He's hit bad," I say. "Don't think he'll make it."

"So long as he covers our six."

"We've lost one nuke," I say. "Can you hold here? I'll go check on Stroud."

Crockett grins. "I got nothing better to do."

I get to my feet. In a crouch, I run back into the cave. The bats mill around, reluctant to flee into the daylight. The echo of Chinese rifle and RPD fire seems weaker. At the end of the tunnel, I flatten myself against the wall, peer inside.

Stroud is trading fire with PLA in the blockhouse. How many are in there? I haven't seen a single scientist emerge. The Chinese brain trust is trapped underground. One nuke will wipe out China's biowar technological capital.

I pull a lemonka from my webbing. Wonder if I can get to the blockhouse without either the PLA or Stroud shooting me. My best chance will be to approach from behind. I slip into the cathedral and run left. When I can no longer see muzzle flashes, I change direction and run to the blockhouse wall.

The fuse on a lemonka is three-and-one-half seconds. I pull the pin, dodge around the corner, and count two seconds. Throw the grenade inside the blockhouse and dive for the floor. There's a splash. I'm soaked in bat piss and shit.

A muffled blast, and the metal door of the blockhouse is blown off its hinges. The firing stops.

"Stroud."

"Breed."

"Don't shoot me."

I get up, brush beetles, roaches and crap from my clothes. I carry the AK47 at my hip. Cautiously approach the blockhouse door. Bright white light pours from inside. I look in, count four PLA dead and wounded. I shoot the wounded and study the room.

There isn't much to it. A guard house, with wooden desks and chairs. At the back is an elevator. To one side, a sturdy metal door with Chinese characters written on the wall above it. Fire stairs.

A bell chimes and the elevator door sucks open. Three men in white lab coats stand inside the elevator. Firing from the hip, I riddle them with automatic fire. They jerk against the walls of the elevator, crumple in a little pile.

I drop the magazine and load another. Pick up a wooden chair and jam the elevator door. I raise the AK47 to my shoulder and shoot the control panel to pieces. Cross the room to the fire door, test the handle. It's locked. The door and metal frame are solid.

"Stroud."

"Breed."

"I'm coming out."

I step from the blockhouse. My night vision is gone. I blink in the red ambient light washing from the tunnels. Lower my NODs, walk to Stroud.

*WHAM!*

Another blast from the Carl G. More hammering of automatic fire from the mouth of the mine. Crockett's having himself a high old time.

Stroud stares at me. His mouth and nose bubble blood. "I'm fucked up, Breed."

"I reckon so, Stroud."

"Fucking bats. I'm sorry."

I won't tell him it's alright. The son of a bitch has single-handedly fucked us all. I take the RPD from him. Lift the bandolier of RPD drums from around his shoulders and slip them over mine. Hand him my rifle.

"You cover that blockhouse," I tell him. "Anybody comes through that door, light them up."

I kick over the useless nuke. Jog through the tunnel to the chapel.

The chapel has gone quiet.

"Stein," I yell. "Ortega."

"Breed," Stein calls. "Back here."

I cross the floor of the chapel. The air is thick with bats, flying this way and that. Fluttering like autumn leaves blown into the sky. I'm sure many have fled through the tunnels. Don't know how many have actually left the mine.

The small blockhouse stands open. I look inside, find three PLA dead. Like the larger structure in the cathedral, this one has an elevator. It looks quiet.

I hurry to Stein. She's sitting at the entrance to the vestibule, protecting the nuke.

Ortega is slumped next to her, his back to the wall. Looks like he is sleeping.

"What happened?" I ask.

Stein's face is pale and drawn. "We took fire from the blockhouse," she says. "Ortega threw a grenade. Before it exploded, they shot him. The whole thing was over in seconds.

"I went inside, made sure they were dead. When I came out, Ortega was gone too."

"The other nuke is toast," I tell her. "How's this one?"

"It's good."

"Get it ready to arm. I'll help Crockett."

"Stroud?"

"He's going to die."

"We're all going to die."

"Yes."

Stein's eyes burn with holy fire. "Let's do it now."

"Not yet."

"Why the fuck not?"

"I need to talk to Crockett."

Stein snatches at my webbing. Jerks me close. "No! Now—before I change my mind."

Like a flagellant, her face shines silver.

I seize Stein by the shoulders. Steady her, thrust the AK47 into her hands. "No. You stay here and hold." I point at the blockhouse. "Anybody comes through that door—kill them."

# 39

## APPLEYARD

### Jiang Shi

Stroud is dead.

He sits with my AK47 in his hands, sightless eyes fixed on the blockhouse. I take the rifle, step to the doorway, and look inside. The elevator remains jammed. No one has disturbed the fire door.

I step outside, hurry through the tunnel, and make my way to the mouth of the mine.

A man can get used to anything. The bats are still bouncing off the walls. The atmosphere still reeks of ammonia. Breathing through my mouth has become second nature.

The rattle of gunfire continues. Crockett is trading fire with the PLA.

"Crockett."

"Breed."

I don't want to get fried by the backblast of a recoilless rifle. "I'm coming through. Hold your fire with that Carl G."

Another armored vehicle straddles the railroad tracks.

Like blowtorches, yellow-orange flames blast from open hatches. Greasy black smoke boils skyward.

"They took a run at me with that armored personnel carrier," Crockett says. "It carries a seventy-five millimeter gun. If they connect with one of those, we're through."

"We have a lot of Carl G ammo," I say. "What's their infantry like?"

Crockett is holding his AK47 in gloved hands. The barrel glows cherry red from continuous firing. "I reckon about a hundred," he says, "but any patrols they have in the area are rushing back now."

I hand him Stroud's RPD. "Take this."

Crockett takes the machine gun, the bandolier of hundred-round drums. I lay on the floor. "Looks like they've occupied the scientists' quarters."

"They've lost a lot of men doing that," Crockett says. "They want to use it as a jumping-off point to rush us."

"When they've loaded it up, let's hit it with the Carl."

"They have more armor," Crockett says.

"We're not getting out of here."

"No, I don't think so."

"This is where Appleyard fought his last stand, isn't it? *You* took his identity. *You* killed Fairchild."

Crockett smiles. "How do you figure that?"

"Spears made modern SOG knives for all of you. So you could use them and put your originals away. Stroud is using a Spears Special. You're using your *original* blade."

"What if I am?"

"You left *your* Spears Special in the chest of one of Fairchild's bodyguards. At the lodge, Heth said you'd taken your knife. It didn't occur to me she meant you'd taken your *original* knife."

Crockett checks the drum on the RPD. Stacks more on

the floor next to him. Along with the Carl G and its ammunition. "Oh hell," he says. "I suppose it doesn't matter now."

"Why did you kill Fairchild, Sam? Why did you torture him?"

"It's complicated, Breed."

"Try me."

"Fairchild was a mole," Crockett explains. "I found out after the war. He approached me and suggested I work for the Chinese. They paid well, and the lodge was in financial trouble. I was going bust."

"So you worked for the enemy."

"Come on, Breed. It's not that simple. The Chinese paid me to kill Vietnamese. Hell, we'd been killing Vietnamese for seventeen years. I was awarded a Silver Star for killing Vietnamese. I saved the ranch, took care of Heth."

"Why did you kill Fairchild?"

"Fairchild went one step too far. He tried to blackmail me into killing Kang."

"Why?"

"That's what I wanted to know."

A dozen PLA make a run for the scientists' quarters. Crockett opens fire with the RPD. Cuts down four of them. The remainder dive behind the building.

"*Think*, Breed. You already know the answer. Phoenix told the Company about Jiang Shi and rabies. Fairchild told his masters. The Chinese panicked and killed Phoenix. At that point, Fairchild knew he was in deep shit if the Chinese decided to clean house. He received instructions to meet Kang and bring all his files. He figured Kang was going to cancel him."

"So he asked you to kill Kang. Why would you do that for him?"

"He threatened to let it be known I was Appleyard."

"So he had to die."

"Yes. But that isn't the only reason. SOG missions were routinely compromised. We could never figure out why the NVA were so well prepared. They often knew where we would be inserted and when. They knew the composition of our teams. By name."

A hail of Chinese rifle bullets blasts the entrance to the mine. Stone chips are scattered in our faces. Crockett rakes the scientists' quarters with the RPD. Shifts his fire to the barracks.

"Think about Guillotine," he says. "Didn't you wonder why General Dung didn't show at 0900 as expected? Was it fluke that a strong force of PLA shot us off Hill 34?"

Crockett twists on his elbow, stares at me. "Fairchild sold us out, Breed. He'd been selling us out for years. The son of a bitch killed our friends for *money*. After the war, I suspected, but I let it slide. Because I *needed* money."

"Why wouldn't you kill Kang for him?"

PLA dodge toward the scientists' quarters from the slope of Hill 48. Patrols returning, drawn by the noise of battle. Crockett fires on them.

"Kang's father was my friend," Crockett says. "We fought together against the Vietnamese in 1977. We worked together during the Sino-Vietnamese war and after. I was a guest in his home when Kang was born. Twenty years later, I worked with Kang after his father retired."

"Taiwan."

"Yes, an aborted mission. You know, I spoke to Kang the night I killed Fairchild."

That surprises me.

"Kang was outside when I left the burning house. He told me to disappear, and he wouldn't kill me. I told him if he came after me, I would kill him."

"You didn't go to France the other week, did you?"

"No, I was in DC. Fairchild would shake his bodyguards and arrange to meet me. Instead, I beat Kang to Fairchild."

"You believed Kang would kill Fairchild."

"Of course. Fairchild believed it. But I wanted my pound of flesh, so to speak. I wanted a confession, and I wanted the truth about Jiang Shi." Crockett smiles. "I hoped Kang wouldn't come after me. When he killed Butler at Salish Rock, I knew all bets were off."

I think how Crockett carved Fairchild before setting fire to him. Then I think of all the soldiers Fairchild sold out.

"Reckon Fairchild had it coming."

"Look over there, Breed. The Chinese are rolling out another Quad 20mm. Soon, they'll attack."

"Yes. I'll take the Carl G."

"No," Crockett says. "You set off the bomb. I'll hold them from here."

"Alright." I pick up my rifle.

"Breed."

"Yes."

"You and Heth would have been good together."

I RUN BACK to the cathedral.

Stroud's gone. Where he sat, a shadow lies against the wall. The red light above the blockhouse door is too dim to illuminate the corner. I flip down my NODs. Rifle at my hip, I edge closer.

The shadow shifts. A frond is peeled away, a bat's wing. The thing it covered is unrecognizable. Outraged at the interruption, the animal turns its head toward me and squeaks. Eyes like silver marbles, canines gleaming like scalpels. One of a mass of bats feasting on Stroud's face and torso. A carpet of roaches and beetles undulates over his legs.

I dodge into the tunnel, keep running.

When I reach the chapel, I find Stein waiting. She's taken the B54 out of its ruck, opened the security cover. Face pale, she swings the muzzle of her AK47 to cover me.

Stein lowers the rifle. "Took you long enough."

"Crockett will hold them off. Let's arm the bomb."

"How long can he hold?" Stein asks.

"Not long enough for us to get through those tunnels."

Stein composes herself. "Alright."

Her long fingers take the primer from the Safe Well and plug it into the Arm Well.

I turn the timer knob to five minutes, the minimum increment.

Stein turns the arming switch from SAFE to ARM. Snatches her hand back as though burned.

The clock starts ticking.

We sit together with Ortega's corpse.

"At least we'll go out with a bang," Stein says.

"I reckon so."

Stein squeezes her eyes shut.

I put my arm around Stein's thin shoulders and pull her close. She buries her face against my chest.

We'll die together. Who would have thought?

# 40

## THE MOUTH OF HELL

### Jiang Shi

"Breed!"

The shout echoes off the walls. Audible over the flapping of bat wings.

That voice.

*Takigawa's alive.*

I get to my feet, step into the chapel. Takigawa's voice is coming from the sinkhole. "Here," I yell.

"What's your situation?"

"We're being overrun," I tell him. "Nuke's going off in five minutes."

"Shit. Can you reset it?"

I look back at Stein. "Yes."

"Get everybody up here! We've got a chance."

"It's me and Stein," I say. "Crockett's hit bad."

"Then get moving."

I turn to the B54's arming panel. Flip the arming switch to SAFE.

The clock stops.

Takigawa throws his rappel rope over the lip of the sinkhole. Borne by its own weight, through the cloud of bats, the thick coil unfurls. The end of the rope splashes onto the floor.

*WHAM!*

I imagine the Quad 20mm firing on the mouth of the mine. Crockett blasting it with the Carl Gustav.

How long can he hold?

I stoop to the bomb. Turn the timer knob to thirty minutes.

"Bring the radio and batteries," I tell Stein. "Drop the rest."

When we reach the surface, we'll run like hell. But we have to climb that rope first. It's a hundred feet, with nothing to help her ascend. With only the ManPack to carry, she has a chance. She weighs a hundred and twenty pounds naked. Get her close enough, Takigawa can haul her the rest of the way.

"Go as far as you can. If you think you can't go further, hang on. Takigawa will try to haul you up."

Stein pulls her gloves tighter. Hurls herself at the rope. She's learned the foot lock technique. Grabs the rope with her gloved hands, wraps it around her feet so she can stand. Straightens her knees and climbs.

I watch her ascend into the blizzard of wings. At the lip of the sinkhole, Takigawa looks down. He won't pull on the rope if he can help it. The exercise is dangerous enough. Military rope climbing exercises rarely exceed twenty feet.

Turn to Stein's pack. Tear it apart for things that could be useful.

Hell, everything's useful, but I have to climb that rope too. I won't do it carrying two rifles and Stein's ammo on top of my own. Disgusted, I kick her ruck into the corner.

*WHAM!*

The blast of the Carl Gustav is so fierce the concussion

travels around corners. Believe me, soldiers suffer TBIs from around corners. The bats go insane. Imagine what those shock waves do to ears a thousand times more sensitive than ours. Worse, bats use their ears for more than hearing. Sensors in their ears provide their brains with pitch, roll, and yaw data. More effective than any jet fighter's avionics, because the animals integrate that information in real-time.

Stein stops climbing. Clings to the rope, shields her face.

"You okay?" I yell.

"Yes," Stein calls. "Give me a minute."

Can't mistake the stress in her voice. She's more than halfway up. I shrug off my rucksack. Tear out my camelback, discard the MREs. I keep the magazines and first aid kit. Signal panels and flares. Shrug the ruck back on. It's lighter. I tighten my gloves.

Stein reaches the lip of the sinkhole. Throws a leg over. Takigawa drags her over the top.

*Fuck me, she did it.*

I turn to the nuke. Flip the arming switch from SAFE to ARM.

Jump for the rope.

It's a race. From here on, every second counts.

The first forty feet are easy. Halfway up, my arms are burning. Without full combat gear, I'd scurry up this rope in no time. The rifle and ruck hanging off my shoulders bow my body. I'm not climbing vertically. Rather, every time I straighten my legs, my arms have to carry more weight than they otherwise would.

*WHAM!*

Crockett is giving them hell. How much longer can he last? I focus all my energy on the rope. Ten more feet. *Climb.*

A bat, disoriented by the concussion, caroms off my shoulder. Another flies past my face, stares at me through angry eyes.

*Climb.*

The higher I climb, the more my muscles stiffen into blocks of cement. My spine is on fire with pain.

Drumbeat of automatic fire. The RPD. Fifteen and twenty-round bursts. The infantry, charging the mine. How quickly can Crockett change out a drum?

Throw my leg over the lip. Takigawa and Stein grab me by my webbing and heave. For a second, I lie on my back. From the mouth of the sinkhole, a cloud of black wings spirals into the sky. Like smoke from a volcanic eruption.

I get to my feet. "We have to do a mile in twenty minutes."

Stein and Takigawa are staring at Jiang Shi.

FROM ACROSS THE SADDLE, Hill 180 glowers at us. Immediately east rises the commanding height of Hill 868. The valley is a bowl. Three tracked vehicles burn, pouring foul black smoke into the sky. Half of the scientists' quarters has been blown to splinters. Bodies are strewn across the landscape.

Another armored personnel carrier crawls from behind the lodge. Chinese troops with rifles occupy the rear passenger compartment. The front has a turret with a short-barreled 75mm howitzer. The kind of gun used against fortifications.

*WHAM!*

The Carl Gustav spurts fire. The round hits the vehicle behind the turret and penetrates the passenger compartment. An orange flash, and a great gout of flame obscures the rear of the vehicle.

The driver and bow gunner bail out of their hatches. The howitzer's muzzle puffs grey smoke. The shell, a small black football, sails toward the mine. Explodes against the side of Hill 180. Splintered trees and shredded vegetation cascade over Crockett's position.

Firing their rifles, the Chinese infantry surge forward.

Crockett's RPD stammers defiance.

"Let's go," I say.

Throwing caution to the wind, I lead Stein and Takigawa south along the ridge. It's all downhill, and I run as fast as I dare. We have to put distance between ourselves and the valley.

I avoid the trails. If one of us steps on a land mine, it's curtains. I thrash through the dense curtain of elephant grass. The blades are taller than I am. Behind me, I hear Taki-gawa gasping.

Stein isn't even breathing hard.

On my left, charging the other way, a body crashes through the brush. A rapid string of shots, seven in all, lash the air. Stein's Tokarev. Lord, she isn't shy about putting a man down.

The first Chinese and I had passed in the high grass. In our hurry, we'd been making so much noise, we didn't notice each other. The man behind him crashes into me, full force. The impact stuns us both, but I'm bigger and he goes down hard. I shove the muzzle of my rifle in his face and pull the trigger.

I sense a shadow in the grass, fire from the hip. Full auto, belly-height. I charge forward, let muzzle climb walk the burst into the man's chest. He screams and falls. I run right over him, spray the grass ahead until the bolt clacks empty.

Drop the mag, reload. Brace for returned fire.

Nothing. I keep running, Stein and Takigawa behind me.

Fifteen minutes gone. The terrain levels out. The wind blows north-by-east. I don't see the sinkhole where we made our original entrance, but I reckon we're close. I stop, allow Stein and Takigawa to catch up.

"Should we turn west?" Stein asks.

"Fallout is one thing," I say. "We need cover from blast. Jungle won't do it. This is the only rock I know around here."

"Over there." Takigawa points to a green gully. "That vegetation covers limestone outcrops for at least two hundred yards."

The sniper leads the way. Stein and I follow.

"I spent hours playing cat and mouse with the PLA in here," Takigawa gasps.

Moss, lichens, and other vegetation cling to the soft rock. I glance at my watch.

"This is far enough," I say. "Dig in."

We drop to the jungle floor. Crouch behind the rock.

"How much time did you leave?" Stein asks.

The worst thing that can happen is—nothing happens.

"Thirty minutes," I say.

She checks her watch. "It's been thirty-five."

The jungle floor ripples. I feel like we're sitting on a boat in a rough sea. We are lifted onto a crest. A second later—we plunge into a trough. We're bounced into each other by the violence of the waves.

I'm on my ass, looking north over the limestone outcrop. Pillars of orange fire burst from the jungle and sear the sky. A massive black gout of rock, earth, concrete, and vegetation is hurled skyward. The debris is flung so high it rises above the jungle canopy and limestone outcrops that shelter us. The bolus hangs suspended in the air while a soft red glare washes over the landscape. The chapel and cathedral have opened into the mouth of hell.

The jungle swells. I put my arm around Stein's shoulders and drag her to the ground. Nose-to-nose, we clutch each other. Trees and vegetation on the outcrop sway with the pressure wave. This is the test. We're over a mile from the epicenter, outside the radius of destruction.

Moments later, a thunderclap strikes us like a physical

blow. It's a wave, traveling at the speed of sound. Takigawa grunts, claps his hands to his ears.

In slow motion, the clot of debris hanging over Jiang Shi breaks up. Pieces fall at different speeds depending on their size, weight and shape. Masses of rock the size of houses fall straight down. The hulk of a tracked vehicle dissociates itself from debris and plunges to earth. Tree trunks, body parts, and other fleshy things disperse in a wide circle around the epicenter.

As the red glow fades, we get to our feet. I half expect to see a mushroom cloud. Instead, the underground blast lifted the earth and set it down in place. Dust and lighter debris seem suspended evenly in the air. Like a rain squall, the mass drifts in the wind. Gravity sorts the cloud's grisly payload.

Takigawa shoulders his ruck. "I'd like to see the headlines tomorrow."

"Crickets." Stein shakes her head. "The Chinese won't say a word, and neither will we."

"We've got some hiking to do," I tell them. "We're stuck twenty-five miles inside China."

"What do we do, Breed?" Stein asks.

I shift my rifle, carry it low-ready. "Head south-by-west. Make for Thailand."

"There might be fighting to do before we see home again," Takigawa says.

"Half an hour ago, we were dead." Stein takes a breath. "Now we fight for ourselves."

# 41

## THE LAST HEROES

### Georgetown

Gilbert's patio isn't crowded. Fall is shading into November, but the afternoon remains warm and pleasant. I'm in town for a week. Tracy and I have agreed to meet on the weekend.

Stein hurries to our table. I rise to greet her, and she gives me a cool hug.

By unspoken agreement, we have parked the moments of intimacy we shared in Jiang Shi. The terror and exhilaration of the night drop, our brush with death. These are not to be spoken of, yet I feel myself immersed in warmth.

She's back to the stern black pantsuit. The sensible polished dress shoes. Brown hair tied into a ponytail. The last time I saw her, we were all dressed in unmarked fatigues. We trekked through the jungles of China and Laos. Avoided trails. Waited all day so we could cross rivers and highways at night. We limped into northern Thailand and unlimbered the HF ManPack.

The Company had given us up for dead. Only Stein's team had continued to monitor our prearranged frequency. Once a day, like dutiful guard dogs. We made contact on our first attempt.

An American unit training with the Royal Thai Air Force at Udorn was diverted to extract us from the jungle. Thailand was a friendly country. There was nothing controversial about our exfiltration.

Thai and American Special Forces stared at the three filthy figures that climbed out of the helicopter. One man, certainly American. Another man who looked Korean or Japanese, but who was too tall to be either. A woman who would be attractive if she only changed her clothes and washed her hair.

We walked past them, carrying Chinese weapons. We looked like hell. Our jungle fatigues were dirty and torn from weeks in the bush. Onlookers drew back instinctively. We hadn't bathed in six weeks. Our stench preceded us.

Secret flights were arranged. Udorn to Clark. Clark to Guam. Guam to Peterson.

Stein was right... there were no stories in the mass media. Geological stations had registered a significant seismic event in southern China. The event, measuring 4 mb or body-wave units, was consistent with a modest earthquake. What was *not* reported, was that it was also consistent with the underground detonation of a one-kiloton nuclear device.

The media was not aware that US and Russian satellites had recorded a thermal bloom from southern Yunnan province. The bloom was consistent with an underground nuclear explosion of one-kiloton magnitude.

US Naval units in the Pacific were placed on alert but ordered to maintain a non-threatening posture. US carriers were withdrawn to a safe distance. Admirals complained they were held so far back the mainland was beyond range of their air groups. Japanese naval assets put to sea and scattered. Chinese and American vessels eyed each other warily.

Telephone lines burned for days between Beijing, Moscow and Washington DC. The matter was quietly dropped. The Chinese licked their wounds.

"How are you, Stein?" I ask.

Stein smiles. She isn't gloating, but she's pleased. "I'm good, Breed. I spent an hour with the Director, and thirty minutes with the highest authority."

"Have you run into Poole?"

"Yes, I have." Stein smiles sweetly. "He's announced his retirement. In six months, Warren Thiel will become Deputy Director of Plans. I was offered Deputy Director of Human Intelligence."

"Congratulations."

"I turned it down. The Company is creating a new unit. I will become Deputy Director of Special Situations."

"Equal in rank to Thiel."

"On paper. I don't have his credentials."

"Harvard Law isn't good enough?"

Stein shakes her head. "I didn't belong to the right secret club at Princeton. Apparently, neither did Poole."

She signals Tracy to take our orders.

"I suppose that stuff matters."

"It's the system."

When Tracy has gone, I turn to Stein. "Maybe you can beat the system."

"No." Stein winks at me. "Breed, you can't beat the system. But—you can win the game. You and I are about winning."

Tracy brings my beer. From a carafe, she pours Stein a glass of rosé.

"You told them about Fairchild and Appleyard?"

"Yes," Stein says. "And Crockett. They couldn't believe Fairchild was a Chinese double agent all these years. They traced his money. That mansion in Chevy Chase was the tip of the iceberg. We've concluded he was responsible for the loss of many SOG teams in Laos and Cambodia. He was paid enormous sums to sacrifice our missions, *especially* Guillotine.

"After the war, he followed the fortunes of a number of SOG operators he could compromise. He knew Crockett was in financial difficulty. He used time-tested Chinese techniques. Exploited the ambiguity of the ask. Crockett had been given the Silver Star for killing Vietnamese. Why should he *not* accept money for doing the same job?"

"Why not Spears or one of the others?"

"We're speculating, now. Mosby was an unreliable alcoholic. Spears was happy. Butler was financially well off. Stroud was a ghost. Crockett was ruthlessly effective *and* in financial difficulty."

"Will the Company close the books on them?"

"Yes. Apart from Fairchild, the Black Sheep are victims of a dirty war. In fact, they were the last of an idealistic generation. They volunteered for infantry. Volunteered for airborne, Ranger, and Special Forces. They *asked* to go to Vietnam. Despite its one hundred percent casualty rate, they *volunteered* for SOG. Those men are unmatched in professionalism and courage."

"I never thought I could live up to Dad."

Stein stares at me thoughtfully. "I think you have."

I say nothing.

"Have you decided about working for the Company?"

I smile. "Stein, I think our current arrangement works fine."

Stein looks rueful. "Damn. I put too many zeroes on that check."

Silent, we sip our drinks.

"What will you tell Heth about Crockett?" Stein asks.

I think of the battle at Jiang Shi. A life spent fighting for his country.

"I'm going to tell Heth her grandfather died a hero."

## ACKNOWLEDGMENTS

This novel would not have been possible without the support, encouragement, and guidance of my agent, Ivan Mulcahy, of MMB Creative. I would also like to thank my publishers, Brian Lynch and Garret Ryan of Inkubator Books for seeing the novel's potential. Thanks also go to Jodi Compton for her editorial efforts, and Claire Milto of Inkubator Books for her artistic efforts, and support in the novel's launch. Not the least, I wish to thank members of my writing group, beta readers, and listeners, who support my obsession with reading every word of a novel out loud in pursuit of that undefinable quality called voice.

If you could spend a moment to write an honest review on Amazon, no matter how short, I would be extremely grateful. They really do help readers discover my books.

Feel free to contact me at cameron.curtis545@gmail.com. I'd love to hear from you.

## References


Alister, D. and Fukiyama, S. "A new methodology for protein sequencing of *lyssavirus*." Journal of Procedural Molecular Biology, 96:123-35

Bhatia, S. "Homology of spike proteins: comparison of European bat *lyssavirus* and Asian bat *lyssavirus*." Journal of Experimental Membrane Research, 6:42-9

Bugolyubov, D. "Strengths and weaknesses of Q50 as a metric of infectivity." Journal of Procedural Microbiology, 105:43-51

Bugolyubov, D. "Alternative metrics of infectivity: substitutes for Q50." Journal of Procedural Microbiology, 105:52-60

Chen, M. and Liu, B. "Methodology for insertion of HIV-1 envelope proteins in *coronavirus*." Lumen, 250: 33-41

Chen, M. "Characterization of *lyssavirus* G glycoprotein spikes." Lumen, 252: 67-71

Chernov, B. "Evidence of enhanced autophagy and *lyssavirus* clearance in bats." Immunology, 152:37-45

Denton, S., Fassnacht, C. and Thompson, A. "An efficient protocol for the high-yield isolation of HIV-1 gp41 and gp120 proteins." Journal of Physical and Biological Chemistry, 105:112-8

Denton, S., Fassnacht, C. and Thompson, A. "An improved protocol for the high-yield isolation of HIV-1 gp41 and gp120 proteins." Journal of Physical and Biological Chemistry, 110:62-0

Dietrich, S., Umlauf, A. and Hessler, R. "A methodology for glycoprotein substitution among *lyssavirus* and some observations on the portability of infectivity." Journal of Procedural Molecular Biology, 102:51-9

Drye, A. "An efficient algorithm for identifying optimal growth media subject to arbitrary parameters." Journal of Microbiological Science, 77:91-8

Emory, C. and Ross, W. "Gain and loss of function in H5N1 avian influenza: molding the relationship between transmissibility and lethality." Virion, 112:55-71

Engle, D. "Monogamy in bat species of south Yunnan: implications for conservation." Natural History, 188:235-8

Fan, Y. "Geology and tectonics of Yunnan Province." Tectonics Journal, 15:75-88

Filovich, D. "Strategic versus tactical biological weapons: factors influencing selection, production, and dispersal." Frontiers of Virology, 155: 37-42

Gordon, J. "Rehabilitation of underground mines: technology, price-points, and microeconomics." Copper, 421:133-55

Gracie, W. "China's Biological Warfare Programs: Historical contextualization and future directions." StratCom Research Q1 2018

Grinkov, V. "Half-lives of solid and liquid microbiological preparations: demands on scalability of production strategies." Frontiers of Virology, 149:235-257

Haberman, A. "Roost selection by diverse bat species in south Yunnan Province." Natural History, 518:226-30

He, Y. and Wang, T. "Development of transgenic bats by retrovirus-mediated gene transfer." Advances in Biotechnology, 12:142-9

He, Y., Wang, T. and Zhang, L. "Attempt to develop transgenic bats by DNA injection: methodology and results." Advances in Biotechnology, 11:326-40

He, Y. "Induction of antiviral RNASL gene in transgenic bats: artificial development of living bioreactors." Immunology, 385:61-9

Huang, Y. and Plaster, R. "Evolutionary development of virion glycoprotein structures with implications for cross-species gain-of-function research." Journal of Evolutionary Genetics, 7:73-81

Horlick, L. "Day of Infamy: Japanese Biological Warfare and the Tokyo War Crimes Tribunal April 29, 1946." Matilda Press, 1994

Irving, J. "Increased expression of heat-shock proteins in bats: implications for host defense capability." Immunology, 284:1273-0

Irving, J. "Heat-shock proteins and *lyssavirus* evolution in bats: enhanced mutation tolerance." Immunology: 290:583-92

Irving, J. and Chernov, B. "Investigation of suppressed inflammasome pathways in bats: reduced NLRP3 and PYHIN and enhanced immune tolerance." Immunology, 284:1280-92

Jacob, R. "Volcanogenic sulfide ore deposits in southern China, Laos, and Vietnam." Copper, 168:57-70

Jobert, F. and Wang, H. "Diversity of bat species in southern Yunnan cave systems: implications for conservation." Natural History, 520:113-120

Joliet, H. "Emergence of novel *lyssaviruses* and zoonotic viral pathogens." Virion, 82:85-94

Kalman, U. "Breakfast, lunch or dinner: effect of temperature inversions on the spread of pathogens." Journal of Procedural Microbiology, 116:55-59

Karpov, B. "Computer modeling the dispersal of selected agents as a function of altitude and wind." Computational Microbiology, 88:123-35

Karpov, B. and Bugolyubov, D. "Distributions of Q50 on projected dispersion fields." Computational Microbiology, 90:15-26

Khoury, S. and Alvarez, C. "Titration of *lyssavirus* and *coronavirus* isolates from the Indian False Vampire Bat." Virion, 86:122-9

Khoury, S. and Alvarez, C. "Distribution of *lyssavirus* in bat species of the Indian subcontinent." Virion, 86:215-28

Korolyev, A. and Bhatia, S. "Serological analysis of distribution of *lyssavirus* genus across Eurasia with granular focus on Russia, India, China, and Indochina." Virion, 120:97-108

Kumar, D. and Pushkin, A. "Selection of nutrient media for transportation of pathogens: a comparative analysis." Journal of Microbiological Science, 131:35-42

Liu, B. "Survivability of *lyssavirus* in abiotic environments: the aerosol transmission of rabies." Epidemiological Projections. Q3 2019

Liu, B. "Factors affecting survivability of virions in abiotic environments: comparison of *lyssavirus*, *coronavirus*, and *lentivirus*." Epidemiological Projections Q3 2019

Mishkin, V. and Bugolyubov, D. "Time decay of Q50 for liquid and solid preparations of selected agents." Journal of Procedural Microbiology, 106:71-8

Musgrave, A. and Krauthammer, N. "Characterization of the alpha-complex envelope proteins in a selection of virus families." Journal of Experimental Membrane Research, 7:33-42

Pankow, H. "Planning efficient adit networks in underground copper mines." Copper, 255:2132-40

Renko, K. "Biopreparat: The Soviet Biological Weapons Industry." VectorTek Publishing, 1997

Wang, H. "Biogeography of tropical rain forest in southern Yunnan." Geoscience, 102:326-30

Zhang, L. and He, Y. "Creation of transgenic bat bioreactors by retrovirus-mediated gene transfer: a progress report." Advances in Biotechnology, 15:125-39

## ALSO BY CAMERON CURTIS

**DANGER CLOSE**

(Breed Book #1)

**OPEN SEASON**

(Breed Book #2)

**TARGET DECK**

(Breed Book #3)

**CLOSE QUARTERS**

(Breed Book #4)

**BROKEN ARROW**

(Breed Book #5)

**WHITE SPIDER**

(Breed Book #6)

**BLACK SUN**

(Breed Book #7)

Published by Inkubator Books
www.inkubatorbooks.com

Printed in Great Britain
by Amazon